11/99

Berkley Prime Crime Books by Katherine V. Forrest

LIBERTY SQUARE
APPARITION ALLEY
SLEEPING BONES

r Kate Delafield Mysteries by Katherine V. Forrest

AMATEUR CITY
MURDER AT THE NIGHTWOOD BAR
THE BEVERLY MALIBU
MURDER BY TRADITION

SLEE
BO

Othe

SLEEPING BONES

BONES

Katherine V. Forrest

BERKLEY PRIME CRIME, NEW YORK

SLEEPING BONES

A Berkley Prime Crime Book
Published by the Berkley Publishing Group
A Division of Penguin Putnam Inc.
375 Hudson Street, New York, New York 10014

The Penguin Putnam World Wide Web site address is
http://www.penguinputnam.com

First Edition: September 1999

Library of Congress Cataloging-in-Publication Data

Forrest, Katherine V., 1939–
Sleeping bones : a Kate Delafield mystery / by Katherine
V. Forrest.
p.   cm.
ISBN 0-425-17029-2
I. Title.
PS3556.O737S44   1999
813'.54—dc21   98-54294
CIP

Printed in the United States of America

10   9   8   7   6   5   4   3   2   1

Acknowledgments

To former Sergeant Mitchell Grobeson for his advice on procedural matters, and for his friendship and continuing involvement in the Kate Delafield mystery series. Most of all, for the pioneering activism that has changed the face of law enforcement throughout this country.

To Montserrat Fontes, novelist extraordinaire, the most "senior" adviser on all my work; to my writer-brother Michael Nava for splendid advice and his own splendid work. Very special thanks to Cath Walker for her candor and for saving my bacon in the poker game. To Sherry Thomas for always astute criticism. To Doreen Di Biagio for the excellent counsel on banking procedures. Many thanks to the staff and volunteers at the George C. Page Museum, Rancho La Brea, Los Angeles.

To my editor, Natalee Rosenstein, with much appreciation for input that always strengthens my work.

To Charlotte Sheedy, with love and thanks.

To my partner, Jo Hercus, for bringing it together and keeping it together . . .

My appreciation is owed to major research sources that form the historical backdrop for this novel: *Ancestral Passions: The Leakey Family and the Search for Humankind's Beginnings* by Virginia Morell, Simon & Schuster, New York, NY; *The Wisdom of the Bones* by Alan Walker and Pat Shipman, Alfred A. Knopf, Inc., New York, NY; *The Story of Peking Man* by Jia Lanpo and Huang Weiven, translated by Yin Zhiqi, Beijing Foreign Languages Press and Hong Kong Oxford University Press, New York, NY; *Inside the CIA* by Ronald Kessler, Pocket Books, New York, NY; and the *Los Angeles Times* archives.

Some locales are factual, as are the historical events surrounding the Peking Man fossils and their attending historical figures. The present-day story, and all of the characters, are a product of the author's imagination.

For Jo—
and in memory
of Cassie

The pool of water, no deeper than a boulder and dark as a tomb, reflects the fading moon and stars but not the surrounding tule reeds. Its surface, coated with leaves and twigs and bark, with feathers and tiny bones, is ruffled with rings.

A dark, thick bubble unhurriedly emerges from the pool's depths, and in a slow, steady distention expands beyond its limit and then vanishes in a whock of extinction, marked only by another spreading ring on the water's surface.

As dawn grays the edges of the horizon, the rounded shoulders of distant hills define a vast bowl of valley, its floor cotton-balled here and there with fog; occupied by a resolute army of manzanita, elderberry, sagebrush, ragweed, juniper, dogwood, poison oak, and thistle; and by studdings of pine and scrub oak. The night-cooled earth is fecund with decomposed flora and fauna, dank with dew, rank with odors of death and decay.

A huge dark form eases its way through the tule reeds toward the water and in the dusky light acquires shape and identity: a bison, massive, seven feet tall at the apex of her thickly muscled shoulders. She moves in guardianship of her young, a four-month-old calf gamboling in her wake, awkward and innocent, but already wary, pulling at tender bits of grass amid the low chaparral.

Other life stirs awake. The tentative first chirp of a

bird echoes with sharp clarity across the valley floor. A cautious rustling of rats, squirrels, and rabbits as they discreetly reconnoiter their surroundings. In a patch of brushy undergrowth, a sabertooth cat remains concealed and asleep.

Another sound: the calf lapping at the water, slurping and meandering its way along the pool border. Its parent follows, edging her bulky body farther into the shallows where she more firmly plants her hooves. Alert, she stands motionless in the ebony water, watching her calf and listening, head raised, curved horns bristling. No dangers seem to be lurking here. Settling herself, she drinks to satiation.

Soon the calf makes its way back up the sloping bank, seeking more of the grass succulent with the night dews. Sensing that its parent has not followed, hearing a flurry of splashing, the calf halts, wheeling around on its spindly limbs.

The bison has not moved because she cannot. Her hooves are held fast. She attempts again, and yet again, to force her way out of the innocuous-appearing pool of shallow water. Concentrating all her muscle power as her calf scrabbles about in apprehension, she succeeds in extracting one tarred hoof. But she lacks the leverage to free the others. Concealed under the water, the substance in which she is mired, shallow though it may be, permits incremental but fruitless movements. The bison is powerless to calm her panicked calf, its bleating and erratic hoofbeats clear signals to predators.

In the undergrowth, the sabertooth cat springs awake, ears pricked to the sounds of distress, and crawls from its concealment. Lithely, soundlessly, it lopes through the grass toward the perturbation.

The bison's struggles become frenzied as the tawny, dappled cat creeps through the dewy reeds into visibility, its yellow eyes fixed on her calf, its enormous curved eyeteeth gleaming in the growing light of dawn.

*Intent on its prey, the cat assesses in cold, swift cal-
culation that the calf is a stray; this first meal of the day
will be a quick and easy kill. Crouching on its haunches,
it gathers itself. The bison bawls her agony and rage.*

*Aborting its spring, the sabertooth cat leaps back,
snarling, bracing itself for what is sure to be a charging
attack from the parent of its intended victim.*

*The raging bellows continue, but the bison does not
emerge from the pool; and the cat, low on its haunches,
tail swishing, cautiously edges its way forward, eyes
fixed on the bison. Why does it not defend its young—
or itself? The bison is much larger and more enticing
prey, well within the cat's hunting capabilities, and a
sumptuous feast now and for many meals to come.*

*The cat snarls in challenge. The bison, struggling with
all its might to extricate itself, can only bellow defiance
and fury.*

*Other predators appear. In the grass behind the sa-
bertooth cat, five dire wolves, drawn by the snarls and
rage of the hunter and hunted, quickly circle the terrified
calf, exposing huge pointed teeth in their powerful jaws.*

*Again the bison bawls its agony. At the edge of the
pool, the sabertooth cat rises to its full height, taunting
its paralyzed quarry. With a roar of triumph, it breaks
into a lope along the border of the pool away from the
bison as if to spare it, then suddenly wheels back to
swiftly crouch and launch itself. Landing on the back of
the bison, it simultaneously seizes her in its claws and
strikes its two saberlike teeth into her thick neck, re-
tracts, stabs again, yet again. Leaping nimbly into the
pool it completes its conquest by dragging the massive
body down by the head.*

*Her life ebbing in a flow of crimson into the black
water, the bison does not see the strings of bright red
blood flying from the snarling, thrashing pack of wolves
who yank her calf into the rapidly reddening pool as
they voraciously feed.*

Some minutes later, the glutting sounds lessen. The cat, sated, one paw on its savagely ripped and mangled prey, rears its blood-smeared head and roars its supremacy. Prepared to stalk grandly from the pool and drag the remains of its prey to its lair, it finds its other three legs mired. Tugging ineffectually, it growls in outrage and plants all four paws in the pool to gain greater leverage, only to become fixed in place, even less able to move than its prey had been. Of the five dire wolves, four are also in distress, mired like the cat, only one of their number able to retreat to safety in the reeds.

As the thrashing, howling, and roaring in the pool continues unabated, coyotes and weasels appear, drawn by the uproar and the metallic scents of blood and butchery, as are more wolves, a lynx, a puma. Eyeing formidable enemies that have become helpless prey, they attack, rending and tearing. A horde of vultures circles ever lower over the carnage; but, deterred by the snapping and snarling of the trapped animals and the eager, opportunistic savagery of the newest arrivals, they flap back out of danger and wait patiently, unaware of the tarry, congealing substance being flung onto their feathers by the thrashings of the victims and victimizers.

When their turn comes, and they finally set themselves to feed on both the living and the dead, they hop into the pool to gain better vantage as they rip and pull at flesh: and they, too, are trapped, unable to escape.

And so they all perish, those who have entered this killing field to slaughter the powerless. Bubbling from the depths of the earth, a deadly, viscous asphalt formation only three or four inches in thickness has seized victims and killers alike.

The dark pool gradually, inexorably closes over all of them, entombing them in its asphalt preservative, conserving their bones and the history of this carnage—for the nearly four hundred centuries to come.

1

Approximately Forty Thousand Years Later

"IT'S the pits." Dropping the receiver into its cradle, Detective Joe Cameron grinned across the homicide table at Detective Kate Delafield. "The world-famous La Brea Tar Pits."

He tucked the follow-up report he was working on into a shelf of his four-tier file and climbed to his feet, stretching his lanky frame to slide his jacket from a hanger on the clothes tree. "DB behind a park bench. Being the stiff's less than ten thousand years old, Sergeant Hansen thinks we should take a look."

"He would," Kate said, slapping the Gonzales murder book closed and sliding the blue binder into a desk drawer. She reached for her shoulder bag, grateful that she and Cameron were number one on the rotation, even if it was odds on the dead body would turn out to be a result of natural causes. Anything was preferable to beating herself bloody over the Aloysius Gonzales fiasco.

The homicide table was devoid of other occupants, and the entire detectives squad room was relatively quiet; except for a group clustered in low-toned conversation beside the burglary table, the men and women at the various tables were immersed in paperwork, obeying LAPD's ever-present imperative of keep up or drown.

In the parking lot behind Wilshire Division, Cameron climbed into the passenger side of the Caprice. "Cremate your balls in here,'' he muttered, yanking his tie loose.

There was no insinuation in the remark; after three weeks with this junior partner, Kate had learned that Cameron seemed inclined toward neither sexism nor homophobia. He left his door wide open, waiting for her to start the engine and the air conditioning, choosing dust over heat. The dust was fierce, a fine silt billowing up from the construction project adjacent to the station where a new facility would add more West Bureau functions and create new parking problems.

Gingerly bouncing her hands on the steering wheel to locate a safe hold, Kate leaned back into the sun-baked seat as if to transmit all the concentrated warmth up her arms. Heat eased the stiffness that seemed to be a permanent souvenir from the bullet she had taken in her left shoulder during a botched arrest a year and a half ago.

As she pulled out of the parking lot onto Venice Boulevard, Cameron extracted a pair of aviator sunglasses from the breast pocket of his jacket and donned them, then studied the Reporting District Map for Wilshire Division. ''Seven-two-two,'' he said, identifying the area for the La Brea Tar Pits.

''Right,'' she said shortly. A transfer from Devonshire, Cameron had just been promoted into Homicide and needed to familiarize himself with Wilshire, to gain a feel for a territory far more diverse than his previous assignment at LAPD's farthest outlying division in the San Fernando Valley. As part of his training, he would be the lead detective for the first time if this investigation turned out to be a murder; he would be put in nominal charge under her supervision and oversight. But she was in no mood to offer her usual mentoring and running commentary whenever she rode with him.

The usually talkative Cameron cinched up his tie as the car cooled, and he peered out his side window; she was left to scowl into the traffic, her mind still churning through the details of the Gonzales morass.

As she turned onto Wilshire Boulevard, she understood that Cameron was restraining himself because of her mood. It was unfair, she conceded, to take her anger out on him. The Gonzales case was none of his doing.

"Never thought I'd get to see the Tar Pits this way," she offered.

Hitching his sunglasses up on his nose as he turned to her, he said incredulously, "You've never been to the most famous place in the whole division?"

Rankled by his response to her effort to be considerate, she retorted, "As far as I'm concerned, the most famous place in my whole division is CBS. And maybe the Farmer's Market."

"Famous only in America," he returned. "You've lived in L.A. how long?"

"Forever." A white-lettered green sign on the median strip of Wilshire announced Museum Row on the Miracle Mile. The miracle was yet to occur along this undistinguished strip of Wilshire, but the L.A. County Museum of Art was indeed a jewel, she thought, and a *real* museum. She remembered when the new La Brea Tar Pits museum had opened in the mid-seventies, and that it hadn't been much of a big deal; there was no reason to think any differently now, even if some stupid movie had recently featured a volcano rumbling up from its depths to obliterate West L.A.

"There's a lot more to the place than you think. It's remarkable." Cameron shook his head. "I bet you've driven past it thousands of times."

"Tens of thousands," she said without remorse. "And every single time, I see the replicas of those prehistoric animals from the street. Tar pits and fossils just don't ring my chimes."

"My dad took me there before they even built the museum. He loved it. So did I."

Another reason not to go, she thought. Parents and squealing kids.

"Body's behind the main lake pit," he said, "so your best bet is Curson."

"Roger," she said, amused that he was now directing her around her own division.

She pulled up behind four black-and-whites parked on Curson, their revolving light bars hurling more brilliance into the radiant sunshine, their radios emitting endless staccato squawking.

Cameron's remarks had piqued her curiosity, and when she got out of the car, she paused to inspect the museum, a structure tucked into the contours of a smoothly mown green hill set well back from the street. Squat and square, it was nonetheless quietly impressive. The roof, separated from the main structure by a complex composition of pillars and crosshatched girders, was a massive, brown-toned stone frieze of carvings depicting prehistoric animal scenes. As she accompanied Cameron under a canopy of shade trees and onto the curving sidewalk that skirted the museum building, a hot, sluggish current of air carrying the pungent, cloying smell of petroleum filled her nostrils. A horde of tourists flowed along a wide, shrubbery-lined brick pathway that angled downward to the museum, toward glass doors over which bold lettering announced:

GEORGE C. PAGE MUSEUM
LA BREA DISCOVERIES

Across from the building was a solid-granite elevated observation platform crowded with young children. Ineffectually herded by a few harried adults, they punched and pulled at one another to gain better position on the platform, shrilling their excitement at what police action they were able to glimpse.

"What's the matter with grown-ups these days?" she

groused to Cameron. "Television's one thing. A real homicide scene is no place for children."

"I don't know that it isn't," he said. "Maybe a dead stranger's a painless way for kids to know the reality of death."

She did not reply. This was hardly the time to argue. Beyond two rows of park benches lining the pathway she had spotted the first barrier of yellow police tape, several dozen onlookers clustered behind it. But Cameron was a fool if he thought anything could prepare you for the reality of permanent loss, and she ought to know.

Sergeant Fred Hansen waited at the perimeter of the tape; Officer Pete Johnson, standing beside him, logged in his posse box her arrival and Cameron's. She returned their nods and pulled her notebook and pen from her shoulder bag. Looking past Hansen to see that four other uniformed officers guarded the scene, she cast the briefest of glances at the figure sprawled facedown on the grassy earth.

"Something special here, Fred," she said. The heated, petroleum-laden air was oppressive.

Hansen shrugged. "Kate, I just think maybe."

She wrote down the time and date, 10:35 A.M., August 21, and the approximate temperature, ninety plus degrees. Then she asked, "What have you got so far?"

"Four New Zealanders found him right after the place opened at ten. Ran in to the museum gift shop. The woman on the information desk called it in. Paramedics arrived a minute after we did, pronounced him. White male, looks to be in his seventies."

"And?"

"Nothing more, except the way he looks."

Kate ignored his gesture toward the body, unwilling to be detoured from her method. "ID?"

"Nothing on that yet."

"Who touched him?" Cameron asked, writing in his

notebook. A left-hander, his wide wedding band glinted in the sun.

"Paramedics. The Kiwis only took a look—that's all anybody needs to do."

"Yeah, you can tell from here," Cameron said.

Hansen said, "They left, real upset. Staying at the Mondrian through Friday, I've got their names and room numbers if we need a statement. No witnesses so far. We're spread out trying to find somebody who saw something, but this place is a real bear—all tourists and kids. That's all I've got, folks."

Kate nodded. After many years of working with her, Hansen knew her approach, and he would now wait until after she surveyed the entire scene for further instructions.

There was not much to take in. On a clean page of her notebook she wrote the compass points from where she stood facing west, then made a quick, rough diagram of an oblong patch of grass perhaps fifty feet by thirty, formed by intersecting pathways, two of which ran off into a parklike distance. She drew rectangles for the four gray wooden benches embedded into the pathway, and forks for three trees with thin, pale bark defaced with initials. She inked in a pole indicating the light standard at the western perimeter, then let her gaze drift upward, taking in several bushy heads of palm trees above a distant cluster of trees, and the soft green facade of the art museum, thinking sacrilegiously that its rooftop sculptures looked like a collection of surfboards. North, across the path, a white pedestal displayed the bust of a man wearing a jacket and tie. Behind him and directly to her right, the orangish Park La Brea apartment complex provided a distant frame for the Page Museum. South of the death scene, to the left of the path on which she stood, a wire mesh fence fronted a pool of water, its dark, ruffled surface visible through reeds and brush. She lightly shaded in an expanse of grass behind the farthest bench, and for the final element in her sketch, inscribed an X for the position of the corpse on the grass. The area was not secluded nor was it off the regular tourist track behind the lake pool; anyone coming from any direction on the grounds could have found the body— or perhaps caused this death.

"His hands," Cameron said from beside her.

"Give me a minute," she said quietly, but she was exasperated at this break in her concentration. A new partner was a royal pain. It had taken a bone-lazy Ed Taylor the better part of five years to respect her methods, and Torrie, whose faults did not include Taylor's sloppiness, had required a year to adjust to Kate's style. Now there was someone else to break in. Not that she would wish to have either Ed Taylor or Torrie Holden back . . .

She pulled her attention back to the scene, focusing on the dead man. Dressed in baggy dark pants and a maroon polo shirt, he lay prone on grass yellowed by the summer sun. In so placid a scene, the body seemed unusually grotesque, one arm bent sharply back at waist level, the other raised and stretched downward over the shoulders, the clawed fingers of both hands straining, for no discernible reason, toward the middle of the back.

"You were smart to call us in right away, Fred," she said, and Hansen's dour face lightened with a faint smile. He lifted the tape as Kate made her first move to enter the scene.

Taking care with every step, Cameron in her wake, she edged her way to the body. There was not much to disturb; the grass seemed devoid of objects other than a few stray leaves. She hunkered down a cautious distance from the corpse. The finality of this death seemed a melancholy contrast to the smell of sun-baked grass and earth, mingled with the odor of petroleum from the tar pits.

The man was gray-haired and gray-bearded, with thin

hair combed straight back and only slightly disheveled, his beard an inch or so in length and well-trimmed. His face was burrowed into the turf from his death throes, but one glazed, staring, milky eye was partially visible. She touched the back of her hand to the dead man's cheek. The warmth of his skin could be from sun but more likely was his true body temperature. In some parts of Los Angeles a dead body could lie on the street for hours while people walked around it, but these were more wholesome surroundings filled with tourists unacquainted with the city's less-than-endearing cultural quirks. This man had died within the past hour.

Mindful that she was Cameron's mentor, she said, "What do you think, Joe?"

Hunkered down beside her, he was writing in his notebook. "The guy's trying to grab at what was killing him. So it's no heart attack unless his heart's in a real strange place."

She peered at the heavy-mesh maroon shirt. "If there's any blood, I don't see it."

"Could be some, though—the shirt's the same color as blood."

"Wet blood would be visible," she argued.

"Maybe his kidney exploded."

She answered Cameron's attempt at levity with a smile. "An interesting hypothesis." Cameron was relatively young, and whatever his prior history in police work might be, he was inexperienced in having to examine corpses and notify spouses and children whose lives would change forever from the calamity of death. From this dead man's age, there might be considerable family, even grandchildren . . .

Cameron said, "Could be something crazy, like a bee sting—the guy goes into anaphylactic shock."

"Now that's a really interesting hypothesis," Kate said. "You could even be right."

She reached to the dead man and pinched a piece of

shirt sleeve between her thumb and forefinger, using it to lift one of the clawed hands. It bore a wedding band thinned and finely scratched by age, and a wristwatch, a Seiko with a worn leather band. Seeing that the palm of the hand was crisscrossed by faint black smears, she examined the fingers one by one, noting black residue under several nails. She lowered the hand and rose to her feet. She moved over to the bench.

It was a common enough park bench, with chipped gray paint, except that it was patterned with dried-out strings of tar, as was the pavement around it. The tar looked old and dry, the bench reasonably safe to sit on, especially in the kind of casual clothes the dead man wore.

"The bench looks like a canvas Jackson Pollock just started," Cameron remarked.

Immersed in her own observations, she crossed the path to the chain-link fence and peered through it to the lake. The opaque surface was pocked with rings—from tar bubbling up, she presumed. She remembered reading somewhere that this particular tar pool was kept flooded with water to reduce its potential as a fire hazard. The surface was imprinted with refracted reflections of the brush around it, the heads of a few emperor palms on Wilshire Boulevard, and the geometric shape of a building. She could make out the long tusks of a huge prehistoric mammoth curving out over the water, one of the replicas for which this place was known; the sculptures were positioned in and around the lake.

"Bizarre," Cameron said from beside her. "This place, so . . ." He searched for a word, ". . . elemental. All this prehistoric stuff and it's sitting right in the middle of a modern, cutting-edge city . . ."

"You're right," she murmured, gazing at the building reflected in the tar pool beside the tusks of the mammoth. "It's an incredible juxtaposition."

"I always imagined Jimmy Hoffa could be dumped in here."

"Why not? Along with Judge Crater."

"Maybe Amelia Earhardt."

"That one's a bit of a stretch." Kate walked back to the park bench.

Examining the dark striations, she suggested, "A freaky high wind blew some of the tar from the lake onto the bench a long time ago."

"Makes sense." Cameron pointed to several faint scrapes in the tar splotches. "Maybe the victim was sitting here when whatever happened to him happened. So first he claws at the bench and then he staggers to his feet. It could explain what's on his hands and under his nails."

"Maybe," Kate said, pleased that Cameron had also seen the residue under the victim's nails. Hearing children's voices again rise from the viewing platform behind her, she thought that unlike an art museum, this place seemed the kind you didn't visit alone. Had someone accompanied this old man? Could a grandson be lost and wandering the premises?

The dead man could have perished from natural causes. But, like Hansen, she smelled something odd here, and it wasn't just the tar. She said to Cameron, "Let's do what we can while we're waiting for the coroner's investigator."

2

"**N**O running!'' ordered a tall, gray-haired woman, clapping her hands at a gaggle of energetic children she was ushering through the lobby of the George C. Page Museum.

Entry to the exhibits was fenced off by an information desk and gift shop filled with light from the glass wall of an atrium through which glowed a vista of plants and trees. Beyond a kiosk that collected a six-dollar adult admission, Kate glimpsed the crouched dark brown skeleton of a predator. To her right were a few fabric-covered benches, and rest rooms and pay phones, and an unidentifiable hexagonal exhibit surrounded by noisy, enthusiastic children pulling at levers. The gift shop, modest but attractively laid out in a semicircle, exhibited its wares under glass counters and in display cases offering plastic replicas of fossils, games and puzzles, toys, coffee mugs, cards, pens and pencils, a selection of books, and the ubiquitous stacks of T-shirts offered at any tourist attraction. A few posters of dinosaurs hung on the walls.

"Are there dinosaur bones in here?'' she asked Cameron. *That* she would find interesting, especially since she and Aimee now owned a videotape of *Jurassic Park.*

"Not in this particular museum.''

Her question had been answered by a young Japanese woman at the information desk who wore a crisp white blouse adorned by an X-shaped version of a black bow tie. "Everyone asks," she said, smiling. "Our fossils go back as far as forty thousand years. Dinosaurs were extinct sixty-five million years ago. We carry dinosaur posters because we get so many requests."

Kate nodded; now she was even less impressed with the place.

"But we do have the world's most amazing and important collection of fossils preserved in asphalt," the young woman continued as if she had read Kate's mind and was trying to change it.

"Such as what?" Kate asked politely, sighing inwardly as she reached into her shoulder bag for her notebook along with the leather case holding her badge and ID. She and Cameron had processed the scene, what little processing they could do, and she had given Hansen her cellular phone so that he could ring her pager when the coroner's van arrived.

"Sabertooth cats," the young woman was saying. "Dire wolves, bison. Huge mastodons, woolly mammoths—"

Kate knew there was no hurrying the busy coroner's office, and any attempt to do so could boomerang into deliberate foot-dragging. Until an investigator from the coroner's office looked at the body of that man behind the park bench and gave an indication of whether the death required investigation, she was stymied.

"Camels, bears the size of elephants. Insects, plants, huge birds. Not to mention La Brea Woman—"

"Impressive," Kate interrupted her, displaying her identification. "I'm Detective Delafield. My partner is Detective Cameron. If we could ask you a few questions . . ."

The young woman's face assumed an expression of gravity; she ran a smoothing hand over her glossy black hair. "This is about the dead guy out there, right?"

Kate nodded, amused that the young woman's switching of gears included slipping into standard slang. "May we know your name?"

"Yeah. Sure. Joanne Takani." Staring at Kate's notebook, she spelled her last name.

Cameron asked gently, "What can you tell us about the man out there, Joanne?"

"Him? I haven't got a clue. A bunch of tourists came tearing in here just after we opened, yelling about finding this dead guy, and I called nine-one-one. That's it. He have a heart attack?"

"Possibly. We're not sure yet. Thank you, Joanne," Kate said, turning away from her.

"Joanne mentioned La Brea Woman," Cameron said. "A replica of her skeleton's in a display case. She died of a skull fracture ten thousand years ago."

"Really," Kate said with a grin. "So she was murdered? L.A.'s first homicide victim?"

Cameron grinned in return. "Offed with an ax is my guess."

"So right here in this building is L.A.'s first uncleared homicide."

"Unless she was buried here as some kind of ceremony, and that's one possibility. Do you know why they've found so many fossils here?"

Kate shrugged impatiently at what seemed an obvious question. "The tar was like quicksand and the animals sank into it."

"They didn't sink—at least not immediately. The tar isn't that deep. Only a couple of inches, actually. Look at this." He led her toward the hexagonal exhibit where children were pulling on handles with all their might— trying to lift them out of tar.

"Shows you how sticky it actually is," Cameron said. "What happened was, an animal would come to one of the tar pits thinking it was water and get trapped. A predator would hear it scream and figure it had an easy meal. It, too, would get trapped. Then more predators would come along and join the festivities and get themselves trapped, then the vultures would swoop down, and they'd get snared—''

"This town's inhabitants haven't changed very much, have they," Kate observed.

Cameron gestured back toward the kiosk where tickets were sold. "How about looking at some exhibits while we wait?"

"Let's see what the uniforms have come up with in their canvass," she countered. She was in investigation mode, not tourist mode, and she could care less about the flipping exhibits.

Her pager went off. "Can't be," Cameron said.

"No way," Kate agreed as she and Cameron went back outside the museum. A coroner's investigator couldn't possibly have arrived this soon from downtown.

But one had indeed arrived, in the person of Walt Everson, who was making cheerful conversation with Hansen while a technician photographed the scene.

"How very considerate of LAPD to arrange back-to-back calls for us in such a nice part of town," Everson greeted them.

"How are you, Walt?" Kate asked, smiling. She and Everson had collaborated on many death investigations and, in her opinion, he was one of the best in his overworked department. "Do you know Joe Cameron from Devonshire?"

"Don't believe I've had the pleasure."

"You have," Cameron said shortly.

"Sorry about that," Everson said with conspicuous insincerity, his gaze fixed on the photographer who was taking rapid flash pictures. "You homicide detectives all look alike."

Cameron replied tersely, "And here I thought I was prettier than Kate."

"Walt," Kate said, puzzled by Cameron's testy tone, "what do you mean, two calls?"

"West L.A. Young fellow with sixteen stab wounds in a nice pattern around his nipple rings." He inclined his head toward the contorted corpse. "Interesting. If he wasn't already dead, I'd say his back was killing him."

Kate said, "Detective Cameron here has diagnosed an exploded kidney."

"Detective Cameron shows great promise as a pathologist." The photographer began to pack away his equipment, and Everson ducked under the police tape.

"A real smart mouth," Cameron muttered as Everson made his way along the tape-designated path to the body, black bag in hand. "I know we all joke around about this stuff, but I think he's got a genuine taste for it."

Kate exchanged glances with Hansen, who rolled his eyes. Everson had never changed his patter in all the years she had worked with him; and the more gruesome the homicide scene, the harder he wisecracked. As grim as aspects of her own job might be, she could not imagine the compartments she would need to divide off and wall away to examine dead bodies all day, every day, as Everson did, some of them children, some of them unspeakable with damage and decay. She said to Cameron, "Each of us—we do what we need to do."

Everson snapped on two sets of latex gloves and knelt, bag open beside him, sitting back on his haunches to evaluate the body on the grass before he touched it. Then he worked loose the portion of the man's maroon shirt tucked into his pants, pulled it up toward the shoulders. He beckoned to Kate and Cameron and waited as they maneuvered their way under the police tape and toward him.

Under the maroon shirt the dead man's chalky skin was liberally peppered with freckles and large liver spots that suggested years of sun exposure. But on his lower back a fist-sized pinkish smear coated the freckles, and within it was a small clot of coagulated blood. Cameron's right, Kate thought. It is a bee sting.

"Detective Cameron, you were right," Everson said.

Kate looked at Everson in bewilderment. No one had mentioned anything about a bee sting to him.

"His kidney did explode," Everson said. "Aided substantially by the implement that was plunged into it."

Cameron said in disbelief, "He was *knifed*?"

"Ice-picked, is more like it." Everson extracted an elegantly thin gold pen from his breast pocket and used it as a pointer. "Look closer. You can see the imprint of an instrument inserted to the hilt."

Crouching down, Kate squinted at the small mound of congealed blood. Surrounded by the irregular pinkish stain, it was exactly centered in a circle perhaps an inch in diameter pressed into the skin. She had seen ice pick homicides, but those wounds had been inflicted during bloody gang fights or had been multiple bloody punctures perpetrated in a rage killing, with blood spatter everywhere.

"How can this be a knifing?" Cameron protested. "There's hardly any blood."

"If you don't hit a vein or artery, very little exterior blood's not unusual with one puncture from a sharply pointed, thin blade. The blade's probably broken off inside, further sealing off the wound."

"You'd think some blood would make it through his shirt."

"Maybe it did." Everson pinched the fabric of the shirt. "This is a pretty heavy mesh . . ." He released the fabric and held up his gloved fingers; they were coated with pink. "The shirt absorbed some of it." With his gold pen, he described a wide circle above the man's back. "Inside is where this dude is one massive hemorrhage. Roll him over and he'll look six months pregnant. Inside he's a balloon filled up with blood."

"Take a look at his—"

Cameron broke off as Kate, knowing he was about to mention the corpse's hands, poked him sharply with her elbow.

"Take a look at what?" Everson said, looking up.

"All those liver spots," Cameron said. "The guy was a candidate for skin cancer."

"An outcome more preferable to an ice pick, is that your point, Detective, excuse the pun?" Everson issued a brief cackle of laughter.

He picked up one of the dead man's hands. Plucking an instrument from his black bag, he peered through its magnifying lens. "Looks like he was playing in the tar pits."

Kate said, gesturing, "The bench over there has old tar stains all over it."

"Does it," Everson said, and looked at her sardonically. "My guess is, you two took a pretty good gander at the deceased before I got here."

Kate said carefully, "We're very aware that touching the body is your province."

"Senior homicide detectives like yourself sometimes tend to take on some arrogance about what they can do at a crime scene," Everson said, pulling a tape recorder and a notebook from his black bag. "I wouldn't want newer detectives like young Joe here thinking that's ever a good idea."

"I hear you, Walt," she said.

He nodded. "We'll bag the hands, find out for sure what's under his nails. After your technicians fingerprint the bench or whatever you plan to have them do, you or your partner sit over there. See how you can fit an ice pick under the bench back at about the same place where this poor son of a bitch got it."

"I already believe you, Walt," Kate said.

Cameron said, "You're thinking maybe somebody came up behind him and did the deed and then he got up and staggered over here and croaked?''

''We prefer to say expired. But yes, I'm betting somebody knew exactly where an ice pick needs to go. Maybe even knelt behind him to get a good angle and lots of leverage, and proceeded to do an Irish jig with the ice pick, yank it up and down and around inside him so it pierced and tore up everything, including his lungs and heart, before the blade snapped off. The victim managed to get to his feet. And then, as you so nicely phrased it, croaked.''

Kate was sickened. Cameron, looking a shade paler, asked quietly, ''Could a woman do this as well as a man?''

''Sure. Doesn't take any strength at all to penetrate the human body with a thin, pointed instrument so long as you're not going through bone.''

''Looks like a pro to me,'' Cameron muttered to no one in particular. ''Like this is a hit.''

''Grandpa here is a Mafia don?'' Everson mocked.

His lips tightening, Cameron shrugged. Everson said to Kate, ''His temperature's dead-on normal, you should excuse the expression, so TOD's within the standard three-hour limit. But you know that already—no way he'd lie out here more than a few minutes before one of these solid citizens found him.''

Kate nodded and dutifully wrote this official pronouncement of the time of death in her notebook.

''Nasty but quick,'' Everson said. ''A better death than melanoma,'' he added, picking up his tape recorder. ''Now, if you two gumshoes will excuse me, I have work to do.''

''Walt, would you check him for ID?''

He looked at her in feigned surprise. ''You're telling me you actually *didn't* sneak a look before I got here? What are homicide detectives coming to these days?'' Grasping the dead man's belt, he angled the right side of the torso slightly upward, patted the front pocket, then reached in and extracted a thin, shabby wallet. Climbing to his feet, he handed it to Kate.

The driver's license was behind a yellowed plastic window. "Herman Layton," she read to Cameron. "DOB eleven, eleven, twenty-one." Which made the victim five months younger than her own father, if her father were still alive. "An address on Tilden in West L.A." She read it off, and he took it down.

"That's where I just came from," Everson said. "Not that street, but close by on Veteran. Over by UCLA. If I'd known, I could have made the notification for you."

"I wish you could have," she said. Relatives in a state of shock tended to be more incautious and forthcoming with information, and she often learned crucial facts; but she dreaded next-of-kin notification. She inspected the bill compartment of the wallet and counted three twenties and four singles. It wasn't a robbery, unless the attacker had been interrupted. Opposite the driver's license was a yellowed photo of a young, patrician-looking blonde wearing a black graduation gown and a mortarboard.

"We'll take possession of the photo," she said to Everson.

He nodded, recording it in his notebook, and she slid the picture out of the wallet and into the breast pocket of her jacket. The same compartment of the wallet held a single white card. Beneath the printed statement, Person to Be Notified in the Event of Death or Injury, was handwritten *Peri Layton, Ph.D.,* with two phone numbers, one of them marked UCLA, the other under an address on Ophir Drive, also in West L.A.

Producing a plastic bag for the wallet, Everson said, "When was the last time you saw one of these notification cards in somebody's wallet?"

"Can't remember," Kate said. "Maybe never."

"Very considerate of him."

"Peri Layton," Everson mused, studying the card over her shoulder. "Name rings a bell."

"You know, it does to me, too," Cameron said. "It really does."

Kate looked at both of them.

"Damn, I can't think," Cameron said.

Everson shrugged. "Me, either. The bell's ringing, but nobody's answering." Again he hunkered down beside the body. "Go get whoever did this poor son of a bitch," he said in dismissal.

3

BOUGAINVILLEA—crimson, orange, white—climbed up over many of the rooftops on Tilden, a lushly landscaped street south of Sunset, its gardens overflowing with roses and impatiens. North of Montana Avenue, the street on which Kate had once lived, it lay tucked between Bentley and Veteran, the avenue that ran alongside the vast, quiet acres of green grass and white crosses in the Veterans Administration Cemetery. The address listed on Herman Layton's driver's license was a guest house at the rear of a white ranch-style house roofed with rough, oversize dark brown shingles. A curtain fluttered in the street-facing house as Kate and Cameron made their way to a mossy flagstone path woven between well-tended shrubbery.

The small cottage in the rear, also white and with the same style roof, bristled with bars on all of its shuttered windows. Kate knocked repeatedly, even as her instincts told her that she would receive no answer.

She and Cameron retraced their steps to the main house, and she rang the doorbell. On the evidence of that telltale flutter of the curtain, Kate rang insistently.

Finally, a querulous male voice commanded in a heavy Yiddish accent, "Go away, I have a religion. I have no interest in yours."

"Police officer," Kate called back. "Please look

through your peephole, sir, I'll hold up my identification.''

As a series of locks scraped open, Cameron muttered, "First time I've ever been taken for a Jehovah's Witness.''

A bearded wraith of a man, suspenders over his hunched shoulders securing baggy pants, edged the door open. Kate introduced herself and Cameron; the man nodded but did not otherwise respond. She inquired politely, "May we come in, sir?''

The man shook his head in vigorous refusal. "Why do the police come to my house?''

"The man in the cottage behind you—''

Again the man shook his head vehemently. "I know nothing about my tenant.''

Kate was accustomed to suspicion and hostility in the eastern and southern areas of her own division but not in this upper-class section of West L.A. where police protection was assumed and welcomed. "This is important, sir. Does anyone live back there with Mr. Layton?''

"No. I know nothing about him. I mind my business, Mr. Layton minds his business.''

"How long has he been your tenant?''

"I tell you nothing.''

"May we know your name?''

"I tell you nothing.'' The old man began to close his door.

"Mr. Layton is dead,'' Kate stated baldly.

The old man froze in place. Then, fully opening his door and standing aside, he pronounced, "If you say so right away, we don't play a guessing game.''

She nodded. He was right, from his standpoint.

She and Cameron followed the man, who shuffled in front of them on slippered feet, into a small, scantly furnished front parlor where he gestured for them to sit, selecting for himself an overstuffed armchair and leaving for her and Cameron the matching sofa, its back covered by a coarsely woven white afghan.

Cameron said, "May we know your name, sir?"

"Meyer Silverman. It's good you don't let this inefficient woman do all the talking."

Cameron's color deepened. "She's my partner," he said. "We both do the talking."

Given so blatant a clue as to who would be most effective in conducting this interview, Kate sat back on the hard sofa, thinking that Cameron's propensity to reveal emotion by changing facial color was a serious shortcoming in a homicide detective. Still, his natty jacket and tie did not diminish the element of toughness in him; and the taut leanness of his body, the tight economy of his features, suggested someone who could take care of himself. Her father would classify him as a man's man.

Cameron said, "Detective Delafield asked how long Mr. Layton had been a tenant."

Silverman stroked his beard as he searched his memory. "He came here the summer of 1970. Twenty-seven years."

"What do you know about him?"

"Nothing. I mind my business."

"Nothing, Mr. Silverman?" Cameron said politely but with an edge in his tone. "In twenty-seven years you know nothing?"

"I mind my business," he said. "He puts his check in my mailbox every month, he goes his way, I go mine."

Cameron jerked a thumb to the curtained windows behind him. "You have no bars on your house. Why the bars on Mr. Layton's windows?"

"He told me he had to have them." Silverman shrugged. "He argued to have me pay. I told him they were his bars, not mine."

"When was this?"

"When he moved in. The same week."

"What was he afraid of?"

Again he shrugged. "We all have things to be afraid of."

Judging that Meyer Silverman was in his seventies, Kate wondered if the origin of his suspicious nature had been an internment camp in World War Two, if he had been a victim of Nazi terror.

Cameron asked, "Did he ever have any visitors?"

"I mind my business."

"Yes, we understand that. But over the past twenty-seven years, you've seen people on the pathway to his house, even by accident."

Silverman adopted the classic posture of reluctant co-operation, crossing his legs and folding his arms tightly across his chest. "Maybe sometimes, yes. I don't know who they are."

"Does anyone else live here in the house with you?"

"Not anymore," Silverman said softly.

"I see," Cameron said, his tone muted in sympathy. "The people you saw, were they men? Or women?"

"Men, different men, two women, sometimes. I know nothing more. Why all these questions?"

Kate fished from her breast pocket the photo she had removed from Herman Layton's wallet and handed it to Cameron.

Cameron leaned forward, holding up the photo. "Is this one of the two women?"

Unfolding his arms to extract a pair of glasses from the pocket of his baggy pants, Silverman donned them; the lenses were so smeared with fingerprints that Kate wondered how they could be any improvement on his eyesight.

"I think maybe . . . yes, the younger one," he said, closing one eye and squinting at the photo with the other. "This is an old picture." He removed the glasses and fumbled them back into his pocket. He said with clear misgiving, "What happened to Mr. Layton?"

"He's been killed," Cameron said.

"Killed? Like in an accident?"

"Not an accident. I'm sorry, Mr. Silverman, that's all we can tell you until we inform his relatives. Is Mr. Layton's name the only one on his lease?"

Silverman nodded.

Cameron said, "We need you to let us into his house."

He held up hands splotched with liver spots. "He put in the bars, he changed the locks."

Kate exchanged glances with Cameron. For at least the last twenty-seven years of his life, Herman Layton had lived behind bars, in a house well-concealed from the street, trusting no one, not even his landlord.

"Ever have any problems with Mr. Layton?" Cameron inquired.

"No. No problems. He seemed a good man. Quiet." He added resignedly, "The city, today they make you keep tenants, you can't raise the rent to what it should be. When you get a new tenant you have to keep who you get no matter if they destroy the place."

Kate nodded to Cameron and rose to her feet. Regardless of Silverman's statement that he did not have a key, she would have an officer assigned to the premises until she and Cameron could get into that cottage and conduct a search. Cameron said, "We'll be back later today, Mr. Silverman, and we'll be going into that house."

"And me," he said dourly, "I need to find a new tenant."

Several blocks away from the address on Tilden, Kate pulled up to the curb across from a beige frame house with a used brick foundation and matching driveway, the house elevated on a low hillside swathed in ice plant and ivy.

"Nice," Cameron said.

"Aren't they all," she returned. This West L.A. neighborhood, tucked in between the western perimeter of the UCLA campus and the San Diego Freeway, possessed the same air of refinement and sophistication as nearby Brentwood had before the O. J. Simpson debacle landed it in the tabloids and on tourists' drive-by lists.

Kate could hear footsteps in a rapid march to the door, and before she could finish announcing herself and hold up her identification to the peephole, the door was wrenched open.

The woman in the doorway was the one in the photo in Herman Layton's wallet, except she was at least twenty years older, and the photo had not prepared Kate for so ascetic a face nor eyes that were willow-green, the color heated to vibrancy by intelligence and the penetration of the woman's gaze. Kate and Cameron extended their badges and ID cards, and Kate, mesmerized by the face and eyes, uttered automatically, "I'm Detective Delafield. This is my partner, Detective Cameron." Remembering the Ph.D. designation on the card in Herman Layton's wallet, Kate inquired, "Would you be Dr. Peri Layton?" This woman on first impression easily matched the distinction of such a degree.

"I would be Peri Layton." The voice was Lauren Bacall–throaty.

Kate wondered if Peri Layton was dressed for an appointment or if she habitually wore a silk shirt, dressy slacks, and desert boots even at noontime on a hot August day. "We need to talk to you, Dr. Layton. May we come in?"

"Only if you drop the Dr. Layton business and call me Peri." She spun on her heel and led them at a brisk pace down a corridor as she continued, "Unless of course the two of you happen to be students in my class and I've somehow failed to recognize you."

Entering a huge, sunlit room, Kate was vaguely aware

of one entire wall covered with framed posters and photographs before her senses were overwhelmed by the riot of flowers in a garden seemingly brought into the room through floor-level windows. The room, comfortably cooled by air conditioning, was perfumed by a profusion of roses in vases on a desk and on several casual tables.

Peri Layton seated herself in a leather chair in front of a bookcase, its contents a tumult, and hoisted her booted feet onto a matching leather ottoman; a jumble of books lay splayed open on the table beside her. "Please sit down and tell me what can I do for the Los Angeles Police Department." Her remarkable eyes settled on Kate and studied her with frank curiosity.

Nonplussed by the compelling gaze, dreading the words she would speak to this clearly unprepared woman, Kate took a seat on the futon, Cameron beside her. "Are we correct that Herman Layton is your father?"

"You are. He is." Peri Layton's face—and her unsettling charisma—shut down so suddenly and completely that Kate thought of a screen saver blanking out a computer monitor. "What about him?" She flipped her feet off the ottoman and sat up, leaning toward Kate.

"I'm afraid we have bad news."

"What bad news? Tell me." The green eyes skewered Kate.

"I'm sorry to have to tell you that his body was found about an hour ago—"

"His body. He's dead, then? My father's dead?"

"I'm sorry, Dr. Layton—"

"I told you to call me Peri," she snapped. "What happened?"

"He's been killed—"

"By a car? In an accident?"

"No. I'm sorry to have to tell you—"

"Will you for God's sake just *tell* me?"

I'm trying to, Kate wanted to shout. "He's been stabbed to death."

"Freaking Jesus." She lifted a long, slender hand briefly to her cheek. "Where?"

"The La Brea Tar Pits."

"Dear God. His favorite place in the world." The smile that fluttered over Peri Layton's sculpted features was ghastly in its mismatch with the shock and anguish in her eyes. "Or at least the world he lived in. He's— he was a regular at Rancho La Brea. He was stabbed? With what? Who did it?"

"I'm sorry, we don't have all those answers yet." Kate offered, "His body was found by some tourists about ten-thirty this morning behind one of the tar pits."

"They're not exactly tar pits, you know. It's actually asphalt. . . ." Peri Layton had leaned farther forward, hands clenched, her slender body taut with tension. "What bubbles up through the asphalt in those pits is methane gas produced by the subterranean decay of organic material." Her voice was a whisper, the struggle to gain emotional control so palpable that Kate did what she could to help her.

"I didn't know that," she said.

"Hardly anyone does." Peri's voice strengthened as she added, "La Brea Tar Pits is not only an inaccurate term, it's redundant. *Brea* is Spanish for tar. The correct name is Rancho La Brea . . ." She cleared her throat and said in a normal tone, "So—was this a mugging, a gang sort of thing?"

Kate looked at her with respect. "It doesn't fit any sort of profile for that kind of assault," she said. "It appears nothing was taken from your father. When you look over his effects, perhaps you'll be able to confirm this to us." It might well be a thrill killing, she thought, perpetrated by one of the monsters roaming the cities of America, striking at random and then moving on, snake-like, invisible, virtually impossible to track.

"How did . . . Did my father suffer?"

"It appears he went quickly," Kate said. She could see no reason to report to this woman Everson's conjecture on how her father's internal organs had been ruptured. "We won't know everything until the autopsy."

"Autopsy?"

"It's required in a murder case."

"Yes, of course it is. A murder case . . ."

Watching Peri Layton struggle to grasp the dimensions of what had befallen her, Kate fended off the sympathy intruding on the dispassionate corner of her mind that knew that the most convincing grief was often expressed by killers themselves. But she needed to establish rapport, and obeying Peri Layton's wish to call her by her first name seemed a good beginning. "Peri," she said, "who would want to harm him?"

"I can't imagine . . ."

"Did your father have any enemies?"

"Any enemies . . ."

Peri's eyes were glazed with thought as well as pain, and Kate looked at Cameron to signal him to wait. But Cameron was fixated on the dozen or so posters and photographs on the walls. Kate glanced at them; they were all of Peri in khaki pants and shirt, in the company of what appeared to be scientists, perhaps geologists, in various attitudes of examining or excavating rocks against a desert backdrop.

Peri finally said, "My father is—was an unconventional man, and a very difficult one. . . ."

"The Footsteps of Time," Cameron uttered. "Are you that Peri Layton?"

"I am," Peri said quietly. "Thank you for knowing my work. It's been a very long time since that book was published."

"It's a privilege to meet you," he said. Pointing at the poster centered among all the others, he asked, "Is that Mary Leakey?"

"It is."

"At the footprints?"

She nodded. "The G2 Trail. If it weren't for my father, I'd have never been there to be part of the excavation of those footprints."

Kate had no idea what they were talking about, but she remained silent to allow Cameron to establish his own rapport.

Cameron said, "Forgive me, Peri, I realize this is hardly the time."

"I appreciate your consideration, Detective Cameron."

In the silence that followed, Kate asked, "Do you have siblings? Are there other relatives?"

"My mother. I'm an only child," Peri replied. "Mother lives in Hollywood. My parents separated about twenty-five years ago."

"I know this is hard," Kate said, "but we need a next of kin to make a formal identification."

"I'll do it," Peri said, her lips tightening. "My mother's a strong woman, but there's no reason for her to go through this—and I deal with death in my profession just as you do in yours."

Not flesh-and-blood-and-guts death, Kate thought. Ancient, scientific, laboratory death, if those photographs are any indication. She asked, "Did you get on well with your father?"

"You mean did I go to Rancho La Brea this morning and kill him?"

Kate glanced down at her notebook, wondering if this response had its origin in indignation at the question or in some sort of self-protection, or was it something else yet again. "You said he was difficult. Did *you* find him difficult?"

Cameron followed up, "Are you telling us that you didn't get on well with your father?"

"My father and I got along fine," Peri retorted. "I

guess I read too many mystery novels where everybody's a suspect.''

Kate was pleased with Cameron; he had not let his esteem for Peri Layton interfere with his ability to ask good questions.

"Why don't we get one mystery-novel issue over with," Cameron said pleasantly. "Where were you this morning?"

Thumping her feet back onto the ottoman, giving Cameron a poisonous glance, Peri muttered, "Here." She gestured to the books on the table beside her. "Right here, preparing my lecture for tonight. I don't have an alibi. So arrest me."

"Peri," Kate intervened, "I asked how you got on with your father because we know nothing about him, and we're trying to put some kind of picture together very quickly so we'll know which way to go."

"I'm sorry." Peri rubbed her face with both hands, then ran her fingers back through her hair. "I'm just really thrown by this. You expect to lose your parents at some point, but for God's sake, not to murder. We were extremely close. He was closer to me than anyone else in his life," she added.

The note of lament in her voice caused Kate to wonder if it was entirely for her father's death or if it was that he had spent so much of his emotional capital on his only child. Her own father had been like that with her, after the death of her mother.

"How old was he?" Kate asked, even though she knew from his driver's license.

"Seventy-six."

"I assume he was retired?" Kate followed up as Peri Layton nodded, "What did he do before that?"

"He was a technical writer. Moved from job to job, quit for the slightest reason. Someone with my father's skills in that occupation could do it." She shook her head in rueful memory. "It drove my mother crazy."

"Did he make enemies at any of those jobs?"

After a pause, Peri said, "I couldn't say for sure, but nothing stands out. My father waded into more than a few altercations in his day, he was very confrontational and never one to back away from trouble. But he never stuck around anywhere very long, either."

"Except for the house he lived in."

"Yes. I couldn't get him to move in with me even temporarily. Him or my mother, either." She gestured to the garden. "Not even into this wonderful house the foundation's given me till I have to be out of the country again."

"Why did he have those bars on his windows, Peri?"

"It's nothing unusual, believe me." She shrugged. "Just the same old pattern. Every place we lived in, he put in triple locks. He was very mistrustful, suspicious."

"It seems there might have been some basis to it, after all," Cameron observed.

"I can't even imagine . . ." Peri did not finish.

Kate asked, "Was he mistrustful and suspicious for any concrete reason that you can think of?"

"Mother always said it was due to the war. Even so . . ." Peri raised her shoulders and turned her palms up in the universal sign of perplexity. "Growing up, I felt more protected than most people. It seemed to me we had government people around all the time."

"Government people? What was that about?"

"Priceless missing fossils. It was about my father being a Marine officer attached to the American embassy in Beijing in 1941—"

Kate heard a smothered sound from Cameron.

"—and he spent World War Two in a prisoner of war camp near Tientsin—"

"Wait," Cameron interrupted as if no longer able to contain himself. "You talked about him in your book." He clapped a hand to his head as if to further break up the logjam of memory. "Your father was one of the company of Marines who tried to get Peking Man out of China before the war started.''

"Exactly right. Indeed he was.''

The last time Kate felt this excluded from a conversation, she had been trapped in a group that had spent the evening avidly discussing classical music. "I'm sorry,'' she said, "but who or what is Peking Man?''

Peri said to Cameron, "Shall I explain to your partner?''

"Who better? Kate, this is so *amazing . . .*''

A semblance of a smile flitted over Peri's features as she gazed at Kate. "Knowing about Peking Man makes your partner the strange one, not you, Detective Delafield. Few people outside my field have any sort of detailed knowledge about our discoveries. My father did, but even so—he came home from the war not fully realizing what he'd come into contact with—''

"It's the most fascinating story, Kate,'' Cameron interjected.

Annoyed by his interruptions, Kate made a mental note to tell Cameron to correct the tendency.

Peri said, "Peking Man is the colloquial term for the fossil vertebrate remains of one of mankind's earliest ancestors. American and Chinese paleontologists discovered the fossils in a series of finds at Zhoukoudian in China, beginning in 1937. They were one of the first really important discoveries in the history of paleontology.''

This information had been given as if excerpted from a lecture, and Kate supposed that it was. Impressed, she nodded. She had begun to comprehend Cameron's reverence for this woman.

"After Japan invaded China,'' Peri continued, "our government promised temporary custody and protection for the fossils. The paleontologists in Peking had them packed up and ready to go. They were put into the care of my father's company of Marines—they were leaving

China, going by train to the coast to board an American ship.'' Caught up in her own story, Peri shook her head sadly. ''The fossils were moved on December 8, 1941. Back across the International Dateline, it was December 7. Pearl Harbor Day, of course. The train got to the coast—it was surrounded and captured by Japanese soldiers. My father went to a POW camp. The fossils vanished. What happened to them has been a matter of controversy ever since.''

''The Japanese confiscated them?'' Kate suggested, needing to ask the obvious question, her detective's mind engaged on the mystery.

''Some people still think so, but the Japanese did such rigorous searches during their years of occupation it pretty strongly suggests they didn't have them.''

''Or maybe didn't know they did,'' Kate said.

''Or maybe didn't know they did,'' Peri agreed. ''After the war, the search expanded worldwide. My father was interviewed time and again by agents from our government and from Taiwan. Dozens of researchers, too, lots of them from Japan. Quite a number of books and articles came out around that time and again in the seventies. My father had a lifelong interest in paleontology, and he never refused an interview. He never stopped hoping some question from someone would dredge up a memory that would somehow lead to the recovery of Peking Man. . . .'' Peri trailed off, visibly caught up in emotion.

Cameron said, ''From your book, it seemed your father was obsessed.''

''Yes. Yes, he was. My poor father . . . When you've had a hand in the disappearance of some of the most priceless hominid artifacts in the entire history of humankind . . .''

''His obsession apparently had no effect on you,'' Kate observed dryly.

''Apparently not,'' Peri answered, equally deadpan.

"Only to the extent that I became a paleoanthropologist."

Kate exchanged the briefest of smiles with her, then dutifully wrote a condensed version of this information about Herman Layton in her notebook. Interesting as it was, she couldn't see that it had anything to do with this case, other than the odd coincidence of Herman Layton dying at a museum dedicated to prehistoric fossils. "Tell us a little about your mother," she suggested.

"Where do I start? What would you like to know?"

"What's her name and address, Peri?" Cameron asked.

Kate glanced at him approvingly. Good strategy—ask a simple question to get someone talking.

"Arlene," Peri answered. "Arlene Rose Layton," she reported as Cameron wrote in his notebook, and she provided an address on Kenmore Avenue in Hollywood. "She kept my father's name—that's all she kept of him. She couldn't live with his job habits, so she went to college, got her teaching credential. I didn't realize how unhappy she'd been till I was graduated from Berkeley. I took off my mortarboard and she filed for divorce."

The photo in Herman Layton's wallet must have been of that graduation, Kate surmised.

Peri continued, "I've never figured out whether I should be grateful or embarrassed that Mother stayed in a miserable marriage because of me. She's been very happy since—in her teaching profession and with her close circle of women friends."

"How old is she?" Kate inquired.

"Seventy-one—five years younger than my father. She's retired now, of course."

"Did she have any contact with your father?"

"Yes, some. They were perfectly civil with each other. Whenever I received honors in my profession, they always attended the ceremonies together. They go—they went to the same bridge club in Santa Monica every

Friday afternoon. My father paid her membership dues there—she never knew it.'' Shaking her head, Peri made a note on the pad beside her. ''I'll need to take care of that now. . . .''

''You mentioned your mother's circle of close friends,'' Cameron said. ''How about your father?''

''Just a few old cronies down at the bridge club. Father was pretty much a loner.''

''I realize we're really reaching here, Peri, but is there any evidence in your father's life to . . .'' Kate searched for tactful phrasing. ''Is there anything that could lead you to believe your father was involved in something he kept from you?''

''Like what? Drugs? Prostitution? You're right, you're really reaching. The thought of my father peddling cocaine . . .'' She grimaced. ''It's ludicrous.''

Kate did not mean drugs. A man of Herman Layton's years was more likely to be in some area of illicit gambling. No fool like an old fool, as her father used to say, and from what Peri had said about Herman Layton being confrontational and never backing away from trouble. . . .

Kate's pager went off. She glanced at the number; it was the station.

''I take it you need to use the phone,'' Peri said and indicated a desk at the far end of the room. ''There's one in the living room if you'd like privacy.''

''Thank you, this one's fine,'' Kate said, getting to her feet. She walked self-consciously to the desk, uncomfortable with the knowledge that Peri Layton's eyes were on her.

''I'm patching through Sergeant Hansen,'' Madge Carter told Kate. ''Also, you have a message to call Aimee at home ASAP. Not urgent but important.''

''Was she informed that I'm on a case?''

''She was.''

''Thanks, Madge,'' Kate said. She was alarmed; Ai-

mee was home with a mild case of the flu, and she knew
not to attempt to reach Kate when she was on an investigation. Had she taken a serious turn for the worse? Or
maybe something had happened with Marcie . . .

"Patching through Sergeant Hansen."

"Kate," Hansen said, "you and Joe should get over
here. They've found something in one of their exhibit
sites. With what happened this morning, it looks like too
much of a coincidence to me. The people who work here
are real excited about it."

"What is it?"

"It's not a body, that I can tell you. But it's not that
easy to describe, Kate. You'll need to see it."

"We'll be right there," Kate said, her mind too occupied with Aimee to insist that Hansen more fully inform her.

Hearing Kate's sign-off, Cameron rose to his feet.
Kate pulled one of her cards from her notebook and
strode back to hand it to Peri. "I'm very sorry, Peri, we
have to leave," she said in genuine contrition. "Do you
have someone you can call to be with you?"

"Right now I need to see my mother before she hears
the news from somewhere else—"

"Your father's identity hasn't been released," Kate
assured her.

"Not by you, I'm sure. These things still get out. I
need to go over and be with her."

"Of course," Kate said, thinking that Peri Layton had
undoubtedly had her own experiences with the sharklike
conduct of the press. "The coroner will be contacting
you."

"Here's the number where I'll be," Peri said, scrib-
bling on the back of her own business card.

Distress was imprinting on Peri's features like a mask,
and Kate said sympathetically, "We'll be back in touch
as soon as we can. We'll keep you fully up to date on
our progress. If anything comes up, if you remember

something, if you want to talk, please call me. Anytime. And tell them I asked you to page me if I'm not at the station. Peri," she added, "I'm very sorry about your father."

"I am, too," Cameron said. "My condolences."

"Thank you." Peri added softly, "I sense that it comes from somewhere other than your official capacity, and I'm very grateful."

4

AS she walked with Cameron toward the Caprice, Kate cast an appraising glance at him. She did not know how much he knew about her personal life. Plenty, she suspected. LAPD's rumor mill worked at the speed of light and never closed; it was by far the most efficient part of the bureaucracy. She had always made it her practice to volunteer nothing about herself, neither asserting nor denying her sexual orientation, deflecting personal questions with light remarks and generalities. Aimee, in a phrase that harkened back to the days of the Nixon-Watergate scandal, sarcastically referred to this as her limited hangout policy. But Aimee did not have to work at LAPD. Kate had given up trying to convince her that any announcement of sexual orientation would focus a spotlight on a senior officer like herself, and the recent, highly publicized coming out of a commander had done nothing to diminish that belief.

Cameron, she had been gratified to discover, operated under the same principle of privacy that she did. Beyond the facts that his wife of twelve years was an instructor at the Police Academy and they shared an enthusiasm for the outdoors, he did not discuss his home life. If Cameron did not feel the need to talk about his wife or lay bare any details of what he did on his time off, why should she?

Although he did not seem to be a homophobe like her

first partner, Ed Taylor, who could tell until he was put to the test? Her last partner, Torrie Holden, had not been homophobic, but she had been, in her own passive-aggressive way, as bad as Taylor.

Kate's thoughts lingered bitterly on Torrie Holden. If responsibility for the Gonzales fiasco lay on Kate's shoulders, the blame belonged with Torrie, who had appeared in court yesterday to testify in a homicide investigation for which she had been lead detective. Kate did not expect any police officer to lie in court under any circumstances—lying was the refuge of the incompetent, of police officers who had failed to do their jobs properly—but the Gonzales case was now in turmoil because of Torrie's admission on the witness stand that a single item of evidence, a torn shirt, had been collected in a room different from the one described in the warrant. Torrie knew better than to enter an area not covered by the terms of a search warrant. Either she should have stayed out of that room, or she should have had the warrant amended. After the court's proper ruling that deemed every item of evidence covered by the search warrant inadmissible, Torrie had compounded her felony by leaving the courtroom without speaking to Kate or Prosecuting Attorney Marlene Dixon.

Par for the course, Kate thought, yanking the keys to the Caprice from her shoulder bag. Torrie Holden was fundamentally gutless, her behavior after her court testimony consistent with her disappearing act after the shooting that had left Kate wounded. Thank heaven for Lieutenant Mike Bodwin, who had taken this problem partner off Kate's hands a month ago in a face-saving move for all parties involved, bringing her with him to Hollenbeck, his new assignment now that he had made captain.

But right now, at this moment, Kate was in a bind. She remembered that Aimee had called her in the middle of an investigation only one other time, when her Uncle

Herbert, the relative closest to her after her Aunt Paula, had suddenly died of a heart attack. These days, Aimee's closest childhood friend was being relentlessly pursued and harassed by an ex-husband. There was really no decision to make; Cameron would think whatever he was going to think.

"I need to make a call," she told him. "Would you drive?"

"Sure," he said and deftly caught the keys she tossed to him.

Scrambling into the passenger's seat, Kate pulled her mobile phone from her shoulder bag and punched in her home number code.

Aimee picked up on the half ring and greeted her with a quiet "Hi."

"Are you okay? Kate said with equal quietness, staring unseeingly out the windshield. "How do you feel? What's happening?"

"Actually, I'm feeling a lot better," Aimee said. "Kate, your aunt's here."

"My *aunt?* You can't mean Aunt Agnes."

"I do."

"She's here? In Los Angeles?"

"More than that."

"She's there," Kate said. "She's there in—" She broke off, acutely aware of Cameron beside her. "She's there, is that what you're telling me?"

"That's what I'm telling you. I'm in the den with the door closed. She's in the living room. And you have somebody with you so you can't talk, right?"

"Right. How . . . did she get there?"

"Kate, be reasonable. What else could I do, slam the door in her face?"

"Hell yes. Tell her to get lost," Kate sputtered. "Tell her I told you to do it. Tell her you're sick. How dare the woman—"

"Honey, I know how you feel about her," Aimee said

placatingly. "I did the only thing I knew to do, which was call a cop. My cop."

"Tell her to leave," Kate commanded. "Tell her to get the hell out. Tell her I don't want to see her."

"She knows that, Kate. She says she has something to tell you, and she's not leaving till she does."

"I don't want to hear it. Judas priest, I'm on a case, I'm—"

"I told her that, too."

"I won't be free for hours—"

"I also told her that. She says she'll wait till you get here, no matter what the hour. She claims she owes it to you to tell you whatever this is. I'm sorry I had to call, Kate, but I didn't want you to just walk in the door—"

"Sure. And I really appreciate it. I'm sorry to put you through this—"

"It's all right. Look, I've made her some tea—"

"Put arsenic in it," Kate muttered heedlessly.

"I could play my Spice Girls album," Aimee offered. "That might drive her out of here."

Kate chuckled in spite of herself at this transparent attempt to lighten her mood. Thank heaven for Aimee, especially on a day like today. The Gonzales mess, a new murder case with a rookie partner, and now Aunt Agnes. "Not bad enough about your flu, and Marcie being harassed," she told Aimee. "I'm really sorry. This is none of your doing. I'm sorry to put you through this."

"Kate, maybe . . . for her to come all the way out here from Michigan, I think this has to be something really important—"

"Only to her," Kate retorted. "I'll be there when I can. I'm glad you're feeling better."

"I'll be fine," Aimee said. "Be careful," she added and disconnected.

Kate folded the phone and replaced it in her shoulder

bag. Cameron had been studiously attending to his driving, staring straight ahead. Now, gazing past her at the Beverly Wilshire Hotel with its flags flying in the hot breezes of Beverly Hills, he said casually, cautiously, "If you need to take care of a problem—"

"It's not a problem, Joe," Kate said, choosing her words. "It's a goddamn nuisance. An aunt who's decided to invade my life. I don't want anything to do with her. But now she's turned up in the city—"

"Where from?"

"Michigan. Where I grew up."

"I take it you got a real beef with her."

"Prime grade. I hate her guts," Kate found herself saying. "From the time I was a little kid she had me convinced I was responsible for my mother's bad health and then her death. Turns out it was all a crock. Mother's leukemia had nothing to do with my birth or any other damn thing connected with me. But all this time I bought the whole damn crock, I couldn't see it any different." As if she were in a vehicle out of control, Kate hurtled on, "She drove a wedge between my mother and me. My mother went to her grave wondering why her only daughter was such a dud and couldn't have a decent relationship with her. . . ." To Kate's chagrin, she choked on her rage, her eyes watery with tears.

"I'd like to feed her the arsenic myself," Cameron said intensely, staring straight ahead. "What adults do to kids. Any idea what the old fart wants with you now?"

"Maybe to blame me for something else. Or to tell me something about my parents I don't want to know." Furious with herself for revealing so much to this new partner, she said savagely, "Dear old Aunt Agnes can drop dead on my living room floor for all I care."

"You got a pretty damn good motive for murder if I ever heard one," Cameron agreed. "Did I hear you say something about somebody being harassed? Sorry, I didn't mean to eavesdrop.''

"Hard not to when you're sitting right here in the car." A chuckle burst from her, and she felt her mood, the arc of her anger, break. Gratified by his sympathy and wondering at her sudden and inexplicable comfort level with him, she sternly reminded herself to be careful. "A friend has an ex-husband after her," she said.

Cameron glanced sharply at her. "Harassing, or stalking?"

"Harassing."

"Better than a stalker," Cameron said, leaning forward to adjust the air-conditioning. "Stalkers are sick. So goddamn crazy—"

"Tell me about it. I've had two cases—"

"Not a damn thing you can do," Cameron said as if he had not heard her, "except hope they come right into your house so you can use a shotgun."

"An ex-husband nuts with jealousy isn't any picnic either," Kate said grimly.

"Yeah, tell me about it," Cameron said with an edge in his tone. "This friend, has she done the drill?"

"Restraining order, police report, the whole nine yards. Her friends can't understand why I can't just pick this guy up and dump him in a cell. I'm as frustrated as poor Marcie. But not nearly as scared," she said somberly, remembering when she had come from work just last Wednesday and found the thin, hollow-eyed woman crouching in slump-shouldered despair outside the door of the condo, waiting for Aimee to arrive.

"Maybe we can figure out something," Cameron said.

"Maybe," Kate answered. There was nothing to be done—he knew it and she knew it.

"Change of subject," she announced as they passed the former May company on the corner of Wilshire and Fairfax, its gold circular facade scruffier than ever; the

store had closed years ago and still awaited a renais-
sance. "What are these footprints you and Peri were
talking about?"

"Do you know about the Leakeys? Louis, Mary,
Richard?" Cameron's voice rose with his eagerness to
answer her question.

"Vaguely. Something about some major discoveries
they made about early man in Africa—was that it?"

"Right. Louis and Mary worked on the same dig for
decades. They made crucial finds before Lucy's skeleton
turned up in Ethiopia. Then Louis died, and Mary was
the one who unearthed a trail of human footprints—they
go back about three and a half million years. Peri was
one of the students working on the dig."

Kate felt gooseflesh creep up her arms. "Footprints
dating back to the dawn of humankind—I can't imagine . . ."

"Me, either. Finding those footprints—that's more
exciting to me than all the skulls and skeletons they've
ever dug up all put together."

"I think so, too," Kate said, surprised at her own
growing interest. "When was this?"

"Let me think. . . . I'd say maybe . . .'78."

Reminding herself of her policy of nonintrusion on
her new partner's personal life, Kate said cautiously,
"You know a lot about all of this, Joe."

"No accident." He shrugged. "I dreamed of being a
paleontologist. Or a geologist. From the time my dad
first took me out to the desert and I found my first fossil.
I took some of the classes in college . . ."

"But you became a cop."

"Yeah, well . . ." He smiled sheepishly. "Security,
you know. Good pay, good benefits. Science is great,
but jobs and budgets come and go. The world always
needs cops."

Kate nodded. This reason, not idealism, was the one
she heard most often from police officers. Security—

along with a dollop or two of idealism—were the reasons she herself had joined LAPD.

"Your father sounds like a great guy," she said.

A shadow of something Kate could not identify crossed Cameron's face. "Yeah," he said shortly, and she knew to abandon the topic.

"I don't understand some of the terminology," she confessed as Cameron turned onto Curson Avenue. "If Peri's a paleoanthropologist, what makes her different from a paleontologist?"

"A paleontologist studies the fossils of prehistoric plants and animals. Peri focuses on prehistoric humans— our origins, the tools we used, cultural development, all that kind of stuff," Cameron answered, pulling the Caprice in between the crime scene van and a station wagon with a *Los Angeles Times* logo on its door. Two black-and-whites remained on the scene, their light bars extinguished.

She and Cameron once more made their way toward the crime scene behind the lake pool. A guitar player, a cigar box at his feet inviting donations, strummed and sang "Tom Dooley." The observation platform across from the museum was still crowded with children, and Kate remarked, "Your death class undergraduates continue to pay close attention."

"I take it you think we should completely protect kids from death," Cameron challenged her.

"Who, me?" Kate said innocently. "Why don't you suggest that the coroner open an office at Disneyland?"

Cameron's chuckle died as *Los Angeles Times* reporter Corey Lanier blocked their path.

"Ah, the great Detective Delafield," Lanier said in a throaty voice. "So who's the victim, what's going on, and are you close to an arrest?"

"No comment, Corey," Kate said, smiling at her.

"Ah, the great and ever-informative Detective Delafield," Lanier said. Propping her sunglasses on top of straight, honey-colored hair, Lanier pulled a notebook and pen from a bulging shoulder bag. Drawing out each syllable, she repeated, "No . . . comment," as she wrote out the words. She gestured to the grinning Cameron. "Anything Smilin' Jack here wishes to add?"

Kate said, "Detective Cameron adds his own no comment."

"No comment from Detective Cameron," Lanier said, dutifully recording the words in her notebook. "May I look forward to similar enlightenment as this case proceeds?"

"You may," Kate said.

"Have a nice day, Detectives," Lanier said and moved on past them.

"Oy vey," Cameron said, turning to watch the lithe, feline figure of the reporter striding away from them.

"We have a little history," Kate said.

"I'd never guess," Cameron said.

"Maybe I'll tell you about it sometime," Kate said. But it would not be for a long time; her involvement with Luke Taggart and the murder in Apparition Alley still aroused too much emotion in her.

Herman Layton's body had been removed, but yellow crime scene tape still marked off the area, its edges fluttering in the hot, oil-pungent breeze. Tourists in shorts drifted by, staring at the tape and the single officer who guarded the perimeter and the white-clad criminalist working on the park bench with an array of sprays, gray powder, and lifting tape.

"This is weird. I can't get over how weird this is," Cameron said. "Here's a prehistoric dig with tar bubbling up and a modern crime lab technician lifting fingerprints."

"Kate, Joe—" Hansen strode toward them. "What it is . . ." He flipped through his notebook and consulted a page. "There's an exhibit here with a lot of bones; it only opens once a day—"

"Yeah, I saw it years ago," Cameron interjected.

"That's where Morella Moore—she's one of the staff, they call her a docent—that's where she found it."

Her patience with Hansen at an end, Kate demanded, "Found what? Dammit, Fred, what did they find?"

"Part of an ancient human skull, a jawbone."

"So? Why is this news?"

Cameron added his own query: "They've already found things like that here. The bones of La Brea Woman—"

"Nothing like this. Believe me, this is news. It wasn't found in the tar, it was placed in a particular area. According to the people here, their fossils are never more than forty thousand years old. This jawbone's way, way older than that."

"You gotta be fucking kidding," Cameron uttered.

Kate asked, "Where's this exhibit?"

Hansen said, edging down the path, "I'll take you. The staff paleontologist is hopping up and down, wanting to move the thing into the lab to protect it, but I wouldn't let him touch it till you got here. He's waiting for you."

Kate did not move from where she stood. "Fred, this is all very interesting, and I'll be glad to have a look, but what does a jawbone, however old it is, have to do with Herman Layton?"

"It's what Jamison—he's the paleontologist—said about it. Look, I'm way out of my depth here, Kate. Let Jamison tell you what it all means, like he told me. Just talk to him, okay?"

"Fine," she said, snapping off the word. She felt out of her depth as well, but Hansen was exacerbating the situation.

"I have a feeling . . ." said Cameron.

Kate turned to him.

"I agree with Fred," he said hurriedly, seeing the look on her face. "Let's talk to the paleontologist."

Thoroughly fed up with both Hansen and Cameron, convinced that the ordinarily stodgy Hansen had crossed the line into theatrics, Kate strode silently between the two men along a wide asphalt path that bordered the graceful, pale green and white curves and angles of the futuristic museum of art. Closed off from the La Brea Tar Pits by an iron picket fence, it sat beyond a low, decorative border of flagstones and a patch of lawn.

Edged with ivy, the cracked surface of the curving parkway on which she walked was overhung with trees and dappled with sunlight and playfully decorated with a set of large yellow cat prints. Just beyond a small brick-lined footbridge, a high chain-link fence, its top garnished with barbed wire, provided security for equipment that was camouflaged as well as protected by green plastic sheets laden with fallen leaves. Kate eyed a line of tourists filing through an open mesh gate into one of the buildings, a neat reddish brown structure, its sign, decorated by a stylized saber-toothed cat, announcing Page Museum Pit 91 Excavation Now Thru September 7, and listing the days and times it was open.

"They excavate in there two months out of the year," offered Cameron.

"The two hottest months," Kate observed, assailed by the potent smell of tar borne on a heated breeze.

He shrugged. "Tourist season."

Several other dark wood frame structures stood inside the fence, and farther within, stacks of oil drums, small sheds, and a tree-shaded ramshackle white trailer apparently converted into an office. Other areas farther on to her right were also fenced off with chain-link, protecting tourists from the oozing pockets of asphalt within. Clearly, this was a working museum where activity was ongoing.

A nondescript circular structure, surrounded by low, concrete benches and partially obscured by trees, came into view; the brick foundation was painted a cream color, topped in one section by metal sheets with paint worn through to its white primer. A chain-link gate had been rolled back; a large brass padlock hung from its lock mechanism. An unobtrusive sign stated that the observation pit was temporarily closed and that La Brea fossils were on display in the Page Museum. The structure's double doors, curtained with brass bars, stood ajar.

"They tell me this place is usually closed," Hansen said, leading Kate and Cameron inside, "except once a day at one o'clock when a docent conducts a tour of the grounds."

"It's well worth seeing," Cameron said.

Cameron's endless hype about this place was beginning to grate on her nerves. She said in a short tone to Hansen, "Anything so far on the FIs?"

"Nothing. We're still interviewing."

Pillars, white brick walls, and a ceiling with several huge skylights came into view. Barred windows were flanked by individual sketched outlines of animals against an amber background: bear, camel, bison, sabertooth cat, a mastodon with elaborately curved tusks like the sculpture in the lake pool. A metal railing that resembled jail cell doors lined a staircase that circled the structure down to a floor that appeared to be a slag heap. Outside the yellow police tape that cordoned off the area where the metal railing ended, a tall, bearded man stood with Patrol Officer Manuel Jimenez.

Kate paused before a large photograph of the slag-heap floor and scanned a lengthy list of animal and bird bones that could be identified by matching them to a letter designation in the photograph. Descending the stairs, she could distinguish bones of all shapes and sizes studding the brownish gray, tar-stained rock. The viewing station reeked of tar.

As she walked closer, she also picked out a glossy bone the size of her palm, stark in its placement on the cement under the metal railing just above the gray beige rock and any encroachment by asphalt. A dark clay color tinged with green, it was lined with large flat whitish molars like a crudely made denture. Beside it lay what appeared to be packing, a box with faint lettering stenciled on its side, containing tissue paper and downy fiber, probably cotton, several layers of gauze, and a thickness of ordinary paper, all of it yellowish and looking brittle with age.

The lanky, bearded man was staring at the jawbone as if he feared it would vanish; Jimenez, arms crossed over his burly chest, watched him.

Hansen said, "The place is staffed with volunteers; Marella Moore's one of the docents. A tourist spotted the bone, asked her about it. Moore took one look and locked up the place, notified Betty Parsons, the lab supervisor. She called Jamison. We got involved almost by accident, our officers were here canvassing and Jimenez mentioned it to me and how excited the staff were, and—I'm getting way ahead of myself."

The bearded man rose and walked toward them on the balls of his sneakered feet, making his way as if he were carrying a brimming glass of liquid. "Greg Jamison," he said. "You're the detectives in charge?"

"We are." Kate introduced herself and Cameron, thinking that the paleontologist, in his baggy jeans and polo shirt and unfashionably long hair, was the perfect image of someone who would happily spend his days in some windswept, ungodly hot place prospecting for fossils. "What's going on here, Mr. Jamison?"

"You tell me." The voice was a husky tenor, as if it, too, had been parched by sun. Jamison jerked his head toward the objects sitting under the railing, his streaked blond hair sweeping forward and then back from his face. "I don't know why your sergeant won't let us take possession—"

"Because a man was killed here this morning."

"I realize that. Everybody including me is pretty

damn shook up about it. What does a hominid mandible have to do with him or the police?'' He hunkered down, carefully, as if his body might produce damaging air currents, and again peered at the jawbone.

Kate turned to Cameron, who knew far more about this subject than she did. But he, too, was staring at the jawbone. Exasperated, she said to Jamison, ''Sergeant Hansen says you've identified this bone as being quite ancient.''

The paleontologist looked up at her, his eyes so pale a blue that they looked sun-bleached. ''That's true only if it's what I think it is. As I told the sergeant here, from its dentition and morphology, it *appears* to be a specimen of *Homo erectus,* which would place it in the two-million-year range.''

''*Jesus!*'' The word erupted from Cameron.

''It *appears* to be,'' Jamison cautioned him sternly. ''It could be just bullshit, too. Like I told the sergeant here, a paleoanthropologist who specializes in hominid fossils needs to examine it. We've got someone in town right now who's one of the best in the world.''

''And who might that be?'' Kate asked, but she already knew and understood now why Hansen had called her

Jamison answered, ''The visiting professor of paleo-anthropology at UCLA: Dr. Peri Layton.''

''You see?'' Hansen said.

''I do see, Fred. And I thank you. Joe and I'll take over from here.'' As Hansen made his departure, she turned to the paleontologist. ''Mr. Jamison—''

''Greg,'' he said.

''Greg, Sergeant Hansen couldn't give you any information about why we have an interest in this find because he couldn't tell you the name of the victim until we notified the next of kin. We can tell you now. The victim is Herman Layton, Peri Layton's father.''

Jamison stared at her, dumbstruck.

She asked, "When was it found?"

"Just after the daily one o'clock tour began." His voice had dropped to a dazed whisper. "This is totally weird."

"Did anyone touch it?"

"No. I was about to move it out of here when your officers took over."

Looking as stunned as Jamison, Cameron said, "If this fossil does turn out to be *Homo erectus* . . . But I can see why you're skeptical."

"I don't," Kate said. "Enlighten me."

His eyes fixed on the jawbone, Jamison said, "Let me put it this way, Detective. Nobody should even think about calling the press."

Kate thought of Corey Lanier leaving the scene, imagining the fury of the *Times* reporter when she discovered the full dimension of the story that had been under her nose.

Jamison continued, "This may be someone's idea of a joke. I'm in a field with lots of controversy, some pretty spectacular fraud. You've heard of Piltdown Man?"

"Sure. Well, what I remember from college . . . Somebody found . . . Was it the missing link? It turned out to be a fake. Or do I have that one confused with Lucy?"

"No, you're exactly right. Lucy's real. Her skeleton was found in Ethiopia in 1974. Piltdown Man was perpetrated in England in 1915. It took a whole forty years to expose it—an enduring embarrassment to my profession. This mandible needs to be authenticated by someone who knows hominids."

Kate said, "We'll need to photograph it, and its packaging, in place. And then collect it ourselves and fingerprint it."

"*What?*" He stepped toward her. "*Fingerprint* it? *Collect* it? You can't *touch* it!"

"We have to," Kate told him sympathetically. "It may be two million years old, but it appears to be related to a murder case in the here and now."

"If it's an actual *Homo erectus* mandible, it's priceless. If it's damaged—"

"I understand. I promise we'll defer to your expertise, we'll have our technician work under the direct supervision of Dr. Layton and yourself."

An hour later, as the LAPD crime scene photographer finished his work, Peri Layton walked into the observation area. Attired now in somber colors, a navy blue shirt and slacks, she did not remove her sunglasses as she made her way down the stairs. Kate judged that she had undergone the stress of informing her mother and had yet to journey to USC County General to identify the remains of her father.

"Sorry, very sorry, Peri," Jamison blustered awkwardly, shaking her hand and holding it.

"Thank you, Greg," she said, patting him on the shoulder.

Spotting the jawbone, she said, "Detective Cameron, when you called me, I didn't believe you."

"Can't blame you," Jamison said, lifting the police tape for her to duck under; he followed, hunkering down beside her.

"Great Jupiter," she breathed.

Kate was interested to see that Peri Layton's attention had immediately shifted from the jawbone to the packaging arrayed beside it.

Peri looked over at Kate. "There's lettering on that box," she said tensely. "I need to look at it. Now," she added in the crisp tone of someone accustomed to being obeyed.

"Baker," Kate called.

The fingerprint technician detached himself from the railing he was leaning against; he had been studying the bones embedded in the floor. Picking up his equipment bag, he strolled over. Kate said, "Dr. Layton needs to look more closely at the packaging. Is that possible?"

"You think I'm some Houdini, I'm gonna print it where it is?"

She expected no less from the irascible Baker, but the logical strategy was always to humor the best fingerprint man in the department. She lifted the tape for him to pass under.

Baker extracted a pair of tongs and a plastic sack from his bag and knelt. With the tongs, he pinched a section of the box to test its weight, then lifted it from under the railing, setting it gently on the plastic sack.

"Greg," Peri whispered, pointing at the faded letters inked on the box. "Look at this."

Hunkering down beside her, Jamison examined the letters. "P-U-M-C," he read. "Peri, I have to confess I don't know what I'm looking at."

"P-U-M-C," she repeated. "Peking Union Medical College. If this mandible came out of this packaging, then it's from Zhoukoudian. It's *Sinanthropus pekinensis.*"

"You can't be serious," Jamison said flatly.

"Meaning what?" Kate said, managing to keep her tone even. She felt ready to explode from the frustration of being excluded from virtually every conversation that had occurred since she and Cameron had been called in on this homicide. "What are the two of you talking about?"

Everyone ignored her. Cameron, looking stunned, said to Peri, "You can't mean it. This . . . is Peking Man?"

"That's exactly what I mean," Peri said. "With a father like mine, you think I don't know every detail of what he saw in China? The way the fossils were packed—I'll have to check the record, but the packing looks exactly right, down to the last fiber, exactly how my father described it about a hundred thousand times."

"I can't believe it." Cameron, on his knees, clasped his hands together as if he were at a shrine. *"Peking Man . . ."*

Kate, too, was awed. She had pieced together the information she had gleaned in Peri Layton's sun room to what she had learned here, and now she understood the significance of this find. "Do you think it's real?" she asked Peri.

"That's the big question here, Peri," Jamison said. "Is it?"

"Only one way to find out. The mandible needs to be authenticated. It needs to be sent to New York. If the Museum of Natural History can match it up with their photos and casts made of the Peking Man fossils in 1941 . . ." Even with her eyes concealed by dark glasses, Peri's face was lighted with excitement.

Kate remained prudently silent. She knew that if the fossil turned out to be a key piece of evidence, it would go nowhere for a considerable period of time, except to an evidence locker and then perhaps to a courtroom.

"Peri," Jamison said, "if it's real . . ."

"It could be a copy, Greg," Peri said reluctantly, as if cautioning herself as well as Jamison. "Maybe this is a new version of Piltdown Man."

"Seems that's a real possibility," Cameron offered. "Otherwise, why was it left here? Why wouldn't somebody just turn it in?"

"True," Peri said. "But if it isn't a copy, then the question becomes . . ." She trailed off, staring at the jawbone.

"The question becomes," Kate supplied, "who put it here and when and why?" And, she mentally added, how is it connected with your father's death?

"If it's real," Peri said quietly, "then to my mind, the big question is, where has this mandible and the rest of the *Sinanthropus* specimens been for the past fifty-six years? Where are the main finds now? Where are all the rest of them?"

5

KATE entered the Page Museum escorted by Baker, whose disposition had improved markedly at the prospect of telling his cronies about fingerprinting a two-million-year-old fossil. Peri Layton, accompanied by Greg Jamison, stalked along behind them; Kate heard her hiss to Greg Jamison, "Stupid, stupid bureaucracy . . ."

Kate understood Peri's anger and the vociferous objections of both scientists at the confiscation of the fossil, but her responsibility permitted no negotiation: "It's potential evidence in a murder investigation," she had stated with finality. "It remains in police custody until we evaluate it." Thus far, Peri had little cause for specific complaint; Cameron, who preceded them by several steps, carried the box containing the fossil and its packing as if it held the Holy Grail.

Joanne Takani on the information desk answered Kate's smile with a frank, unsmiling stare, then fastened her gaze on the box in Cameron's arms as if it held a severed head—which in a sense it did, Kate realized in bemusement. Obviously, word had spread of the find in the observation site, and that the body behind the park bench was that of a murder victim.

Waving away Kate's offering of identification, the plump, gray-haired woman tending the ticket kiosk addressed Jamison: "Greg, what on earth's going on?"

"Oh not much at all, Eileen," he answered wryly, and ushered the group through and into the museum.

Kate took in the general details of an expansive, carpeted exhibition area with replicas of large animals, darkly gleaming mounted skeletons, glassed-in illuminated displays of other skeletons and birds, and walls covered with photographs and murals. A large, circular, glass-enclosed display came into prominent view, a laboratory that had been turned into an exhibit in itself. Kate paused to survey the half-dozen white-clad men and women who sat at counters facing the windows, heads bent in concentration as they worked on trays of bones amid a clutter of equipment and multiple additional trays of fossils.

"Volunteers," Jamison said. "Couldn't exist without 'em. They're cleaning and sorting fossils." He led her to two large double doors to the left of the laboratory.

Inside, a middle-aged blond woman wearing green cotton pants and a white pullover strode quickly up the corridor as if she had been waiting for them. "Betty Parsons, our laboratory manager," said Jamison, and he introduced her to Kate, Cameron, and Baker.

"Pleased to meet you," the woman said perfunctorily, not offering to shake hands. Sympathy etched on her face, her attention was given to Peri Layton. At Jamison's request, Kate had permitted the identity of Herman Layton to be disseminated to the museum's staff. Betty said awkwardly, "Dr. Layton, we're all very, very sorry to hear about your father."

"Betty, I appreciate it." Peri reached to her and gave her arm a brief squeeze.

Cameron's procession with the box continued behind Betty's lead, past an entryway to inner offices, past floor-to-ceiling shelves stacked with labeled boxes holding fossil specimens and cabinets whose tops displayed skeletons and miniature sculptures of animals, past benches where fossil parts were being reassembled into full skeletons.

A large circular table covered with a disorderly array of newspapers and coffee mugs was situated between a plain green sofa and a bookcase chaotically stuffed with books and other publications. Cameron eased the box onto the table as if it were a fresh soufflé. Baker, watched closely by Peri and Jamison, removed a tray from his bag, along with his kit.

"Make yourselves comfortable," Betty said. "Anybody want coffee?"

"I'd love some," Kate said gratefully.

As Betty searched among a selection of mugs hanging from hooks in an alcove that also held a coffeepot and the makings for coffee, Jamison wandered over and slopped a quantity of coffee into a huge mug shaped into a cat's paw. Betty muttered to Kate, "I can't guarantee any of these mugs are clean."

"I'll take my chances," Kate said, moving to the shelves along the wall and peering at a wooden box loosely shrouded with a dusty plastic sheet and labeled Elephant Foot Material, an additional handwritten sign stating, Mammoth & Mastodon Phalanges Mostly Pit 9. Maybe Rancho La Brea *was* something special, she thought; from this room and that open laboratory, it seemed a cornucopia of active prehistoric discoveries.

Addressing Jamison, she said, "We'll talk to Marella Moore, of course, but can you suggest a scenario of how a fossil got placed in an exhibit that's closed except for a few minutes once a day?"

"Two ways," Jamison said promptly. "It was put there yesterday, or today right after the pit opened up."

"When was the last time you were in there?" Cameron asked casually, and Kate looked at him in approval. It was a very good question; despite Jamison's protestations over not calling the press about the jawbone, some sort of a bid for personal publicity by a paleontologist was not out of the realm of possibility.

"Been months," Jamison said after a slurp of his coffee. "With our budget cuts, who has time? Don't have all that much reason to go in there, anyway."

"I was in the place just last week," Betty contributed. "How it works is, the docent unlocks the gate and lets people go in and down the stairs to look around."

Kate asked, "Would Marella Moore have been the docent yesterday as well as today?"

Betty nodded. "She's a regular, very involved and a real student of what we do here. Most of our volunteers work a few days a week."

"In that particular exhibit, would the docent stay with the tour group at all times?"

"Not at all. She'd stay upstairs and answer questions. It's not like anybody has to be watched. There's not a lot anybody can hurt in there." Betty added with an ironic smile, "You'd need to get yourself over that railing and for all your trouble, you'd get stuck in the asphalt."

"So someone could have lagged behind . . ."

Kate did not finish voicing her thought nor did Betty reply; she, along with Kate, was watching Baker lift the bag holding the jawbone from the box and set it on the tray. Peri looked on grimly; Jamison flung himself into a chair and gulped his coffee, staring at the fossil as Baker edged it from the bag with a pair of rubber-tipped tongs.

Cameron, at a bulletin board with the sign Volunteer News across the top, chuckled as he read from a flyer: " 'This job is a test, it is only a test. Had this been an actual job, you would have received raises, promotions, and other signs of appreciation.' "

"It's true," Betty said, pouring coffee for Kate. "Have you heard about our budget cuts?"

Kate shook her head. Money had been allocated to increase police ranks, to rebuild or improve decaying station houses, to replace inadequate cars and obsolete equipment; it had not occurred to Kate to wonder at whose budgetary expense these improvements were being made. "Pretty bad, I take it," she offered.

"Cut to the bone," Betty said, "to make a bad pun."

"Nice," mumbled Baker approvingly, examining the fossil's surface with a photographer's loupe. "The packing's a no-hoper—too porous. But this is painted with resin. Nice slick surface for latents."

"The resin's a preservative," Peri said.

"In more ways than one." Baker dipped a brush in a bottle of black fingerprint powder.

"Wait," commanded Peri. "Are you going to coat the mandible in that stuff?"

"Sure. Can't possibly do any damage."

"I believe you." She turned to Kate. "Before he does that, if I give you my word of honor that I won't touch it, may I examine it?"

"Under that condition, you may," Kate said.

"Mr. Baker, could I borrow your magnifying glass?"

Looking gratified by the request, Baker handed it over, and Peri removed her sunglasses. Her slender body in a taut curve over the table, she peered through the loupe at the fossil, scrutinizing its every exposed surface.

Jamison, watching her face, said, "It's the real thing, isn't it, Peri."

"Greg, it needs testing, it needs to go to New York," she murmured. Then she straightened and looked down at him, donning her sunglasses once again over red-rimmed eyes. "It could be a stunningly good copy. Thank you," she said to Baker. "Proceed with your work."

Baker delicately tapped his powder-laden brush with a finger until most of the particles fell off, then, with light, curving strokes, applied the remainder over the entire surface of the fossil. Nodding with satisfaction, he pulled a fixed-focus camera from his bag and snapped photos of the jawbone from different angles. Then he cut off an inch or so from a roll of clear cellophane tape. "Won't touch the surface," he assured Peri; she and Jamison were looking on closely, tension in their faces. "It'll adhere just to the powder."

"Thank you, Mr. Baker."

Baker affixed the tape on the outside of the jawbone, smoothing it down with a finger, then lifted it, inspecting his handiwork with another satisfied nod. He repeated the operation inside the bone. "Whoever picked this thing up to put it where you found it," he said, holding up the two pieces of tape, "I'd say we got their thumb and index finger."

"Excellent," Peri said. "Now, we'll take the mandible and safeguard it in our—"

"No, Peri," Kate said regretfully. "We still have to retain possession." She added firmly, raising her voice to cut off Peri's objection, "It's potential evidence until we know the relevance of the prints. We're accustomed to safeguarding evidence of considerable worth." But never anything like this, she thought. Drugs and drug money and burglarized jewelry hardly compared with a two-million-year-old fossil.

Baker had resealed the jawbone in its bag as Cameron filled out the evidence tag. Peri gestured to Baker. "I fail to understand why you need custody of this specimen when Mr. Baker's taken the evidence that's on it."

"It has to do with what we call the chain of evidence," Kate explained. "When we find whoever did this to your father, and if the fingerprints are relevant and the case goes to court, we need to prove the chain of evidence is unbroken—that it couldn't have been tampered with because it was never out of our custody."

"If it's connected with my father's death, the mandible needs to be authenticated," Peri argued.

"With or without authentication, it's connected with

your father's death, Peri,'' Kate said quietly. ''How can it not be?''

Peri sighed her concession. ''It's my father I'm thinking of. I don't understand this either, but if it turns out to be *Sinanthropus,* its value is beyond—''

''We still have to do our jobs,'' Kate told her. ''Perhaps you could have your New York experts come out here.''

''Impossible. First it needs to be tested, then it needs to be matched up with fragile plaster casts and photographs of an extensive collection that won't possibly be moved here just for comparison purposes.''

''I'm sorry,'' Kate said, spreading her hands. ''There's nothing I can do till we know more and can safely release it from our custody.''

''Where does it go from here?'' Peri asked in a tone that contained not a hint of defeat.

''To an evidence locker.''

''An evidence locker,'' Peri repeated with distaste. ''I need to accompany it, to make sure this . . . locker is adequate. To make sure the mandible is packaged and stored and safeguarded properly.''

''I'm happy to have you accompany Sergeant Hansen,'' Kate said, concealing a smile. The meeting between Peri Layton and Sergeant ''Iron'' Jane Iverson, whose adherence to evidence regulations placed her in the first rank of bureaucratic zealots, would be a confrontation to behold. But there was too much work to be done before the trail to Herman Layton's killer grew cold.

The smell in the cottage on Tilden—close and musty, with overtones of a faintly sweet moldering—was familiar to Kate from her years of death investigations in airless rooms like these, occupied by solitary old people like Herman Layton. Sweat immediately formed on Cameron's brow and upper lip in the stifling heat, and he shrugged out of his jacket, as did Kate. She wished she could also remove her shoulder holster; its leather straps felt heavy and hot against her body.

Cameron followed Kate around in her initial survey of the place. The tiny living room was combined with an alcove kitchen; the bedroom was just large enough for a double bed and nightstand and a dresser; the closet-size bathroom offered a shower but no bathtub. Furniture was scant but all that a man living alone would require: a flimsy two-seater sofa, a worn but comfortable-looking leather Lay-Z-Boy recliner across from a no-frills portable television on a stand, a small coffee table and end table, several bookcases, an old-fashioned desk with an orderly array of letters spread over its surface. Nothing looked unusual or out of place; the rooms were meticulously neat, the only discordant note a corner of the bedroom where clothing had been tossed into a pile, apparently to be laundered.

The walls were covered with memorabilia of Peri Layton, this collection carefully framed and arranged, in contrast to the casual posters Peri had tacked up on her own wall at the house on Ophir Drive. In unspoken agreement, Kate and Cameron walked over to peruse photographs of Peri on digs, articles written by her and about her, the centerpiece an eight-page *National Geographic* photographic spread. In a shadow box frame was a polished skull of a horse that reminded Kate of a Georgia O'Keeffe painting.

"Something's been taken down," Cameron said, indicating a pristine white square on the dingy wall.

"I wonder what it was," Kate said. "It hung here for a good long time."

"Yeah. I remember this," Cameron said, indicating the *National Geographic* piece. "And the TV special they did years ago on her dig in Tanzania. The heir apparent to Mary Leakey, they said . . ." He shook his head. "I don't know why, don't ask me, all my dreams of being the next Louis Leakey were long gone by then, but she captured my imagination. I went out and bought her book.''

''I completely agree with you, she's truly impressive,'' Kate said. And so magnetic that she had to remind herself that she was happily married to a woman every inch as striking as Peri Layton, albeit differently so.

She returned her attention to the job at hand. In her experience, a good many closely held secrets were often revealed in bedrooms, and she directed Cameron to begin their search for information about Herman Layton's death, and his life, in this room.

Kate took the closet, and after pausing to inspect a collection of small, framed photographs of Peri at various excavation sites, Cameron busied himself with the dresser. In her notebook, Kate did a rough inventory of Herman Layton's apparel: six pairs of shoes, two pairs of slippers, eight sport shirts, seven pairs of pants, two white shirts, and two gabardine suits, one navy, one gray. She heard the buzz of a fly and saw a blue-bottle butting up against the barred window. It must have come in with her and Cameron, Kate thought, walking over to let it out of this hot, airless place. But she could not; the window had been nailed shut. She looked more closely at glass streaked from an ineffectual cleaning, and bright nail heads in the frame that suggested they had been hammered into place recently. Nails, in addition to bars. Had this man been paranoid? Or justifiably frightened?

''Underwear, socks, sweaters,'' grunted Cameron from the dresser, writing in his notebook. Perspiration had spread on his blue shirt between his shoulder blades and had formed above the nine millimeter holstered at his waist. Lifting a stack of sweaters in the bottom drawer, he exposed some magazines. ''Porno,'' he said, flipping through them. ''Guess you're never too old . . .''

He got down on his knees and peered under the bed and the dresser. "Dust balls and two safety pins," he announced.

On the closet shelf more than two dozen neatly stacked shoeboxes were labeled with a marker pen by the year, dating back to the seventies. Kate opened one and rifled through its contents: canceled checks, bills, receipts, pension check records. "Herman kept everything connected with money," she said to Cameron, "even grocery lists."

Cameron scanned an address book on the nightstand, then replaced the book next to the phone. "Peri didn't exaggerate about him being a loner. The guy knew about ten people, and most of those names are crossed off."

He opened a drawer of the nightstand beside the double bed. "Bingo," he said.

With his pen, he lifted a gun by its trigger guard. "Paranoid as this guy was, am I surprised it's a loaded three fifty-seven?" he asked. He held the gun at eye level to scrutinize it, sniffing the barrel. "Clogged with dust. Hasn't been fired in this century." He slid the weapon into a plastic evidence bag.

There seemed nothing else of interest or note in the nightstand, save a scrapbook of Hawaiian vacation photos with a young Peri and a shorter woman who bore so strong a resemblance to her that Kate was sure she was Peri's mother.

In the kitchen, the tiny cupboard was stacked with canned foods; the refrigerator held lunch meat, bread, butter, and mayonnaise; the freezer, trays of ice cubes and cheap frozen dinners. Herman Layton's diet was a depressing reminder to Kate of her own indifferent eating habits during the lonely years after Anne's death, before she met Aimee. Six half-gallons of Ancient Age crowded the cupboard under the sink; there were two empties in the trash.

"Heavy solitary drinker?" Kate suggested.

"Yep," Cameron said and opened a cutlery drawer. "Just like dear old dad. Right down to the same brand of bourbon."

Kate did not reply; something about his tone told her he would not welcome a response.

In the living room, Cameron knelt in front of the bookcase, head cocked to one side to read the titles. "Jesus, Kate. Nothing but books on paleontology. And a whole subsection: *Searching for Peking Man, Peking Man, The Peking Man Is Missing, The Story of Peking Man* . . ." Sitting back on his haunches, Cameron copied the titles in his notebook.

"We know from Peri how obsessed he was," Kate replied, surveying the desk and the letters arrayed on its surface.

She opened the top desk drawer. It was stuffed with packets of letters that matched the ones sitting on the desktop. Still in their envelopes and carefully tied together with thin ivory ribbon, each packet contained twelve letters festooned with colorful stamps from Kenya, Tanzania, and Ethiopia, each letter neatly slit open and fat with its onionskin contents. Kate counted fifteen packets of them. She felt a rush of melancholy. This treasured correspondence, obviously the letters Peri Layton had written to her father regularly each month from her overseas postings, were symbolic of Peri's importance to him, that she had been the essence and central joy of his life. Kate wondered if Herman Layton's last act in this sterile cage he had inhabited for twenty-seven years had been to reread them. She slid the cache of letters into an evidence bag with the pleasurable, guilty thought that they would probably hold more clues to the fascinating Peri Layton than they would to any killer of her father's, and it was Kate's right as a sanctioned snoop to look through them.

The desk's cubbyholes held nothing unusual: a supply of onionskin and ballpoint pens and paper clips. Reaching into one of the nooks to pick up a pocket-size, spiral-bound calendar, Kate felt a papery stiffness brush the top of her hand. She rummaged in her shoulder bag for her penlight, crouched down, and shone it on the upper portion of the cubbyhole.

"Joe," she called softly to her partner, "take a look at this." He came over and knelt next to her.

The key was fastened to the top of the cubbyhole by a piece of cellotape. Some of the tape had come loose, which was what had brushed her hand.

"There, right there." She shone her penlight onto a faint image in the raw wood next to where the key was fastened. "Somebody used the key and put it back but made the mistake of using the same piece of tape."

Cameron picked up the calendar. The July page had not been turned over to August. "What do you reckon? Herman—or someone—"

"My money's on him," Kate said.

"Mine, too. From the calendar not being turned over to August, Herman used the key sometime last month and never reached into the cubbyhole again. He had no idea the tape was loose."

"Sounds about right to me." Kate worked the bronze key loose from its hiding place with her pen and slid it into a plastic bag.

"Safe-deposit box," Cameron said, peering at the key. "The plot thickens. Too bad they're never marked to identify the institution they come from."

"Maybe there's some further clue in the desk," Kate said without conviction. If Herman Layton had gone to such pains to hide the key, chances were slight that he'd leave easy evidence of its location.

"No way," Cameron said in confirmation, "not a guy this paranoid. After we go through every one of those damn boxes you found in the bedroom and don't find anything, we'll have to go to every damn bank in the city." He pulled his damp shirt away from his body.

"But they'll be air-conditioned. Can we go right now?"

"Let's go talk to the ex—Mrs. Herman Layton," Kate said, grinning sympathetically. "Maybe she's got air-conditioning. Maybe she knows something about this." And, Kate thought, maybe this ex-wife would not match Peri's good opinion of her.

6

ARLENE Layton lived in a two-story apartment building half a block up from the white stucco church that sat at the foot of Kenmore Avenue on Wilshire. The neighborhood was old and settled, with front porches on most of its single-dwelling homes. As Kate parked the Caprice, she eyed five jean-clad, bare-chested male teen-agers leaning on the hood of a battered black Oldsmobile, passing a joint among themselves.

"Don't let that fancy house Peri lives in fool you," Cameron said, reading her mind about the jeopardy in this neighborhood for an older woman. "The Leakeys spent most of their time trying to finance their digs, begging for grant money. I'm sure Peri's life isn't much different."

Kate nodded. "I remember she said something about a foundation making that house possible."

"Foundation, yeah," he said sardonically. "With a chairman who's probably summering in Europe and figured out how to get himself a high-class house-sitter."

Getting out of the car into glaring sunshine, Kate flexed her left shoulder; it felt virtually normal. If she appreciated the healing power of sun, she hated the accompanying smog assaulting her nostrils, at its worst this time of the year and more acrid and thickly ferrous inland from the ocean and the west side where she lived and worked.

"Pigs," she heard one of the boys sneer, to laughter from his companions.

"Assertive females," Cameron joked as they walked across Kenmore. "Your body language gives us away every time."

"Couldn't possibly be that Police Academy strut of yours," Kate parried. The truth of the matter, she thought, lay in the fact that anyone wearing a jacket on a day like this qualified as either a certifiable nut or a plainclothes detective required by protocol to conceal a weapon.

The beige stucco apartment building, a faded chartreuse palm tree decorating its facade, was classic old Hollywood, its units a U-shape around an interior courtyard. But entry to this building was restricted by tall bars across a gate that had been either installed or reinforced recently; the footing on the two anchoring pillars appeared to be freshly dried cement. The intercom system also looked new; a touch tone pad rang the phone in the tenant's apartment. Kate punched in Arlene Layton's three-digit code.

"Yes." The voice was of indeterminate age, but its resonant, chesty timbre told Kate that this was Peri Layton's mother.

"Police," said Kate. "Very sorry to disturb you, but if you could spare us a few minutes—"

"Of course. I've been expecting you. Top floor, two nineteen." The buzzer sounded.

"Doesn't waste any time, does she?" Cameron remarked.

A large, kidney-shaped garden bordered with tile and planted with evergreen shrubbery occupied the center of the paved courtyard. "It's a swimming pool," Cameron exclaimed, pointing out its contours. "Somebody filled it in with dirt."

"Rent control strikes again," Kate observed.

"You have a problem with rent control?"

I have a problem with you challenging the most casual remark I make, Kate thought. She said, "Some landlords use it as a convenient excuse for abandoning amenities."

"Ain't that the truth."

This building, however, did not look to her in any way abandoned. The evergreens in the swimming pool–garden and several large pots overflowing with daisies were well tended; the hedge bordering the foundation was neatly trimmed. And the owner had cared enough about the safety of the tenants to reinforce the security systems.

She and Cameron made their way up a staircase to the second floor. A slender woman perhaps an inch or two over five feet tall, her short gray hair swept back from her face, her bluish green eyes magnified by thick lenses, stood stiffly erect in the doorway of apartment two nineteen. Kate extended her identification, thinking that Peri Layton should be grateful for inheriting her mother's ascetic features and arresting presence. "I'm Detective Delafield, my partner is Detective Cameron—"

"Yes, yes, I'm Arlene Layton. Do come in, please."

Surmising that this woman's anxiety not to have any business conducted or witnessed in public was probably due to the prominence of her daughter, Kate entered the ovenlike interior of an apartment darkened by closed pale gold drapes. A rotating fan on the breakfast bar whirred softly. Condensation spilled down the side of a pitcher of lemonade that sat on a tray, along with several glasses, on a small coffee table that appeared to be sculpted from a single piece of glass.

Kate looked around with interest and appreciation. A slender, translucent, cobalt blue vase held pride of place on a chrome pedestal. A piece of primitive African sculpture, a warrior in a defiant pose, stood as if in totemic protection of the hallway to Arlene Layton's bedroom. On top of a small bookcase, two ceramic vases of highly polished gold and blue and green bookended a collection of slipcovered books. A small quilt of subtle geometric patches hung like a tapestry on one wall; needlepoint flowers covered the seats of two chairs visible in a small dining alcove. Except for the African warrior, undoubtedly a gift from Peri, these objects fit into the apartment in so striking and beautiful an arrangement of color and placement that Kate knew they had been selected with exceeding care.

There was some memorabilia of Peri: a poster on the wall and a photocopy—Kate presumed it was a photocopy, although if so, it was a very good one—of Peri's doctorate degree from Berkeley in a shadow box frame, and two small framed photos on an end table, one of them the same graduation photo of Peri that Kate was now carrying in her jacket pocket, the one that Herman Layton had carried in his wallet. Several highly polished fossils were scattered around on surfaces as conversation pieces, but it was not a fraction of what was displayed in Herman Layton's cottage.

"This is a difficult time," Kate began, seating herself on the sofa beside Cameron. "Thank you for seeing us." Remembering that Herman Layton had worn a wedding ring, she noted that his ex-wife did not.

Arlene Layton replied to this opening with a regal nod. "May I pour the two of you some lemonade?"

"Wonderful," Cameron answered for himself and Kate. "Thanks."

Waiting to be served, Kate evaluated Herman Layton's former wife. Well-groomed, her navy blue linen pants and sleeveless white blouse crisp in the wilting heat of this top-floor apartment, she did not appear to be red-eyed or in any other way distressed by the news of her ex-husband's death. However, like her daughter, this poised, dignified woman might resist public displays of emotion; plus, she had been divorced for over two decades. Still, she had borne an only child with a man who had just been murdered. Kate reminded herself that she felt no lingering trace of affection for the aunt who had been an omnipresent and fondly regarded family member during her childhood. Her animosity to Aunt Agnes was new, but it sprang from long-standing and deep-rooted reasons. What were the deep-rooted reasons, if any, behind Arlene Layton's calm?

Kate took a swallow of the tart, refreshing drink, then asked, "What can you tell us about the death of your ex-husband, Mrs. Layton?"

"I was hoping you could tell me. My daughter either couldn't or wouldn't give me many details."

"Did she inform you as to the manner of his death?"

"She did."

"Can you think of anyone who would want to harm him?"

Arlene Layton shrugged and sipped from her lemonade. "Perhaps you know that I haven't been a part of Herman's life for many years."

Feeling as oppressed by the heat in this apartment as Cameron, who was fidgeting in discomfort beside her, Kate resigned herself to intermittent relief from the oscillating fan and to excavating for answers. "But you did see him from time to time."

"Of course. We went to the same bridge club. But we didn't interact; we were in different foursomes."

"When was the last time you saw or spoke with him?"

"Let's see, that would be . . . I guess last week, at the bridge club."

"He was in a regular foursome?" Cameron asked with interest. "Do you know their names?"

"Sam, Barney, and Russ," Mrs. Layton said with a faint smile as Cameron wrote in his notebook. "I have no idea as to last names—you know how it is with casual acquaintances. You'll have to check with the club— it's called The Grand Slam."

"I hear you," Cameron said, smiling back at her as he finished a note.

Arlene Layton possessed some of her daughter's charisma, Kate observed, and Cameron was succumbing just as he had to Peri. She herself was hardly immune; she found that she was steeling herself as she asked, "Just for the record, Mrs. Layton, where were you this morning?"

"Are you accusing me?"

Another element in common with Peri: defensiveness. "Certainly not," Kate answered. "We're just trying to develop information."

"I was here."

"Did anyone see you? Call you?"

"I'm afraid not. But all of us were here this morning."

"All of us?"

"I'm sorry, of course you're not a mind reader. The older ones who live here, eight of us. We call ourselves the Gang of Eight." As Kate and Cameron chuckled, Arlene Layton said loftily but with the hint of a smile, "We may be in our seventies, but we're plenty feisty. We never go anywhere unless there's at least four of us, whether it's to the grocery store or catching a bus or going down to the bridge club. Sometimes we take Marie's van, but she gets terribly nervous in all this traffic. We don't carry purses, but we do carry pepper spray. In plain sight." She added serenely, "I don't believe we appeal to much of anybody as a target."

"Good for you and the Gang of Eight," Cameron said, grinning.

"Life in Los Angeles in the nineties," Kate murmured.

"It's all happened so gradually," Arlene Layton said mournfully. "The drugs, it's all the drugs—but you police know that better than anyone. My daughter's begged me to move, but all my friends are either in this building or nearby. The church, my entire social circle's here. I'd rather stay and enjoy the years I have left than go off somewhere and die of boredom.''

''I'm sure your daughter's happy you've made such good adjustments to take care of yourself,'' Kate said, and then gestured to the poster and to the graduation photo of Peri. ''You must be very proud of her.''

''I most certainly am,'' she declared. ''But Peri's achievements owe everything to Herman and nothing to me. I did everything I could to discourage her. I told her she couldn't possibly fulfill her crazy ambitions—''

''My mother gave those exact same messages to me,'' Kate interrupted, unwilling to allow this self-flagellation to continue. ''She was your age and a product of her generation, too. You were being protective, you did what you thought was best.''

''Yes. True.'' She spoke emphatically: ''I've always been protective of her above all else. Perhaps your mother was inspired by you as I was by my daughter. Her independence of spirit led me back to school to get my teaching credential. Isn't it ironical when your offspring turns out to be your role model?''

''Irony of the best kind. I see too many parents who don't have a single reason to be proud of their kids, and vice versa.''

She had succumbed, just like Cameron, to this woman's charm, and Kate caught herself up with the harsh thought that maybe Peri's independent spirit had also inspired the divorce between Herman and Arlene Layton. There had never, thank God, been any hint of such a rift between her own mother and father. A divorce would have crushed her.

''I do take what credit I can.'' Arlene Layton's smile was ingenuous. ''Peri's the single reason I kept my husband's name. I enjoy a lot of reflected prestige from my daughter.''

''Mrs. Layton—''

"Yes. Back to the business at hand."

She seems very casual and cavalier about this, Kate thought. "Peri told us the extraordinary story about Mr. Layton and his encounter with the bones of Peking Man during World War Two."

"She did?"

The tone was polite, but there had been a flash of something behind Arlene Layton's eyes, passing so quickly that Kate could not classify it. She asked, "Did Peri tell you yet about the prehistoric find that was made this morning at Rancho La Brea?"

"No. She didn't." All the casualness had suddenly left her manner. Her stare pierced Kate. "Today? It was found today? How prehistoric is it?"

"It was found this morning." Kate glanced at Cameron; this was clearly his area of expertise.

He said, "Peri's tentatively identified it as *Homo erectus.*"

"She what?" Arlene Layton's eyes were wide behind her thick lenses; she looked utterly astonished.

"The packaging found with it—it needs authentication by a museum in New York, but your daughter seems to think it might be a part of the long-lost Peking Man fossils."

Arlene Layton's face drained of color as she listened to these words. "Too late . . . Oh dear God," she whispered. She raised a trembling hand to her cheek. "Herman . . . This was found today? At Rancho La Brea?"

"Yes." Kate watched her. "What do you mean by 'Too late,' Mrs. Layton?"

She responded in a stricken voice, "Herman's gone, and now this happens. I can't believe it. What an incredible . . ." She searched for a word.

"Coincidence," Cameron finished for her, to Kate's intense annoyance and disapproval. She made a note on the last page of her notebook.

"An incredible coincidence," Cameron repeated. "Can you give us any explanation?"

"Me? I can't imagine . . . Was there anything else, was there any indication of who . . ."

"Who put it there? We don't—"

Kate coughed, and Cameron obediently broke off. "The investigation is ongoing," she said, wanting to throttle Cameron. "The discovery's far too coincidental not to be connected," she said, and waited.

"Of course it is. It must be," Arlene Layton finally answered. She leaned over and picked up her lemonade and took a long drink of it.

Kate said confrontationally, "Do you know who placed it there, Mrs. Layton?"

"Of course not. How could you possibly—that's preposterous."

"Then where did it come from?"

"What did they find?" Shaking her head, she asked fiercely, "How much was there?"

"For the time being, it's evidence, and we can't release any details."

"But I have a right to know!"

Kate kept her tone courteous. "Why, Mrs. Layton?"

"Because I have a *right.* We had goverment people haunting our lives for years. I have a *right.*" Then, abruptly, she waved a hand in dismissal of Kate. "Never mind. If Peri looked at it, *she'll* tell me."

Kate found her intensity about the find interesting, in view of her apparent lack of grief over her dead husband. "You claim you can't recall any enemies your husband might have had—"

"I can't," she said sharply. "Are you always this unpleasant, Detective, or does your job require it?"

Kate said evenly, "Both, I expect. I don't mean to upset you, Mrs. Layton, but we're looking for a connection here. And there must be one. Please try and help us. Think all the way back. To the war, and this episode from when he was in the Marine Corps.''

"It was a very long time ago,'' she said in a mollified tone. ''The government looked into everything thoroughly. Herman did his level best to help them find those fossils. There's nothing I can add.''

Kate's instincts told her that something more lay behind Arlene Layton's agitation. She paused deliberately and for some moments wrote in her notebook, but nothing further was forthcoming.

Kate shifted to another topic: ''Did you know that your husband possessed a firearm?''

"That thing.'' Arlene Layton thumped her lemonade back onto its coaster, her mouth a moue of disapproval. "With all his safety precautions we hardly needed it, but I could never persuade Herman . . . The worst thing, he always kept it beside the bed in an unlocked drawer, fully loaded. I was terrified Peri would find it.''

"Did he ever have occasion to use it?''

"Never. Never even took it out of the drawer, to my knowledge.''

"If your daughter's safety was paramount,'' Kate prodded, ''why didn't you insist he get rid of it?''

"Herman spent four years in a Japanese prisoner of war camp under unimaginably brutal conditions,'' Arlene Layton said quietly. ''My husband needed that gun to feel truly safe, and it was very hard to argue in the face of what he went through. Peri was forbidden to come into our bedroom. To my knowledge, she never did. I did my best to persuade him, but I could hardly insist.''

"Why did Mr. Layton have a safe-deposit box?''

"A safe-deposit box?''

Assessing the amazement on Arlene Layton's face, Kate concluded that she didn't know her ex-husband as well as she thought she did. ''Did you not have a safe-deposit box when you were married to him?''

Arlene Layton laughed shortly, bitterly. "What would we have kept in it?"

"So you have no idea what valuables your ex-husband could have stored in there?"

"Valuables . . ." Again the laugh. "Herman and I were a classic case of the grasshopper and the ant. When it came to money, I couldn't persuade him to look beyond next week. Understand me, I don't blame him. It was the war, of course—he'd learned to live day-to-day as a POW. I wouldn't have even minded all that much except for how it affected Peri. I was the foolish one, believing he'd change, thinking I could change him. I waited too long to get started on my teaching career. This late in life, I'm just thankful I can squeeze by with my pension and savings. I don't have to cannibalize my daughter."

"What about your ex-husband?" Kate asked. "Did he ever feel entitled to cash in on Peri's success?"

Arlene Layton hesitated, then finally said, "Peri's been as generous as she could manage to be with both of us. Beyond that . . . I think Peri's the only one who can answer you."

"Thank you, Mrs. Layton. We'll have other questions." Kate rose to her feet and handed her one of her cards. "Will you call us if you think of anything?"

"Yes, of course."

Kate knew she would not hear from her.

Out on Kenmore Avenue, the young men who had been passing a joint among themselves had moved on. In the car, Kate started the engine, then sat unmoving as the air conditioner labored to cut through the blistering heat.

"Joe," she said, "never put words in the mouth of an interview subject. Let them finish their own sentences and their own thought process, no matter how tedious it is or how obvious the answer may seem to you."

Struggling out of his jacket and yanking his tie loose,

he nodded. "I know, Kate. I knew it was wrong as soon as I did it. It's how I try to connect, and I really need to watch it and stop myself. I've got a lot to learn."

"You're doing lots of things right. What do you think so far?"

Cameron said promptly, "I think Arlene did it. Her and her Gang of Eight."

"Really." Kate grinned at him. "And the motive?"

Cameron waved off the challenge. "Motive, schmotive. People are killed by people they know. In any good mystery, the least likely one's the killer. Arlene's least likely. So that's two good reasons why it's her."

"Sad to say, the first part of your statement is no longer true. Today most people are killed by perfect strangers. As the lead detective in this case, Joe—"

"Call me the *lead* detective," Cameron said dolefully, pronouncing the word to rhyme with *dead.*

"Okay, as the *lead* detective, where are we in this case?"

"Screwed. Even though the coroner's investigator all but called me a dipshit for saying it might be a hit, the killing's so callous I still think so. Either that," Cameron added somberly, "or somebody felt like sticking an ice-pick in him for kicks. And walked away whistling."

"So you don't think we have much of a chance."

"Not much." He shrugged. "You asked."

"It'll go against your clearance stats," Kate needled him. "Your first case—a net zero. Joe," she said, "we've only talked to a handful of people."

"Yeah, but how many more are there? The guy lived like Robinson Crusoe. You think his cronies at the bridge club wasted him?"

"Who knows? We need to talk to them. What about the jawbone?"

Cameron ran his fingers through his hair, creating darker rivulets in its fine, thin texture. "Yeah. That part doesn't fit. So what do you think, Kate?"

"I agree it could be a thrill killing. I don't think you're a dipshit to suspect it could be a pro hitter. Let's run with that for a minute. What is there in Herman Layton's life to bring in the heavyweights?"

Cameron whistled softly. "His connection to a priceless scientific treasure missing for half a century."

"Bingo. You say the jawbone is the part that doesn't fit. I think it's the one part that does fit. Don't you think this murder has everything to do with the appearance of that fossil?"

Cameron said with sudden animation, "We've got prints on that jawbone—"

"—to run through our database. We'll have the post in a couple of days and maybe learn something more from the pathologist. You never know. If the victim was a regular visitor at Rancho La Brea like Peri says he was, some of the staff know him and may have seen someone with him at times other than today. This investigation's just begun."

"There's that safe-deposit box key to check out," Cameron said. "Which means twenty-seven years of shoeboxes in Herman Layton's cottage to go through for some clue. Let's get going, Kate."

Kate pulled away from the curb.

A few minutes later, as she wove her way through traffic on Wilshire Boulevard, Cameron broke the silence to murmur, "About your friend Marcie . . ."

Surprised—and disappointed—that Cameron's mind was not fully focused, like hers, on the puzzle of Herman Layton's murder, Kate answered tersely, "What about her?"

"Her ex—how dangerous would you say he is?"

"According to the officer who responded to the four-fifteen," Kate said flatly, "Marcie's ex is a pussycat. Charlie Grissom is a Sacramento boy and couldn't be a nicer guy, and things got just a little out of hand—"

Cameron leaned his head against the backrest, making a gagging sound.

"Charlie swore on his mother's grave he'd never come near her again. Charlie said he just loved her too much. He just had to figure out a way to stop loving her."

" 'I can't help it, man, I just love her too much,' " Cameron mocked in a guttural growl, then said in his normal tone, "The wife beater's motto. Ever met this guy?"

"Haven't had the pleasure. Marcie had filed for divorce when she moved to L.A."

"How long has it gone on?"

"The abuse? Thirteen years, worse each year."

"Escalation from verbal?"

"You got it."

"Typical pattern," Cameron said. "And Marcie never pressed charges. . . ."

"Not till a broken arm and three cracked ribs and our zero tolerance policy for spousal abuse. She paid a big price for waiting. The court only gave him thirty days, suspended most of it, and ordered treatment. A friend helped her move again while he was incarcerated." The "friend" of course being Kate's own partner, Aimee.

"Where does Marcie live?"

"West Hollywood. He's found her again—which figured."

"Out of our jurisdiction," he said, obviously thinking aloud since she would know that West Hollywood was patrolled by the L.A. County Sheriff's Department. "How much are you involved?"

"Zero. What can I do? He's been fronted twice by our Threat Management Unit, including on his job, and lectured by a judge. His behavior's cost him visitation rights to his seven-year-old son, which only sent him farther around the bend. Her friend Aimee wants me to throw him against a wall and shove my .38 up a nostril."

"No use," Cameron grunted. "He knows you and the gun'll go away and he can get back to business as usual."

"That's what I told her. I told her Marcie has to let the TMU advise her how to take herself and her son out of L.A. and disappear. But Marcie's already moved twice."

"Today anybody with half a brain can find anybody. Unless you're in Witness Protection."

Kate said with interest, "Seems you know a lot about this stuff, Joe."

"You could say that. You know I started my police career in Victorville?"

"I knew that, yes." She remembered this detail from the briefing given to her before he became her partner. "I'm not much for desert country, but I've been there a few times. It's a really pretty town."

"I guess it is . . ."

Cameron broke off to gesture toward a storefront where a bearded homeless man lay on the pavement, shampooing and rinsing his hair under a tap normally used for hosing off the sidewalk.

"Enterprising fellow," Kate commented.

"Worst thing I ever saw was in Victorville," Cameron said. "Sam Raddich. Another Charlie Grissom, exact same MO. I was on patrol, we got called out to the Raddich place for the umpteenth time, only this time Rita was dead, and Josh, too, their eight-year-old boy. Raddich used a shotgun on his son and himself, brains and gore splattered all over everywhere. The wife—he'd tied her up and taken hedge clippers to her. We found parts of her in every room of the house."

"God," Kate breathed, her hands gripping the wheel as if for safety. "How come I never heard about this one through the grapevine?"

"Murder-suicide with mutilation, that's all that got released, how the *Daily Press* carried it. Everybody just covered their eyes, none of us went leaping out of that house wanting to talk about it, least of all me. Raddich'd managed to isolate his wife from every friend she'd ever had. He was a mean, moody bastard nobody liked. You're right, Victorville is a real pretty town. But for me, those murders turned the place into a charnel house.''

''So that's why you left.''

He said, ''I guess you don't know that two years ago I was in the Threat Management Unit for a minute or two.''

An item not mentioned at her briefing about Cameron. The formation of the TMU had been given impetus by a series of celebrity stalkings, but incidents involving the famous had turned out to be a small fraction of its work. ''Only a minute or two? Sounds interesting and challenging and like you could actually accomplish something.''

''I was frustrated as hell.'' His voice was low and intense. ''I was a glorified guidance counselor, and yeah, sometimes I could help women understand the danger they were in and how to protect themselves, but most of them couldn't see why they were the ones who had to uproot their lives and give up their friends and their careers and sell their houses and take their kids and disappear. They couldn't see why they were the ones who were going to jail, not their victimizers—'' He broke off and then asked, ''Can you get me this asshole's address, his car description and license number?''

''Why, Joe?''

''I have an idea.''

''You know that running his license could show up on a department audit.''

''If Marcie's a friend of a friend, I figure you can probably do it another way.''

''What do you need the info for?'' She said facetiously, ''You know a pro hitter?''

"Sure. Don't you?"

"Seriously, what do you have in mind?"

"Seriously, you'll have to trust me on that score."

"No way," she stated, turning the Caprice onto Veteran Avenue. "There's not a thing we can do till he's caught violating his restraining order, and we both know it. Sure, I'd love to see this bastard get his knees busted—"

"Busting his knees wouldn't do anything but ratchet up his rage. Kate, I take it Marcie's pretty close to this friend of yours, am I right?"

"All the way from grade school days."

"You know how the scenario's gonna play out—the pattern's all in place. He'll go on terrorizing her and the kid, it'll get worse and worse. You want to just sit there and let him do it? You want to let him turn into Sam Raddich? When it happens, you want your friend to see you as part of the system that let it happen? You want to drive by the place where Marcie buys it and know what happened to her in there?"

Kate asked, "Is this why you left Victorville? Driving by that house?"

"There were some other reasons why I had to get out of there," Cameron said with clear reluctance, "but yeah, that was a big one."

Kate understood that her growing comfort level with Cameron had caused her to step over a line. He had not answered the question the first time she had asked it, and now she had forced him to reveal more of himself than he had wanted to. She said, "The worst thing in my career, Joe, was a child murder. The rape-torture of a nine-year-old girl. I spent the most horrific two hours and fourteen minutes of my entire life listening to her killer describe everything he did to her and how he went about killing her."

"Jesus. And you could stay in Homicide after that?"

"I wasn't in Homicide," she said. "It's why I left

Juvenile to go into Homicide. I knew I couldn't deal with crimes against children day after day. This was way back in '78. The man was Victor Schmidt.''

"Victor Schmidt? You actually took the confession from that monster? Jesus, talk about nightmares . . .''

"I had them," Kate said.

"I appreciate you telling me, Kate," Cameron said, his face grim.

"Up till about a year and a half ago, I couldn't tell anybody. Somebody helped me break through it," Kate said. "Somebody I came to trust. Joe, I need you to trust me enough to tell me what you have in mind about Charlie Grissom."

"Doesn't work that way."

"It has to work that way with me," she stated, turning onto Tilden and searching for a parking place. "I won't be a party to having anyone physically harmed—"

"I'm telling you, physical harm doesn't come into it. This is a matter of trust, too, Kate. When and if you decide you can trust me, then get me the info I asked for."

7

At 3:30 A.M., Kate pulled into the parking lot of her condo and turned off the engine. Head bowed with exhaustion that seemed to reach into her bone marrow, she remained in the Saturn, her fingertips massaging her face, wincing at the needlelike pain under her eyelids.

She and Cameron had spent most of this past afternoon and evening in painstaking scrutiny of the contents of Herman Layton's shoe boxes, sifting through bank statements, canceled checks, utility bills, credit card statements, medical bills, bus transfers, grocery receipts: all the detritus of a man compelled to save evidence of the day-to-day passage of his solitary life. By her estimation, the net results of their search remained ambiguous. The bank statements revealed monthly deposits of social security checks and a military pension, and an annual interest withdrawal taken each December from a five-thousand-dollar savings account, indication that Herman Layton had reformed from his previous carefree, shortsighted fiscal ways. Neither the statements nor the records of the Bank of America accounts exposed what she and Cameron had hoped to find: a paper trail leading to the safe-deposit box that would fit the key she had found hidden in Herman Layton's desk. Later today she and Cameron would check out the bank branch listed on his accounts, but the lack of evident record told Kate that either the box did not belong to Herman Layton, or he was a coholder, or, more likely, it had been rented under an alias and registered to a post office box for receipt of any correspondence relating to its existence. All that conspicuous flotsam in the shoeboxes to the contrary, from what she had discerned about Herman Layton and his well-guarded life, he had been a man who would cover his tracks well if need be.

Afterward, she and Cameron had returned to the station and, under Kate's direction, had begun the official murder book for the case, the preliminary report and investigator's summary, plus the crime scene chart and summary reports of their interviews, bringing this paperwork into an exemplary state of completeness for Lieutenant Walcott when she came in this morning. As Cameron was about to transcribe the evidence inventory list for Herman Layton's cottage, Kate took mercy on him and sent him home.

Afterward, knowing that her aunt and Aimee were waiting for her, she had deliberately and perversely taken up the Aloysius Gonzales murder book and for the next hour had studied and reassessed its reports and photographs, seeking some avenue that would lead away from what Torrie Holden's negligence and subsequent court testimony had set up as a certainty: acquittal and the inevitable condemnation heaped on an incompetent police department by the press, and worse still, by the grieving family of a victim whose fatal misstep had been to innocently walk in on a major drug transaction.

Not to mention Carolina Walcott's withering scorn. Compared to her predecessor, Mike Bodwin, this new lieutenant was an altogether different kettle of fish. After the obscenity-laden tirade flung at Kate by Assistant District Attorney Marlene Dixon over Torrie Holden's transgressions in court, Bodwin would have offered aid and comfort. Carolina Walcott had interrupted Kate's explanation of the fiasco with the biting assessment, ''Bottom line is, this is a royal fuckup and you're the supervising detective. Good luck explaining this shit to the victim's wife and children.''

Kate had felt a glimmer of possibility stir as she re-read the witness interviews, but she had been unable to engage with it and finally closed the murder book, her concentration shut down by exhaustion. Or maybe it was conscience, she thought wryly, punishing her for the procrastination over her aunt. When she slept—if she managed any sleep this night—a new direction in the Gonzales morass might spin its way up out of her subconscious.

Kate squared her shoulders and then let herself out of the Saturn, quietly locking its doors.

A few minutes later, she just as quietly let herself into the condo.

In the darkened living room, in a pool of light from a single lamp, Agnes Delafield sat slumped in the arm-chair—Kate's own green corduroy armchair—in front of the flickering, murmuring television, feet up on the ottoman, head drooped off to one side, rimless glasses low on her nose, emitting a bubbling burble with each exhalation of breath. A lap robe was tucked neatly around her ample figure—undoubtedly Aimee's work. Miss Marple, paws tucked up under her head, lay curled up asleep on her expanse of lap.

Her aunt looked jarringly the same as when Kate had last seen her perhaps two decades ago. Aunt Agnes had seemed old to her then, and the passing years seemed to have ingrained her age like the weathering of a fence post.

Another source of light slanted into the room from beneath the door of the den, and Kate tiptoed her way toward it, mouthing to the cat, ''You philandering little wretch.'' Miss Marple opened her jade eyes, blinked once at Kate, and without a trace of compunction, closed them again.

In the den, Aimee, wrapped in her favorite plaid flannel bathrobe, sat at the computer engrossed, occupying this late night hour in one of her Internet chat rooms. After closing the door to the den softly behind her, Kate moved toward Aimee, whispering, "Honey, I'm home."

"Thank God." Aimee rose, embraced her. "Everything okay?" she murmured, smoothing Kate's hair, cupping Kate's face in her hands. "Those eyeballs could pass for a road map."

"Thanks. How do you feel? You look a lot better."

"Compared to you, I am. I think the flu's passed on through. I slept some today, too."

Kate could faintly smell apricot scents from Aimee's shampoo, and she leaned toward her and inhaled as if from smelling salts. She smiled into Aimee's violet eyes. Never was she more grateful for Aimee's presence in her life than when another homicide victim certified the fragility of life and of happiness.

Aimee asked, "How's the case?"

"Nowhere. At least not yet."

"We saw coverage on TV. A long-distance shot of you and Cameron at the Tar Pits. Peri Layton—wow. Aunt Agnes is very impressed."

Kate shrugged her impatience at this transparent attempt at peacemaking. "Sweetheart, it's three-thirty in the morning, this is beyond ridiculous."

Aimee stood back from her, her hands sliding down to Kate's shoulders and arms. "Just let the woman say her piece, Kate. That's all she wants. Then we'll put her in a cab."

"Like I have any choice," Kate muttered.

Aimee released her, turning back to her computer, and Kate asked plaintively, "Aren't you coming in there with me?"

"If it's what you want." Aimee half-smiled. "I've learned my lesson about blundering into your personal space."

Kate understood that she was referring to an emotionally charged, traumatic weekend in Washington almost three years ago when Aimee had clandestinely engineered attending a disastrous reunion of the men and women with whom Kate had served in Vietnam. "That was then, now is now," Kate stated. "I want you with me."

Aimee said wanly, "Aunt Agnes thinks I'm your roommate."

"You lecture me all the time about being in the closet," Kate said in vexation. "Why the hell didn't you tell her the truth?"

"I didn't think it was my truth to tell."

Kate reached for Aimee's hand. She marched into the living room, pulling Aimee after her. "Aunt Agnes," she trumpeted.

The old woman started; Miss Marple leaped from her lap. "What on earth—Kate. How are you? What time is it?" Aunt Agnes swung her feet off the ottoman and shook her head, fumbling at the blanket, adjusting her glasses, and patting at her disheveled white hair.

Kate held up both hands as her aunt struggled to rise from the armchair. "Stay there, Aunt Agnes. It's late, and we're all tired. Just tell me what this is all about."

"It's ah . . ." Her glance fell on Kate and Aimee's joined hands. "It's . . . I'm afraid one of those dreadfully complicated and personal . . . things." Gripping the lap robe, she fixed her watery blue eyes beseechingly on Aimee, strands of her disorderly hair drifting above her head like antennae. "My dear, you've been so sweet to me, I hope you understand—"

"I—" Aimee broke off as Kate tightened her grip.

"Aunt Agnes," Kate said curtly, "this dear, sweet girl is my partner. She shares every part of my life and this is our home. I have no secrets from her." At least nothing vital, she amended mentally.

Her aunt's pale, deeply furrowed lips quivered. "Be that as it may, I'm no more fond of this than you are,

Kate. I must say I can't begin to fathom your behavior.'' Her head shook so briefly that it might have been from a tremor. ''All of a sudden no Christmas or birthday cards. My every call goes into an answering machine. Aimee won't tell me anything, other than it's something to do with your mother. Well, I have no idea what that could be, and Eva was closer to me than a sister, and you've been dreadfully unfair not to tell me. I can't imagine what I've done to deserve—'' She broke off, then added in a shaky voice, ''You've been inexcusably cruel to an old woman.''

''You've been even more inexcusably cruel,'' Kate told her. ''If that's what you've come here to find out, Aunt Agnes, I'll tell you.'' With implacable coldness, she said, ''Thanks to you, I blamed myself for Mother's death. Thanks to you, I spent my life believing I was responsible for her every illness. Thanks to you, I took it all on myself when she died.''

Her aunt said in an appalled whisper, ''What in the world are you talking about?''

''Drop the naïve act, Aunt Agnes. It won't wash. How can you have no idea? You think you're going to walk in here and change history?'' She imitated her aunt's breathy intensity: '' 'Eva almost died when you were born, Kate. Eva was never the same after you were born, Kate.' That's what you told me. And told me and told me. Every time Mother had so much as a headache. What did you expect me to think?''

As Kate spoke, the old woman lowered her head and clasped her white curls between her two plump hands. ''The messages we give and we don't know we're giving them . . .'' She looked up at Kate through tearful eyes. ''I was only trying to tell you how much you meant to her. How you took it isn't at all how I meant it. I didn't have an idea in the world you'd take it so literally.''

Aimee eased her hand from Kate's and moved quietly

away; she took a seat on the sofa, tucking her legs up under her. With the physical connection to Aimee gone, Kate's anger burned into her. She strode to her aunt, standing over her; she wanted to heave this criminally stupid woman out onto the street. "How in God's name was I supposed to take it? What other interpretation could—"

"Kate, please—what I meant—I couldn't tell you . . . Eva . . . your mother was in torment, Kate. Before you were born. Even more so afterward. You were a living reminder of Eva's . . . secret. She couldn't have any more children, you see."

"I don't see. Everyone knew she couldn't have any more children. What is this melodramatic crap?"

Visibly shrinking from Kate's fury, Agnes Delafield raised both hands. "There *was* a secret. She made me keep it. Made me swear it on the Bible. I was the only one who knew, the only one she ever told. Kate, you know when I give my word—"

"Yes, I know." Having successfully intimidated her aunt, she did not relent. "I've grown up, Aunt Agnes. I have zero respect for somebody who throws away all common sense and compassion because of some stupid, rigid principle." She knew she was being unfair; everyone in the family including herself had taken advantage of Aunt Agnes's trustworthiness. But she charged on: "And now you see your way clear about breaking your word over this so-called secret."

"I have no choice. Eva's secret is coming out, no matter what."

Kate pulled the ottoman away from the armchair and sat down in front of her aunt. "All right. Let's get this over with. Tell me whatever it is you think you need to tell me."

"Kate," Aimee said, a soft plea for calm.

"You're not . . ." Kate's aunt did not appear to have heard Aimee; her watery gaze was focused entirely on

Kate. She cleared her throat as if the words were stuck there. "Kate, you're not . . . an only child."

So that's what this was about. Kate asked, "Is that what you came here to tell me?" She was gratified by the calmness in her voice.

"Some of it. She had a boy. But—"

"A boy. So I have a half-brother. Living?"

"Yes, living. Not a half-brother, Kate. He's Eva and Andrew's child."

Impossible. She went into full interrogation mode: "When did this happen?"

"September of '42. September sixth, I believe, but I'm not sure of the exact date." Her aunt's voice had strengthened. Now that she was finally able to deliver her news, she gathered herself and sat up straighter in her chair.

A deeply retarded child, Kate decided. Or with some other severe birth defect; otherwise, no way would her parents ever give him up. And even if they did . . . "I can't believe they wouldn't tell me," she said.

"Your father didn't know. Only your mother knew."

This was crazy. "How on earth could he not know?"

"Did they ever tell you anything about their court-ship?"

"For God's sake, Aunt Agnes. You know they did. They talked about it all the time. How they met through Uncle George and got married two months after Dad came home from the war because Dad pursued her till she gave in—"

"Of course I knew they'd told you that much," her aunt said defensively. "But Andrew and Eva met before the war. Did they tell you that?"

"Dad did," Kate said. When that revelation came about was one of her favorite memories of her father. He'd taken a clandestine day off work, and she'd played hooky from her junior high school classes. Her father had sworn her to secrecy over stealing this day together, and also about the topic that had come up as they sat in a rowboat making lazy, desultory conversation in the tender early spring sunlight as they waited for the perch to bite. She said now to her aunt, "He told me they'd had a wonderful whirlwind three-day romance. He told me he had a strong premonition he wouldn't come back from the war, and the time with her was all that kept him going while he was fighting. He'd been so certain he'd die, he didn't confide in a soul, not even Uncle George. He still could hardly believe he'd survived. He was just thankful he hadn't left anyone a widow—"

Kate broke off, mortified by her blunder. The woman sitting before her had been widowed a year after her marriage to George Delafield. He had been lost in the Pacific, his ship sunk during an attack by waves of Japanese aircraft. Aunt Agnes had been left devastated, according to Kate's mother, swallowed up by grief.

But Aunt Agnes was calmly nodding her agreement. "That's right, that's what happened. You know how close Georgie and your father were—"

"Like twins," Kate offered. Her aunt's presence was evoking more and more memories. Images from the treasured albums of snapshots she had seen innumerable times, the endless reminiscences of her father, story after story about George and Andy and their escapades. So inseparable had they been, they might have emerged from the same egg, their one divergence—provident in its own ironic way, as it turned out—the branch of the military each had chosen to serve his country, Kate's father enlisting independently, and later than his brother, to lessen the possibility that they might be assigned to the same area of battle.

Kate looked over to Aimee, who was faintly smiling; she had heard many of these stories along with a detailed description of the photograph that had hung over the mantel of the house in Greenleaf, Michigan: George Delafield in a formal, full-dress white naval uniform that only enhanced the deviltry in his eyes. Aimee knew how pervasively Kate had felt this dead uncle's ghostly presence during her childhood.

"Those boys were so close," her aunt was saying, "so close I believe to this day the death Andy foresaw so clearly wasn't his own but Georgie's."

Struck by the sageness of this insight, Kate said, "You could be right, Aunt Agnes. You still haven't answered my question: How could Dad not know?"

"Kate—" Fingers twisting the fabric of the lap robe, her aunt looked away. "Eva never told him."

Kate started to speak, then closed her mouth. Best to allow her aunt, who was not an interview subject needing to be prompted, to explain the incomprehensible.

"Like Andrew told you, Kate, he did have an affair with your mother before the war. Lots of young men and women did in those days—the war'd turned all of our lives upside down, and so we turned around and broke all the rules. Why not, when there might not be a tomorrow? I'd have done the same thing as Eva if I hadn't already married Georgie."

Kate remained silent, imagining stringently brought up young men and women recklessly throwing off the shackles of those simpler, more rigid days.

Her aunt said, "And then she found out she was pregnant."

"Why didn't she tell him?"

"What was she supposed to tell him? She'd known him three days. By then he'd shipped out overseas. Besides, you remember how your mother was. Her pride."

"Yes," Kate said softly. "I remember." Her mother's quiet, determined dignity was, to this day, the one characteristic Kate most wished to emulate.

"Eva wouldn't tell anybody. Back in those days it was such an awful disgrace—"

"That I know. It was terrible." She mused, "Having a child out of wedlock—you might as well have a scarlet letter on your forehead. It all but got you stoned in the village square.''

''You think it's any better today with all these child-mothers?'' her aunt said tartly. ''We could teach some good lessons about how to behave if the young people today would stop and listen.''

Kate was not interested in this side issue. ''How did Mother keep it a secret?''

''She went to Chicago. Remember her talking about that?''

''Sure, I remember,'' Kate said wonderingly. ''She lived there for three years—''

''That's right. Everybody in Greenleaf thought she'd taken a factory job for the war effort. A lot of women did just that.''

''For sure. Like you, Aunt Agnes,'' Kate said. Her aunt's own wartime contribution had been to drive an ambulance.

Her aunt acknowledged Kate's remark with a nod. ''Myself, I couldn't figure out why she didn't go to Detroit. We had relatives there.''

''No one knew about this? Not even Granny?''

Aunt Agnes shook her head. ''Not even Granny. It must have been so hard. Nobody knew except Doc Randall.''

The family doctor. Keeper, like her aunt, of the town's deepest, darkest secrets.

''Doc Randall helped make some arrangements for her in Chicago,'' Aunt Agnes said.

''When did you know about this?''

''After Andrew came back.''

''After he came back . . . I remember Dad saying she didn't want anything to do with him at first.''

Her aunt's voice was almost a whisper as she asked, ''After what she'd been through, can you blame her?''

Kate reflected. A whirlwind affair ending, except for the agonies of producing and giving away a child. Then the creator of that child blithely skids back onto the scene . . . "I guess not. But he finally did wear down her objections, didn't he."

"Not exactly. I went to her. Told her I couldn't imagine why she was playing so hard to get when anybody could see they were plain as day meant for each other. Well, she got terribly upset with me. I never saw Eva in such a state. After she told me to mind my own business—you know your mother—she said she wasn't playing at anything, and that's when she swore me to secrecy and confessed about the baby. She had to tell someone, she had to have somebody understand. Somebody she could trust."

Kate was struggling to picture her mother in such circumstances. "You must have been shocked."

"Shocked! I was heartsick for her. Bawled my eyes out. She knew for sure I understood. But she and Andy were still meant for each other, and I told her she could have more babies with Andy."

Kate nodded. "This baby . . . she had it all by herself?"

"All by herself." Her aunt sighed. "At some sort of home. For women in her situation. She never would talk about the details of what it was like, what went on there. She bought herself a wedding ring and of course she did get a job—before and after she had the baby."

"The baby was okay? Healthy?"

"Perfectly healthy. Perfectly beautiful, according to her, the very image of your father." Her aunt's eyes narrowed, the network of wrinkles around them deepening. "Eva had no choice but to give that baby up, Kate. Back in those days, it's what young women had to do. These antiabortion fanatics today, they tell young women to give their babies up for adoption like nothing could be easier, like it's the same as giving away a bag of jelly beans. They make me . . ." She clenched her fists. "They make me so angry. Eva—she truly didn't have any choice."

"I know that. I understand." Growing up with the deadly secret of her own lesbianism, who understood better about secrecy and hiding than she did? Rubbing her face, she said tiredly, sadly, "Dad would have so loved a son. Oh God . . ."

Her aunt said in a melancholy tone, "When she couldn't have any more children after you—"

Kate murmured, "So Dad went to his grave believing the Delafield name and line ended with him."

"He did. You can't imagine how much that haunted your mother up to the very day she died."

"Aunt Agnes, why couldn't she . . . why didn't she tell him? Especially on her death bed?"

"What would that have done except maybe kill him for his part in it? The adoption records were sealed. That baby—his son—was gone beyond recall. As if he'd vanished off the planet or never been born."

"They unseal records now—"

"Kate, your mother died in the early sixties," Aimee interposed, speaking for the first time from where she sat on the sofa. "They didn't open records to anyone. Not like they do today."

"Exactly right," Aunt Agnes said emphatically. "Andrew would have suffered such agony knowing—"

"Yes, of course you're right. Why tell me now? Why is this coming out now?"

"Because of what Aimee just said." Her aunt went on in increasing acerbity, "Because in this day and age, nothing is sacred and nothing is secret and the child your mother gave up half a century ago, he's hired somebody, he's tracked us down. I gave him no information about you, Kate," she said imperiously, "you know I wouldn't do that. But he says he's already onto you—as he put it. I felt I owed it to you for Eva's sake, to give you some advance warning, explain why it happened, how your mother came to—''

''What a horrible tragedy,'' Aimee murmured, arms tightly crossed as if she were trying to warm herself.

''If only he'd turned up before Dad died,'' Kate murmured. She asked, ''Have you seen . . . this man?'' She tried out the phrase: ''My brother?''

''I have not. He called me yesterday. And that's when I got on a plane and came out here. Since you gave me no other choice as to how I could talk to you.''

Kate ignored the remark. Her aunt had plenty of time and resources to make this trip. ''What's his name?''

''Dale Harrison.''

''How . . .'' She did not know how to phrase the question. ''How did he sound? How did he . . . seem?''

''I don't know, Kate.'' She sighed. ''Nervous, I guess. Curious. Eager.''

''What does he do for a living?''

''I haven't the vaguest idea.''

''Where does he live? Did he leave a phone number?''

''I didn't ask. I was so thrown—''

''I understand. Thrown is how I feel right now myself.''

''Kate, this other business about your mother, I never meant to—I know I can never make it right—''

''It's all right, Aunt Agnes, it really is.'' Sighing, Kate again rubbed her face. The pain behind her eyelids was worsening and her shoulder ached. ''You're right, I should have written you and explained how I felt. I was just too angry, it was all too close to me—''

''She was your mother. Believe me, I understand.'' Her aunt looked suddenly and completely fatigued, her face seeming to collapse in on itself like a balloon losing air, the lines of age even deeper. ''We can talk more tomorrow. I need to let you get some sleep before the night's over. Would one of you be good enough to call me a cab?''

''I'll drive you,'' Kate said immediately. ''Where are you staying? Are you here by yourself?''

''At the Days Inn. Janice, you remember my friend Janice? She came with me. But you'll by no means drive me.'' Her aunt waved a hand. ''I'll leave you to yourselves. A brother you've never heard about suddenly barging into your life—Kate, you've got a lot to think about.''

Aimee answered for both of them: ''We do.''

8

KATE stepped from the shower, then got back in, turning the hot water tap off and shuddering under the cold spray. She had slept little; her head was reeling with tiredness. "My brother, Dale," she said aloud, hearing the words echo in the shower stall.

Roughly toweling skin nubby with gooseflesh, shocked into alertness, she stared at her image in the mirror. "Too old for this," she muttered. Then, leaning forward to examine her bloodshot eyes: "Too tired." She flexed her shoulder. "Too beat up." Then, inspecting her chunky torso in the mirror, she concluded her grumbling litany: "Too damn fat."

Had Dale, her brother, grown up to resemble her father? Kate thought, He might even look like me.

Through the slightly ajar bathroom door, a hand appeared holding the portable phone. A yawning, barely intelligible voice mumbled, "Your lieutenant."

"Sorry," Kate whispered in apology to Aimee, who had been roused out of a much-needed and well-deserved sleep. She said into the phone, "Yes, Lieutenant."

"Kate, I know you were up till all hours," Walcott said without preamble. "This is important. I need you at the station."

"I'm showered, twenty minutes from being there," Kate replied, disturbed by the additional curtness in

Walcott's usually curt tone. Was she being called on the carpet officially over Torrie Holden's screwup of the Gonzales case? Or had something else gone wrong?

"It's Layton," Walcott said.

Something she'd missed in the reports? Something Cameron hadn't done, or done wrong, and she'd missed it? "Should I call Joe?" she offered.

"This concerns you alone," Walcott said. "Detective Cameron is to remain off duty until he hears from you. Just get in here ASAP."

"Right," she said, and heard a buzzing dial tone.

What the hell was this all about?

Twenty minutes later, after pausing in the hallway to give a final tidy to her jacket and pants, Kate rapped on Lieutenant Carolina Walcott's closed office door.

"Come in," Walcott called.

As she entered the office, a man, gray-haired, gray-mustached, and gray-suited, glanced up from a blue file folder. He raised and then lowered bushy gray eyebrows from behind his spectacles as he evaluated her, then laid his folder on Walcott's desk and rose to his feet, uncoiling an aristocratically lean body. A briefcase gaped open on the floor beside him.

Walcott, crisply attired in a navy blue linen jacket and a white blouse, nodded to Kate from behind her desk, her features revealing nothing. "Would you close the door behind you," she said quietly.

Obeying, Kate noted that Walcott and the gray-haired man apparently had not been speaking to each other; Walcott's hand remained frozen over the file she had been leafing through, and her visitor had been reviewing the blue folder, its cover embossed with the head of an eagle and a crest with a starburst.

"Kate," Walcott said, "this is Case Officer Nicholas Whitby of the Central Intelligence Agency—"

"A pleasure, Detective Delafield," Whitby interrupted Walcott, leaning forward and extending a hand.

Recovering from her surprise, she took his dry, cool hand. "My pleasure as well," she said.

"Grab a seat," Walcott said.

Kate pulled the remaining chair back to an angled position in front of Walcott's desk so that she could observe Walcott and the CIA officer. Her immediate impression was that Whitby looked past retirement age, too old to be a member of any government agency, much less the CIA. His narrow face looked drawn and tired, yet he seemed more confidently at ease in his chair than Walcott did in her position of authority behind her well-organized desk.

The fourth Lieutenant Kate had reported to in this office, African-American Walcott had followed the pattern of her predecessors in installing family photographs on her desk and reconfiguring the office to her own specifications. Her predecessor, instant-reactor Mike Bodwin, had thrived amid a constant rearrangement of priorities, the continually shifting politics and chaos of police work, and dispensed with paperwork as fast as it arrived in his in box; but Walcott allowed paper to accumulate until she could comfortably get to it, and had added two four-tiered file trays to her credenza, each layer neatly labeled for the reports and memos demanding her attention. Her style was to work methodically, and Kate had learned that the variables falling outside Walcott's demarcated lines of order and organization drew her impatience if not her ire.

Clearly, Nicholas Whitby was a spike of chaos. A telltale crease of annoyance between her dark eyes, Walcott said, "You may have guessed what this is in regard to, Kate."

She nodded; it would take a particularly unobservant detective not to notice the Herman Layton case file and murder book that lay open before Walcott, Kate's and Cameron's signatures on the visible reports.

"I'd like you to brief Case Officer Whitby," Walcott said.

"Gladly," Kate said. "I thought CIA people were called agents, same as the FBI," she said temporizingly, searching Walcott's impassive features for any clue as to how condensed or thorough she wished this briefing to be.

"If I were a CIA agent, you wouldn't want me sitting in this office," Whitby answered, his voice a low but penetrating monotone, his pale blue eyes, slightly magnified by his steel-rimmed glasses, surveying her dispassionately. "The people recruited by CIA officers to betray their country are called agents, or assets. Officers are staff employees. We consider ourselves patriots."

Instantly detesting his arrogance, his unapologetic dismissal of his agency's infamous history, Kate wished she could say that millions of people held an opinion far different from his. His attitude was identical to what she had observed in FBI agents, an almost cultlike we're-right-everybody-else-is-misguided mentality that treated agency doctrines and practices as infallible, and detractors as the enemy. That Whitby's agency had destabilized and toppled foreign governments would be a source of pride to him, and the downright bungling of its own internal processes that had produced a lethal traitor in its midst, Aldrich Ames, would be a trifle. To this overweening man, humility was the ultimate foreign concept.

"Your fullest cooperation will be appreciated, Detective," Whitby said, his precise, monochromatic voice like a buzz saw in her ears. "You may consider your reports models of clarity, but please conduct your briefing in an even more detailed manner."

Antagonized in double measure by Whitby's condescension and his assumption of authority in her own lieutenant's office, Kate again glanced at Walcott, who responded with a tightening of her lips and a barely perceptible nod. "Yes sir," Kate said.

Taking her notebook from her shoulder bag, she related her observations of the crime scene and the circumstances surrounding the discovery of the jawbone at Rancho La Brea and the interviews she and Cameron had conducted thus far with Herman Layton's next of kin and some of the personnel at the Tar Pits, observing with interest Whitby fidgeting in his chair, his rising impatience. As she went into more detail about her interview with Arlene Layton, Whitby interrupted her.

"Layton's cottage," he said. "Let's flash forward to that. You conducted a search."

"Detective Cameron and I did so, yes," Kate responded.

"Anything out of the ordinary?"

An imp of perversity told her that he would be most interested in the safe-deposit box key. "A three-fifty-seven magnum," she said. "Some pornographic magazines."

He shrugged. "This information is not in your reports."

"No, sir. Work on our reports took us until three o'clock this morning, so we did not fully complete the inventory list."

"Your industry is commendable," he said. "Your handwritten notes, please. I'll need to see them."

"Yes, sir." She curled her fingers protectively over her notebook. "Since they may be called into evidence at a trial, I'll have copies made."

Massaging his long chin with the tips of his bony fingers, he contemplated her. And finally said, "I suppose copies will do."

Kate said, "Detective Cameron's notes are with him."

"Of course. You'll get them for me, won't you, Detective."

"Detective Cameron will certainly cooperate with you, sir."

"No, he won't," Whitby said. "He's not to be aware of my involvement."

"Sir, he's my partner."

"And so you trust him?"

"He's my partner," Kate repeated. "And he's the lead detective on this case."

"In name only. How long has he been in homicide?"

"Three weeks."

"And how long as your partner?"

"Three weeks."

After a pause to let her know how ludicrous any concept of loyalty would be under such circumstances, he followed up: "How long have you yourself been a homicide detective?"

"Fifteen years," she replied, knowing that all of his questions had been rhetorical and that he had the answers.

"We prefer to deal directly with you, Detective."

After a cautious glance at Walcott, Kate ventured, "Am I allowed to ask questions here?"

"Ask away," Whitby said expansively, folding his arms across his chest and settling his long frame back into his chair.

"Why is the CIA involved?"

"Next question," Whitby said.

"Since the CIA is involved for whatever reason," Kate said doggedly, "doesn't investigation of this case fall under the guidelines for transfer to Robbery-Homicide at Parker Center?"

"Good question," Whitby said.

So was my first question, Kate wanted to say.

"As I understand it, your Robbery-Homicide unit investigates unusual or high-profile homicides. At all costs, we need to prevent the Layton case from seeming unusual or becoming high-profile. And that requires the utmost discretion and judgment. One does not need to live in Los Angeles to know that your Robbery-Homicide people have proved themselves to be a sieve of indiscretion, even before the O. J. Simpson debacle. Robbery-Homicide is out of this equation, as is Detective Cameron because he's an unknown entity. You, on the other hand, have a fine record and a fine reputation.''

Unimpressed by the compliment and realizing that authorization for Whitby's pronouncements and decisions had come from echelons of rank light-years above herself and Walcott, Kate said, ''Sir, am I to understand that I work solo on this case?'' Which would turn the investigation into a nightmare of unwitnessed interviews, should it ever go to trial.

''Absolutely not. That in itself would be a red flag. We want you to work with Detective Cameron but report directly to me.''

''Detective Delafield is to report directly to me,'' Walcott said sharply. ''I'm still a major part of this equation.''

Kate wanted to applaud. She strongly suspected that sexism was an element of Whitby's condescension; he was a member of the generation that had never ceased its scorn of women in law enforcement. Not to mention African-American women.

''Of course you are, Lieutenant,'' Whitby said easily. ''Through you to me. I thought that went without saying. Detective, we need you to develop information very quickly.''

''The post mortem,'' Kate said, ''I'll try to have it moved up.''

Whitby waved off her offer. ''It's scheduled for one o'clock this afternoon.''

Looking wonderingly at this man who could so easily circumvent all the normal bottlenecks of police work, Kate stated baldly, ''I assume this urgency has to do with the prehistoric find made at the La Brea Tar Pits yesterday.''

''Assume what you wish,'' Whitby said, picking up the blue folder from Walcott's desk and dropping it into his briefcase. Kate now recognized its embossed eagle and shield as the insignia of the Central Intelligence Agency.

''Do you have any special instructions, sir?'' she asked with cold politeness.

''Continue your investigation as you normally would. Discuss this case with no one outside of those directly involved. Your only contact, as stated, will be with your lieutenant, whose only contact will be with me.'' Whitby snapped shut his briefcase and then glanced up at Kate and then over at Walcott. ''Are we clear on this?''

''Perfectly,'' Walcott said, a razor edge in her tone.

''Clear,'' added Kate.

Whitby rose to his feet and moved unhurriedly from the office, leaving the door ajar behind him.

''How nice of our Captain Delano to drop this asshole in my lap,'' snarled Walcott.

''Careful,'' Kate said facetiously, ''Whitby might have planted a bug.''

''He probably did. He's still an asshole. Issuing orders like he's Moses with the tablets, like he's holding aces and us poor schmucks need to make do with deuces.''

Gratified by her disdain, Kate asked, ''Are you any further enlightened as to who this guy is?''

''Of course I am,'' Walcott snapped. ''You think I just roll over anytime some snotty asshole strolls in here and waves fancy credentials under my nose?''

She yanked a lined yellow notepad from her top desk drawer. ''I know all about the Whitbys of the world. Their stock in trade is intimidation. I grew up in a Southern town full of assholes like Whitby. I know I don't have to take anybody's shit. And that's the secret: knowing you don't have to take it.''

Looking into a milk chocolate face made darker by anger, Kate judged that Carolina Walcott would go places in LAPD, as long as she chose carefully when to exercise this hard-won wisdom.

"The CIA's the exact same kettle of shit as the FBI," Walcott snorted. "They think every goddamn thing they do has to be a secret. Whitby called me from a chartered goddamn plane over San Francisco at six o'clock this morning, so one thing I knew coming in is this dude is in one hell of a hurry. We have a victim dead less than a day, and we've got a CIA wiseass busting in here—"

"How could they find out about Layton so fast?"

Walcott nodded at Kate's question. "Believe me, I asked. He said the information was classified. I figure they pulled it off the *Times* wire services. Something got triggered in their computers, and that triggered Whitby. So I asked Whitby what I knew he could tell me. I told him I wanted background, his background, before I'd even think about cooperation. I told his royal high-ass that if he didn't tell me who the hell he was and what he was doing in my office, I'd throw so many roadblocks in his way it'd take him all day just to work his way past Venice Boulevard."

Kate smiled, pleased to see Carolina Walcott's abrasiveness turned on someone other than herself.

"This is what he told me he could tell me," Walcott said sarcastically, consulting her notepad. "Case Officer Nicholas Whitby has served in India and Bangkok, and as chief of station in Taiwan and Tokyo. He's been with the CIA since 1958—retired now, as you might have guessed, and living in San Francisco, but he still serves under the national intelligence officer. Apparently, retired operatives are quite often brought back in for special assignments. I'm glad they haven't thought up the same dumb scheme for retired cops."

"Lieutenant, do you know what this is all about?"

Walcott let out an exasperated sigh. "Beyond what I've just told you, I know as much or as little about it as you do. Whitby may be dissatisfied with your reports, Kate, but I'm grateful as hell for the work you did last night. You saved me from embarrassing myself this morning."

Kate felt scalded by the praise, felt heat rise to her face over this unimaginable compliment from Walcott.

Studying another note on her pad, Walcott said, "It's connected with that prehistoric fossil, there's no other possibility. Beyond that—"

"Why is the CIA in on this? If this is something in the national interest, why isn't the FBI involved? Don't they handle all the federal domestic stuff? I thought the CIA wasn't even allowed to operate in this country."

"Believe me, I mentioned that very issue," Walcott said, tapping a roller pen on her notepad. "Whitby claims the CIA's domestic operations absolutely do not involve spying on the domestic activities of Americans." She imitated Whitby's monotone and precise diction: "Under the CIA charter, we may not exercise law enforcement powers or undertake internal security functions in the United States, but that does not mean we cannot operate within our borders or gather intelligence so long as the target is foreign. Codified by Executive Order blah blah signed by Almighty God Reagan on blah blah date."

"I don't like this," Kate muttered.

"Neither do I, goddammit. So then I asked how he got Captain Delano's home number, much less calling me at home from a plane at six this morning. He told me those sources were classified information."

"I don't like this at all," Kate repeated, in escalating alarm.

"We're stuck with it."

"Do you realize—" Kate sat straight up in her chair. "This means they suspect a foreign power is involved with Layton's death. Holy hell, Lieutenant. If they actually think this could be one of the bones from Peking Man, then . . . it must be . . . China.''

"Maybe so."

In her agitation, Kate ran both hands through her hair. "I think maybe I just made a major mistake with Whitby." She braced herself: "I need to tell you. I didn't tell him Joe and I found a safe-deposit box key in Layton's house."

But Walcott laughed, a rich laugh from deep inside her. "Good. Unless you're dealing with God herself, always keep some leverage. Where's the box located?"

"We don't know yet," Kate said, relieved by her reaction. "He taped the key to the underside of his desk and we couldn't find any paper trail to it. Tracking down the box was on the docket for today."

"It still is. If he hid the key, it was for a damn good reason." Walcott made notes on her pad, ruminating aloud as she wrote. "We'll need a search warrant. Given that Layton divorced his wife, Peri Layton's next of kin, so we'll need her to sign a Consent to Search—assuming we find the box, and let's hope he didn't do too good a job covering his tracks and it's God knows where." She glanced up at Kate. "You foresee any problems with consent from Peri Layton?"

"No," Kate answered. "I think she'll be cooperative."

"Good. I'll have her furnish us with a photo of the victim for canvass. For now, let's assume the box is somewhere on the west side and begin there. We'll do the work. We'll track it and page you if we find it, a uniform will deliver the paperwork. We'll tell Whitby you found the key today, or something. Don't worry about it." She made more notes on her pad. "Obviously, we need a uniform at the Layton house. You and Cameron get over there and go over the place again. This time with an even finer tooth comb. Photograph it, have the lab print it.''

''Will do, Lieutenant.'' Kate said, ''You must have been one hell of a detective in your day.''

''I was one hell of a detective but not a very good one,'' Walcott said, finishing a note. ''Not at South Central. Nobody had time to do a decent job, not in that place. Besides, my partners were assholes.'' She looked up at Kate. ''I want things different here.''

''I hear you,'' Kate said quietly. ''Lieutenant, I'm not comfortable keeping this from Joe Cameron. It's a bad way to start off a new partnership.''

''I know that, Kate. But for now, we have to stay at least within hailing distance of their guidelines. Assert our independence too far, and my sense is we'll bring a whole shitload of trouble down on our heads.''

9

IN the Wilshire Division parking lot, Cameron climbed out of his Jeep Cherokee, scuffed his way through the dust from the adjacent construction project, and got into the Caprice where Kate waited for him, engine running. "Another pisser of a day," he growled by way of greeting. "L.A.'s a ring of hell this time of year."

So move somewhere else, she wanted to say. She was sick of his bitching about the heat.

Loosening his tie, he peered over at her as she silently wove her way out of the parking area. "Cat got your tongue? I've seen better-looking faces at an autopsy."

"I'm sure," Kate returned, thinking that Cameron, freshly shaven and neatly attired in his dark brown jacket and tie and beige pants, seemed not only rested but energized.

"Pretty rough time with your aunt?"

"My aunt," she repeated dully as she mentally switched gears. The events of the meeting with Walcott and Whitby had shoved aside everything else in her consciousness.

"Your aunt," he repeated. "The cat's got your brains. The woman you wanted to run out of town on a rail yesterday. No big deal, I take it."

"Just yesterday's news," she responded facetiously. About to add some innocuous explanation for her aunt's visit, she hesitated, then stated baldly, "I have a sibling

I didn't know about. According to Aunt Agnes.''

He jerked around toward her. "No shit. What—''

"A brother. A blood brother.''

"Jesus. *That's* a news item, Kate. Is it true?''

"The evidence looks pretty persuasive.''

From the time she had left Walcott's office, she had been focusing on how best to handle the next steps in an investigation whose full dimension she must conceal from this new partner. Neither dislike for Nicholas Whitby nor contempt for the CIA gospel that a rookie homicide detective deserved no one's faith or trust eliminated the fair question as to how much confidence she could actually place in Cameron, personally or professionally. Revealing personal information made her feel less guilt over concealing the new direction of this murder case, and as she drove up La Brea, she willingly outlined the parental history she had gleaned from her aunt.

"What a story,'' he said. "So what are you going to do about him?''

"Nothing,'' she answered, turning onto Wilshire and immediately cutting over to the far right lane and away from a city truck that was painting fresh yellow lane-separation lines on the boulevard. "I'll be hearing from him. According to Aunt Agnes.''

"How do you feel about this, Kate?''

"Weird,'' she admitted, touched by the concern on his face and in his voice. "Thrown. He's a total stranger, Joe. Yet he's somebody with a . . . connection to me.'' She managed a brief laugh. "The poor devil might even look like me.''

"Things could be worse.''

"Thanks. Do you have brothers or sisters?''

"One of each,'' he replied. "Jean's in Phoenix, we're real close.'' He said in a flatter tone, "Jack's still in Victorville.''

Was he estranged from Jack? She knew she could not

pursue her curiosity and instead remarked, "Joe, your parents like names beginning with J."

His shrug signaled an end to that discussion. Pulling his notebook from his inside breast pocket, he said, "I figure today's agenda is we run down the safe-deposit key, find the bridge club, and see about interviewing the victim's card-playing partners. Follow up on the Kiwis who found the body. Hey," he said as they came up to and passed the turnoff to the Tar Pits, "are we headed somewhere?"

She cast a lingering glance at the prehistoric mammoth in the lake pit fronting on Wilshire as if to glean some new clue to solving her problems of the day. "According to Lieutenant Walcott, the agenda for the day starts with another search of the Layton cottage. The post is this afternoon."

"This afternoon? Isn't that sort of unusual?"

More like astounding, she thought, grateful for Cameron's inexperience. She decided that her best strategy was to shrug.

But he persisted: "How come so soon?"

"I wondered about that myself," she responded in wry understatement.

"How come we have to search the cottage again? Didn't we do a good enough job yesterday?" He added tersely, "What the hell's going on, Kate? I thought I was supposed to be lead detective on this case."

"The agenda's been set for us," she answered, feeling his stare as she drove. "Walcott's directly involved herself and speeded up the investigation. Including assigning officers to canvass the banks."

"Jesus, Kate. If she has no confidence in me, that's one thing—"

"What makes you think you're the one getting the no-confidence vote?" Kate fixed her eyes on the Cadillac in front of her, unwilling to meet his gaze. She loathed having to be a part of this subterfuge.

"If you mean the Gonzales mess—"

"What else?"

"That one's not your—"

"It is, Joe. Torrie Holden made the mistake, but I was the supervising detective."

"I guess Walcott's new to both of us," he conceded. "I never thought I'd be in the same boat as a D-three with all your experience, but right now I guess we both need to prove ourselves."

"I guess we do." She relaxed her hands on the steering wheel. He had bought it. For the time being.

"Is there some method to Walcott's madness? What the hell does she think we'll find at the Layton cottage?"

"Maybe more clues to Herman Layton. She wants a fine-tooth-comb search, prints, photos, the works. Won't hurt. Maybe we'll find prints to match up with something interesting—like the ones on the jawbone."

"Maybe, assuming we ever match anything up with anybody. My money's on that safe-deposit box key." Flipping closed his notebook, he slumped back in his seat.

Kate squinted as a flashbulb of sunlight reflected off the bumper of a Honda changing lanes in front of her. How, she wondered, would she explain the necessity for confiscating Cameron's notebook to copy it for Nicholas Whitby? She'd cross that bridge when she came to it. Best to cross all her bridges when she came to them.

The curtain in Meyer Silverman's front window moved in the same way as when Kate and Cameron had first come here to check out Herman Layton's address. "The unobservant Mr. Silverman who knows nothing, sees nothing," Cameron muttered as he and Kate made their way down the mossy flagstone path.

The officer assigned by Walcott to guard the premises had not yet taken up his post, but Shapiro had arrived; the photographer was slouched against the whitewashed exterior of the cottage, smoking a cigarette. Over the years, Kate's opinion of Shapiro had not changed; she considered him a barely competent sloth, while he thought she was an obsessive perfectionist. They exchanged unsmiling, scarcely civil nods, and she unfastened the police tape seals on the door.

"The usual everything, I assume," Shapiro said caustically, following her inside the cottage.

"Everything," she confirmed. "Plus video. Bedroom first."

"Place is a fucking sauna," Shapiro griped as he set down his camera cases.

Kate sucked in her breath; the interior of the cottage seemed more ovenlike than yesterday, the sweet moldering smell more intense. That blue-bottle fly she had seen in Layton's bedroom yesterday had been sensible, she thought, in trying to butt its way out through the window.

Making exaggerated suffocating sounds, Cameron shrugged out of his jacket and hung it neatly on the back of the desk chair. "We section the whole place off like a crime scene," he said.

"You got it," she replied, removing her own linen jacket and draping it on top of Cameron's. "We look at everything, do a full inventory. Let's follow the same blueprint as yesterday."

Within the pattern formed by the exterior bars on the windowpane in Layton's bedroom, Kate noticed a dark, crescent-shaped blob she did not remember from the day before. With Shapiro's camera strobe-lighting the room, she moved closer.

It was the fly. Crushed flat against the glass.

Squelching an automatic exclamation of astonishment, she composed herself by donning her plastic gloves. Then she followed Shapiro around the room, examining it carefully. The bedroom looked undisturbed to her; it looked exactly the same as it had yesterday.

After Shapiro completed his work in the room, she conducted her part of the search methodically, retracing yesterday's steps as best she could remember, a prickling between her shoulder blades, her senses fully alert to any other discrepancies. Going through the pockets of Layton's clothing, she surreptitiously observed Cameron to see if he noticed anything out of synch, off kilter. He gave no sign, whistling tunelessly under his breath as he removed bedding and turned up the mattress, as he dumped the contents of dresser drawers, holding the drawers by their edges in his plastic-gloved hands to check underneath. She was certain of only one fact: that their search was a useless exercise. Whoever had been here would have already found whatever was to be found. Unless she and Cameron had found it yesterday.

In the kitchen, she perceived a faint scattering of either salt or sugar in the sink and thought she would have noticed it yesterday, but she couldn't be sure. She had never believed it possible that someone could conduct a clandestine search and not leave traces. There would be subtle disorder—the contents of a cupboard replaced illogically, a photograph imprecisely recentered within its lighter imprint on the wall—something would be amiss. Whoever had performed this search was a master at his trade and had undoubtedly been here all night, evidenced by the fly, which would have renewed its quest for freedom at first light. Save for a loss of patience over the persistent buzzing of that fly, the intruder would have come and gone undetected.

Who had been here? The expertise of this search rendered two possibilities. One was that no expertise was involved at all—cottage owner Meyer Silverman had come in and simply looked around. But Silverman had said that he didn't have a key, and Kate now believed him. The second possibility was that Nicholas Whitby had made at least one phone call much earlier than those he had placed to Captain Delano and Lieutenant Walcott this morning.

"Keep on with this, Joe," she said. "I'll take a minute to see if Mr. Silverman's memory has improved since yesterday."

"I wouldn't bet on it," he said absently, lifting a tray of ice cubes to eye level and then shaking them out into the sink.

Meyer Silverman answered her ring promptly but planted his small frame in the doorway, stroking his beard with a thumb and forefinger as he peered up at Kate. "Where is the young man detective?"

"Busy at the moment. May I come in?"

Hooking his thumbs through his suspenders, he shook his head.

"Mr. Silverman, I have just a few questions."

"I know nothing."

"They're very important questions."

"To you. Not to me."

"Let me explain. I can sympathize with your suspicion of the police. But that rental unit will be sealed until my questions are answered. I won't be the only one asking them. Police officers will be here constantly—"

He turned and shuffled away; she closed the door quietly and followed him into the front parlor.

"Ask," he said, not seating himself.

"Mr. Silverman," she said, standing by the window and holding its curtain aside, "who was here during the past few weeks or so? I need to know about everyone you observed visiting Mr. Layton."

"The man who's there now."

Shapiro. She asked, "Who else?"

"Two women, this week. One old, the other tall, blond, no-nonsense." He made a pretense of walking, swinging his arms vigorously.

Concealing a smile, Kate nodded; it was a more than passable description of Peri Layton.

"She was in the photograph you showed me yesterday," he added in confirmation.

"Were the two women here together?"

"No. Days apart."

"What did the other one look like?"

"Old."

"Tell me more."

He shrugged. "Old."

"A white woman? What color was her hair? Did she have trouble walking? What was she wearing?"

"White woman, short gray hair." Stroking his beard as he gazed at her, he added, "Even with the glasses, these days I don't see so good."

She smiled, glad to alter her opinion that old women were just as invisible to a male peer like Meyer Silverman as they were to most of the rest of the population. "Try and remember when they were here, what day."

He leaned back against the wall, contemplating her. "The young one, Monday. The old one, the next day."

"Did you see anyone else today, or this week?"

"A policeman yesterday. Tall, fat."

That would have been Donaldson, with skeleton keys to open Layton's door. "Anyone else?"

He shook his head. "Only the other detective."

"*What* other detective?"

He looked at her in exasperation. "You don't even know who comes here from your own police station?"

Recovering her balance, she asked, "When was this?"

"After you and the young man detective came here the first time. Tried to sneak his way in," he said indignantly.

"How do you mean?"

Up on his toes, he took a few mincing steps. "Sneaking down the path like this, looking this way and that."

"Did you confront him?"

"I confront no one. People trip my alarm, I look to see who's there."

"Can you tell me what he looked like?"

"Older." He shrugged. "Big. Big for Chinese."

Chinese. "How did you know he was a detective?"

"The clothes." He plucked at his gray cardigan. "A suit and tie, like the other young man detective. He showed me identification. Like yours."

She took out her badge. "Like this?"

"Of course like that. I'm not blind, Miss Detective. You think because I'm eighty-five years old I am a fool, Miss Detective?"

"Not at all, Mr. Silverman." She knew she should offer other conciliatory statements, but her eagerness to ask questions was paramount. "You mentioned he tripped the alarm. What alarm is that?"

"On the path to Mr. Layton's place." He spread his liver-spotted hands. "A simple beam that makes a buzz in my house when someone crosses it. I can understand about a man who fears, who puts bars on the windows of his rented house and changes his locks. But I wonder what Mr. Layton fears, and I take no chances. You see?"

"I see. Do you know if this Chinese man tried to get into the cottage?"

Anger pinching his face, he said, "He came back and *ordered* me to give him keys. I was glad not to have them to give him." He peered at her suspiciously. "Are you telling me you don't know this Chinese man?"

She said cautiously, "If my police department sent him, I don't know about it. Did he leave when you told him you had no key?"

"He left."

And returned later, or sent a replacement, she was certain. "Did anyone else trip your alarm?"

"No one."

The prickling returned between her shoulder blades. Someone else had known how to detect and circumvent Silverman's simple alarm. Had been waiting in concealment outside the cottage until she and Cameron had left. To begin his own work . . .

She glanced at her watch. The autopsy was scheduled in forty minutes. She could not call Lieutenant Walcott in Cameron's presence, nor did she have time to call from elsewhere.

"Thank you, Mr. Silverman."

He nodded. "You keep your part of the bargain, Miss Detective. I need a new tenant."

10

KATE and Cameron, clad in gowns and booties and gloves, padded into pathologist Dr. Geoff Mitchell's autopsy station. Pulling down his mask, the lean, gaunt-faced Mitchell staggered backward in mock astonishment. "Where's Chief Parks? How come it's just two peons, one of you being a peon I don't even know?" He addressed Cameron: "Or are you the head of a foreign state?"

"Peon Joe Cameron at your service," Cameron said.

Kate noted that Cameron's gaze had dropped from Mitchell's face; he was staring apprehensively at the naked, waxen body of Herman Layton, which lay ready on a stainless steel gurney with a perforated top.

"I'm Geoff Mitchell, Joe." His gloved hands hovering over the corpse, Mitchell said to Kate, "I lack board certification to touch royalty. Who the hell is this guy? Nicole Brown Simpson didn't get moved to the top of the list this fast."

Nor did the poor sad woman have Geoff Mitchell as her pathologist, Kate thought. In a factory like USC Medical Center, where several hundred bodies were always stacked waiting in in-wall cooling units or in shrouds on tiered cots in the crypt area, where thirty to forty bodies a day were autopsied seven days a week amid a never-ending din of activity, not only had this post mortem been moved up, it had been unerringly assigned to the pathologist judged by those in the know as one of the best in the country.

"Come on, Kate, give," Mitchell wheedled. "We've worked together too long for you to hold out on me now."

Kate's focus was on the greenish-looking Cameron, who had attended only four autopsies thus far in his career, and had admitted a dire aversion to this requirement for homicide detectives. To give him something else to think about besides his nausea, and with a hint of mischief amid her motives, Kate said to Cameron, "Joe, fill Geoff in."

"Okay, guess we have to," Cameron said, lowering his voice to a dramatic gruffness. "This guy—he's Raquel Welch. The secret's finally out."

"Har, har," Mitchell said disgustedly.

"I'm just another peon, too, Geoff," Kate said, appreciating Cameron's poise under these circumstances. "We're just doing our jobs."

"Sure." His hazel eyes fixed cynically on Kate, Mitchell pulled his mask up over his nose and mouth and adjusted his protective eye gear.

Looking at Kate, Cameron said, "If you find out anything, we'd sure like to be among the first to know."

"Nothing stays secret for long in this hamburger joint. Does it, Gary?" he added. His gowned assistant, a husky African-American man, had entered the area.

"Not even the existence of new detectives. You must be Joe Cameron. I'm Gary Robinson," he said to Cameron.

"A pleasure," Cameron said with more than a touch of irony.

As Kate greeted Robinson, Mitchell turned his attention to the body on the gurney. "Gary," he said, "this is Raquel Welch."

"Whatever you say," Robinson replied, pulling up his mask. He picked up a clipboard.

Kate knew that the body of Herman Layton had already been fingerprinted, had had hair samples collected and the nails pared for analysis, had been photographed with clothing on and then off, had been washed, and, because of the nature of the fatal wound, X-rayed.

Surveying the grayish white body, its sagging pockets of desiccated flesh a stark contrast to the distended, blood-filled stomach, Mitchell intoned, "An elderly, poorly nourished male with indications of weight loss, five feet ten and three-quarters in height, one hundred and . . ." He peered at the scale built into the table, "forty-eight pounds."

Pulling down an overhead light and peering through a magnifying glass, he pored over the entire visible surface of the body, then pronounced, "No cuts or stab wounds on the arms, hands, or fingers." He beckoned to his assistant. "Let's roll Raquel over."

Kate saw the pliancy in the body and that the rigor mortis stage had passed. Again, Mitchell studied the body. Then, framing the wound in Herman Layton's back between his gloved hands, Mitchell muttered, "A single perforation in the skin corresponding to location of a single puncture in the clothing. Edges of the wound are sharply cut, indicating perpendicular entry, tissue dented from the force of the thrust, and a deepening of the wound internally. Epidermal abrasion suggesting the implement was rotated in the wound. The exact location . . ." Mitchell turned to a clipboard on the steel table behind him and marked a diagram on the autopsy check sheet and made several other lengthy notes as Robinson photographed the wound.

Mitchell and his assistant rolled the body over onto its back again, and Mitchell picked up a scalpel.

Kate looked away. In the arctic chill of the place, glints seemed to emanate like sonar notes from the stainless steel gurneys and sinks, from the neatly arranged rows of instruments on the autopsy trays. The white-handled knife for cutting large organs, the smaller one for dissecting neck organs—the tongue, larynx, thyroid; the shears for opening the rib cage, the forceps for picking up organs, the scissors for opening vessels and hollow organs; the Stryker saw, the pliers, the bottles and containers for blood and tissue samples.

After fifteen years of attending this grisly ritual required in all homicide investigations, she still had to work at maintaining a professional calm, still had to breathe through her mouth to endure the charnel house smells mixed with the acrid chemical solutions employed in the analysis of death in all of its forms. She no longer watched the slicing open and gutting of a body, nor the Stryker saw when it whirred its high-pitched, screaming way through the thick casement of the brain and the chiseling open of the skull for inspection of its cranial contents. She tuned out everything except the observations and assessments of the pathologist; they were the rationale for her being here.

As liquid sloshed into the channels beneath the perforated surface of the gurney, Kate glanced back to see Mitchell peering through his magnifying glass into the Y incision he had made from breastbone to hipbone. "An ice pick shaft of—" Mitchell reached for a ruler, "—five inches exactly, resting at an oblique angle upward and to the right, a deep tract into the internal viscera, penetrating to the lung and pericardial cavity."

He again turned to his check sheet, recording location and measurements, then picked up another instrument and returned to probing within the incision. "Extensive internal hemorrhage . . . Organs and principal tissues penetrated are the liver and kidneys . . . Wounds also of the aorta, inferior vena cava, iliac vessels. A severe pericardial hemorrhage of perhaps three liters in volume, extending into the peritoneal cavity, the wound in the renal artery resulting in acute blood loss . . ."

"So are you saying this poor bastard died from an ice

pick wound in the back?'' Cameron said in a strained voice. In this cold room, beads of perspiration had formed in faint, curved lines across his forehead.

Kate deliberately looked away from him. He had enough problems without having to deal with sympathy from his partner.

"Pick your own proximate cause of death,'' Mitchell said. "With the effusion of blood into the tissues, there's lots to choose from.'' He was working carefully with a pair of forceps. "But death caused by this particular object occurred within a very few minutes.'' He extracted the blood-covered ice pick shaft and dropped it with a *plink* into a basin. "He died from hemorrhage.''

"Well, no surprises here,'' Cameron said to Kate, pulling down his face mask. "Will this do it?'' Pale-faced, he edged away from the table as Mitchell, his hands filled with a gory, yellow-coated mass, slid it into the basket of the scale hanging over the table.

After a swift glance at Cameron, Mitchell said, "No reason for you to stay for hours more of this fun. Full tox screen in the usual two weeks. Tell President Clinton we can't speed that up, even for him. There's one more thing.'' As he gazed at the mass in the hanging scale, Mitchell's mask distorted slightly as he spoke. "Your guy had advanced renal cell carcinoma, spreading into the liver and adrenal glands.''

"Cancer?'' Kate gagged as she forgot to breathe through her mouth, and she had to recover herself. "The man was dying of cancer?''

"Terminal kidney cancer,'' Mitchell confirmed and pulled away his mask to give her a mordant grin. "Check with Dr. Kevorkian, Kate. Maybe he came out from Michigan and did Raquel here a favor.''

In the car, as Cameron picked his way through the sluggish downtown traffic toward the Santa Monica Freeway, Kate pulled off her jacket and tossed it into the backseat of the Caprice. Cameron had already discarded his own, and with even more celerity, yanking off his tie as well and hurling both items into the rear of the car as if they were abhorrently soiled. Cameron was the first partner she had worked with whose behavior after an autopsy was similar to hers, and Kate gave him a gratified glance. They would both go home now for a shower and a change of clothes—she to perform the obsessive ceremonies necessary to continue with her workday; her skin was already itching as if the smells and atmosphere of the autopsy room would sink inextricably into her pores if she did not soon stand under a scalding shower.

His collar loosened and his sleeves rolled up, Cameron drove left-handed and slid an arm along the back of the seat behind her. Understanding his need for an elemental closeness to human warmth, Kate did not mind the arm that encroached on her space.

"Layton's cancer," he said, "do you think Peri knew?"

Kate countered with, "What do you think?"

He shook his head. "It's not logical. A father with terminal cancer—why wouldn't she tell us?"

"I agree." Kate asked the question that had been echoing in her own mind: "What about Arlene Layton?"

"Ah, Arlene. A horse of a different color."

Kate nodded. "She seems more guarded than Peri."

"Yeah. Some of her ex-husband's paranoia rubbing off on her?"

"Could be. Peri told us Arlene and Herman had a very civil relationship. Maybe Herman didn't want to upset his daughter but didn't mind confiding the news to his ex-wife."

"Telling somebody I've got terminal cancer," Cameron mused, "I sure wouldn't do it by phone. Or in a restaurant or even a bar. Kidney, liver cancer—that's the real quick and nasty. Maybe it's why Arlene came over to see him. She figures to be the older woman Meyer Silverman saw.''

''I agree. Okay, let's assume Peri didn't tell us because she didn't know. So why wouldn't Arlene tell us?''

''Because either she didn't know or, if she did, she still doesn't want Peri to know, through us. Most people don't realize an autopsy report's a public record. Maybe she's protecting Peri, trying not to upset her any more than she already is.''

Kate nodded. ''It's a reasonable theory. Pride in their daughter seemed the one area of agreement between the Laytons.''

''I'd say Herman a lot more so than Arlene.''

''Maybe.'' And maybe not, if her own relationship with her mother was anything to judge by. She had worshiped her mother, despite the distance created by Aunt Agnes's meddling. ''We'll check his phone records, see about phone communication between the two,'' Kate said. And between Herman and anybody else, she mentally added. Judging by the expedited autopsy, CIA man Whitby would have already set those wheels into motion.

''If Arlene knew Herman had terminal cancer, then kiss your prime suspect good-bye,'' Kate teased Cameron. ''Why kill a dead man?''

''To beat out the grim reaper,'' he teased back. His face grew somber. ''So how do we handle this? Hard enough to lose a parent . . . I know all bets are off in a death investigation, but if Herman and Arlene Layton tried to keep this from Peri, maybe we could use a little caution about how this news item gets dropped on her.''

A sensitivity she heartily agreed with. ''Let's verify our hypothesis, first.'' She pulled her mobile phone out of her shoulder bag and searched for the business card on which Peri had written Arlene's number.

Moments later, she folded the cell phone. ''Four rings

into an answering machine,'' she reported.

''Arlene and her Gang of Eight are out terrorizing the neighborhood,'' Cameron joked. ''Give me her number, I'll keep trying her.''

Peering intently out the windshield, he pulled his arm from behind her to gesture to the gray Honda Accord in front of them. ''That car's been on Wilshire Boulevard this morning.''

A prickling between her shoulder blades, Kate studied the Honda and its indistinguishable male driver, then asked casually, ''What are you, clairvoyant? It looks like every other car on the road.''

''Yellow paint on the back left wheel. They were painting the lanes on Wilshire this morning, remember?''

''Probably dozens of other streets, too,'' she said dismissively.

She kept a surreptitious eye on the car. Any police professional knew that one of the sophisticated techniques of surveillance was to occasionally drive alongside or in front of the subject, as the Honda was doing.

Just before the on ramp to the I-10, the Honda dropped behind them, and Kate tried to covertly track it but quickly lost it amid the heavy freeway traffic.

A few minutes later, sitting in her Saturn in the Wilshire Division parking lot, Kate watched Cameron drive off in his Cherokee. She picked up her cell phone and called Lieutenant Walcott; then, with extreme repugnance, donned the jacket she had discarded into the backseat.

A minute later, Kate walked into Walcott's office and closed the door behind her, yanked a chair in front of Walcott's desk, and dropped her body into it.

Leaning back in her chair, Walcott propped an ankle on the edge of her desk and steepled her fingers. She asked, ''Why do I have this idea you're pissed off?''

''What could I possibly be pissed off about,'' Kate

returned. "Because a pro came in and tossed Layton's cottage after we were there last night? Because another pro—a Chinese, yet—is passing himself off as a homicide detective? Because yet another pro is tailing Cameron and me? Because I can't tell my own partner one goddamn thing about what's going on?"

Walcott removed her ankle from the desk and sat erect, her pencil-thin eyebrows lifted so high that Kate could count six distinctive creases in her forehead. "Fill me in."

Kate did so, in full detail.

"Shit," Walcott muttered as Kate concluded.

Walcott sat silent for several moments, drumming her fingernails in a furious staccato. Then she picked up her phone, consulted the blotter in front of her, and punched in a number.

"Case Officer Whitby," she said, "Lieutenant Walcott here. I have three items of information for you. One: Autopsy results confirm death by stabbing, and also the presence of terminal cancer . . . Yes, cancer . . . Yes, terminal. Kidney and liver cancer. Second item: A Chinese male passing himself off as an LAPD detective tried to gain entry to Layton's house yesterday . . . Yes, Chinese. Older, well-built—we have no further description. Item three: Sometime between the hours of approximately eleven o'clock last night and dawn this morning, a clandestine search of the Layton residence was performed after my detectives left the premises."

She smiled sardonically at Kate as she said into the phone, "Since you're not asking me to repeat anything about item three, I assume that last bit of information doesn't surprise you . . . Yes, of course—national security," she said with unconcealed sarcasm. "Sir, you told me there would be surveillance on Peri and Arlene Layton to ensure their safety. You made no mention of surveillance on my own people—"

She listened for several moments, then said crisply,

"We had an understanding as to how this case was to be handled. Pull surveillance off my detectives. Right now. Or I'll order arrests. Hindering the process of a murder investigation and interfering with the legitimate duties of a police—"

Again she listened, then said in a voice oozing with politeness, "I'm sure Captain Delano—or even Chief Parks—would be delighted to hear that our detectives are being followed around by the CIA to make sure they perform their jobs prop—"

Walcott held the phone away from her ear, looked at it, then hung it up.

Kate was laughing, and Walcott grinned ruefully. "I'm just barking at the moon, Kate. I wonder if it makes a dog feel any better. I don't know what the hell else I can do. How much does Cameron know?"

"I'm not sure," she admitted. "I don't think he saw the crushed fly in Layton's cottage, but Joe's very sharp. I had to fill him in on my interview with Meyer Silverman, of course, except for the part about the Chinese male. I don't know that Joe made the Honda out to be a tail . . ." She sighed in frustration.

Walcott spread her hands. "If Cameron finds out, he finds out."

"And when he does," Kate muttered, "I'm dead meat as a partner."

"We'll see."

"What does Captain Delano say about all this?"

"The orders from Captain Delano are to obey orders. To the letter. No questions asked."

That figures, Kate thought.

Studying her, Walcott said, "I heard that thought."

Kate shrugged.

"Look, Kate," Walcott said, "the timing of this thing is part of our problem. You know that virtually every single officer above the rank of sergeant, including me, was at the Police Academy watching Chief Parks being sworn in yesterday. So we have a police chief with exactly one day of experience on the job and a whole heap of career officers including the ones in this station trying to figure out how to rearrange their deck chairs.''

LAPD politics was the last subject Kate wanted to discuss. Her shoulder ached, and she wanted to get the hell out of here and take a scalding-hot shower. ''Nothing back on the safe-deposit box canvass, I assume,'' she said.

''Not yet.''

''Probably the CIA's already found it,'' she said glumly.

''Not likely. If they want to keep this under wraps, they have to let us do our jobs.'' Her chuckle was without mirth. ''I'm sure they're frustrated as hell. We have to follow all these silly rules and regulations they don't have to pay any attention to. What's next on your agenda?''

''Talk to Arlene Layton, see if she knew about her ex-husband's cancer and if so, why she kept it a secret. Talk to the people who found the body, talk to the people he played cards with. See if anything leads anywhere.''

Walcott's phone rang, and Kate got to her feet and moved to the door. ''Wait,'' Walcott called, gesturing emphatically to her. ''Sorry, repeat that,'' she said into the phone. ''Thank you. Thanks.''

Dropping the phone into its cradle, she rubbed her face, then looked up at Kate. ''What do you make of this? The prints on the jawbone—they match up with Herman Layton.''

Kate sank back into the chair. ''Holy heaven,'' she finally said.

''There's more.'' Eyes narrowing, Walcott said, ''I'm not supposed to tell you this, but I will. The jawbone is being removed by order from our evidence locker.''

''*What?*''

"In the interests of national security, apparently they can do damn well anything." Walcott flipped open a blue folder and pulled out the single sheet of paper within. "This arrived by special courier from Washington an hour ago. Would you like to see the signature of the chief law enforcement officer of the United Sates of America?" She held up the paper, the round gold and brown seal of the Department of Justice prominent, an eagle poised on a red, white, and blue shield. "Our attorney general signs her name very legibly, just as you would figure."

Kate said faintly, "What are they going to do with the jawbone?"

"Whitby, as per usual, refused to answer."

New York, Kate thought. Test it first, then bring it to that museum where they have the copies of Peking Man. To see if it matches up. "I don't want any part of this," she muttered, shaking her head.

Watching her, Walcott said softly, "You and me and Cameron—we're very tiny cogs in this particular machine. Just remember: They need us, and they need to keep this under wraps. It's pretty good leverage."

11

SHUCKING off her clothes, Kate toed the door of the condo closed behind her. Miss Marple, curled up on the sofa, opened one eye and then closed it. Aimee would not be here unless she'd had a relapse; even after a night of virtually no sleep, she had declared herself well and had returned to work over Kate's protests.

As she slung her shoulder bag into an armchair, Kate noticed the blinking answering machine light and glanced at the machine: five messages. Odd. Very odd. But curiosity could not overcome the more imperative need, particularly after the lengthy delay in Lieutenant Walcott's office; her skin felt as if it were trying to crawl off her body.

She turned the hot water tap in the shower full on, finished stripping naked, stuffed her clothes into a plastic bag, and flung the bag into a corner of the closet for delivery to the cleaners. Her shoes followed; it would be weeks before she would be willing to wear them again. Seizing the shampoo and her toothbrush and the container of pepper she kept in the medicine cabinet, she inhaled the pepper. Scarcely managing to replace the container before she doubled over in a convulsion of sneezing, she stumbled into the shower and immersed herself under the steaming-hot cleansing spray.

Ten minutes later, feeling decontaminated of the autopsy room, she padded naked into the living room, vigorously toweling her hair, and pressed the Play button on the answering machine. The first two messages had come in at 10:08 and 10:10 A.M., according to the timer on the machine; they were hang-ups. The third was timed at 10:38A.M.:

"Kate my dear, Janice and I are leaving for the airport in about twenty minutes. I wanted to call and say good-bye to you and Aimee . . ."

Listening to her aunt with one corner of her brain, Kate was thinking about the two hang-ups. Twice someone had listened all the way through her taped voice inviting the caller to leave a message or send a fax. She was sure the caller would not have been Aunt Agnes. She tuned in fully to her aunt:

". . . I hope you'll give me a chance to—well, I know I can't make up to you the damage that was done, Kate, but if it'll make any difference, if you can find it in your heart to forgive me, I can find it in my heart to . . . accept . . . you and Aimee."

She strode toward the machine, glaring at it as if it were a living entity she could stare down. "What a trade-off, Aunt Agnes!" she snarled. "I sink to my knees in gratitude!" Miss Marple leaped from the sofa and stalked in annoyance toward the bedroom. Snapping the towel between her hands, Kate whipped it behind her to dry her back and fumed through the rest of her Aunt's message without listening to it.

The fourth call, at 11:38A.M., exactly an hour after her aunt had called, was another hang up. The fifth one was three minutes later.

"Uh . . . This call is for Kate Delafield. This is Dale Harrison."

Kate stood frozen in place.

"I guess you heard from Agnes Delafield that I'm your, uh . . . brother. Maybe this isn't the best way to introduce myself, but then I was thinking . . . maybe it is."

The voice was baritone, with a hint of nasality; but she thought she heard a similarity to her father's voice in its hesitancy and inflection.

"I don't know how you feel about all this. I went to a lot of trouble to find you, a detective agency and all, but maybe you don't want to have anything to do with me and you should have some say in this and I . . . Maybe I . . . Well, I shouldn't put any pressure on you. I'll be in Los Angeles Saturday, at the Vagabond out at the airport. The Triple A book says it has a coffee shop and cocktails. I thought we could meet there, like, say at nine, for breakfast. Ah . . . If this isn't okay with you, then I understand—"

After a lengthy pause, the voice continued.

"I'm just under six feet tall, gray hair a little thin on top, blue eyes. I guess that doesn't tell you much, does it. I'll wear a suit but I'm not a tie sort of guy. The jacket's got a gray and blue pattern in it, gray pants. I hope . . . I hope we can meet."

Kate snatched up the phone, dialed Aimee at her office.

"Aimee Grant." The voice was whispery and still held congestion from the flu.

"It's me. At home. You okay?"

"Hi, you." The voice strengthened, brightened. "Yeah, I'm okay—a lot better than I sound." She asked cautiously, "How about you?"

"I have to leave right away. Would you call our phone and listen to the messages? There's one from . . . my brother."

"Jesus, no kidding. He doesn't waste any time."

"He wants to meet. Would you listen to him, help me think about what I should do?"

"Honey, what's the worst thing that can happen if you go ahead and meet him?"

Kate asked plaintively, "Can we just talk about it? Tonight?"

"Sure. How's the case going?"

"Oh," Kate said, rolling her eyes heavenward, "just routine. I'll be home as soon as I can."

"Right. See ya later, investigator," Aimee said, and hung up.

As Kate put the phone down, the one in her shoulder bag rang. "Pagers, cell phones, fax machines—oh, for the good the old days," she grumbled as she fished it out.

"It's Lieutenant Walcott, Kate. We caught a break. Layton's safe-deposit box—it's at a B of A branch near Museum Square."

The locale of the La Brea Tar Pits. It figured . . .

"One of the bank personnel recognized our photo. Get right down there. The paperwork's on its way."

"Peri Layton—"

"Has waived her right to be present and trusts you'll advise her of the contents. She says he was an obsessive record keeper, and there'll be nothing except some old papers and maybe his will, and she's his only heir, anyway. She's busy preparing a public lecture for tonight."

Peri may well be right, there might be nothing of consequence in the box, Kate thought as she took down the location of the bank. Yet, somehow she knew better. "If there is something there," she said quietly, "then I'll have a problem with Joe."

"No, you won't," Walcott said crisply. "You mentioned you need to talk to the people who found the victim. I'll have him handle that. You go, I'll tell him you're checking something out on our other mess, the Gonzales case."

As Walcott uttered the word Gonzales, the connection Kate had thought she had seen the night before in the Gonzales murder book emerged from her subconscious and clicked into place. "About that case, Lieutenant, I think there's a way out."

"Fill me in and make it quick. I want you right on this."

With effort, Kate switched mental gears. "When we made the arrest, we found vials of crack in open view and also busted Jose Lopez, along with his brothers, for possession with intent—"

"So?"

"So we didn't need to put any heavy muscle on Jose about the murder—we had a bloody shirt belonging to the trigger man."

"Till Detective Holden got our iron-clad evidence tossed out of court," Walcott said acidly.

"Jose has a single prior with a couple of felony counts on it. The DA's added up the counts instead of just the convictions and nailed a third strike on him." This was the latest draconian wrinkle in the fight against career criminals, and Kate viewed it with mixed emotions, even though it swept the genuinely bad guys off the street for twenty-five years to life. With every felony being considered a strike regardless of its nature, society's dirty little unannounced agenda was to give up entirely on young men scarcely out of their teens.

"He's a good possible, Kate," Walcott said. "I'll check with the DA about dropping the strike if Jose gives us our trigger man. Now, get right back to me with what's in that box."

Kate hurriedly pulled her clothes on. But as she strode through the living room, she halted in her tracks as though snapped back by an elastic band. Once more she played the message from Dale Harrison, listening intently to the voice of the man who was her brother. He sounds like a nice, regular sort of guy, she thought. And in a rush of inchoate emotion, she realized that his voice was indeed similar to that of her father.

The elm-shaded bank branch on Masselin was small and quiet, with only three customers at its teller windows.

In the rear of the facility, oblivious to Kate's approach, Patrol Officer Larry Siegfried leaned with both arms on the marble counter of the Notes and Collections Department making flirtatious conversation with a dark-haired young woman in a soft pink tunic-style dress.

"Hello, Larry," Kate greeted him.

"Detective," he said and jerked erect, looking embarrassed. "Nice to be inside where it's cool."

She smiled. "Indeed it is." Displaying her badge and ID card, she said to the young woman, "I'm Detective Delafield. May I know your name?"

"Veronica Turner," she said, staring at Kate out of wide brown eyes neatly lined with mascara. A tiny diamond glinted on the side of her nose.

"Ms. Turner, you were the one who identified our photograph?"

"That's me. I really remember the guy, and I'll tell you why. His entrance ticket was old as the hills and clean."

"Clean?"

"I mean, it's the first time he ever came in since he had the box, and he had the box the whole time this branch's been here and we've been here like, thirty years. Imagine having something that long and paying for it and never coming near it."

Kate nodded. "I see what you mean. When did he come in?"

"Tuesday. Noon. Just before I went to lunch."

"Do you remember anything else about him? Did he say anything to you?"

"Nothing special, nothing I remember."

"How did he act?"

"Act? Well, jeez, normal. I mean . . . What did this guy do?"

"Nothing that we know of. But we need access to the safe-deposit box."

"Let me get Ms. Fernandez, the bank officer." She

turned, and then stopped; a middle-aged Hispanic woman smartly attired in a lime green linen dress was already walking briskly toward them, carrying a folder.

"Hilda Fernandez," she replied after Kate identified herself. "You walked in here like you just might be with the police," she said, approval in her voice. She tapped the folder. "I have a copy of the death certificate, a completed affidavit, the subpoena for removal of contents. All I need is for you to sign your name and title on the entrance ticket along with your badge number."

Kate smiled. "Sure. I also need a copy of the rental agreement for our records."

"Ronnie, will you take care of that for the detective?"

"Sure, Ms. Fernandez."

Hilda Fernandez pressed a buzzer, which opened a gate leading to a flight of worn gray-white marble stairs. Kate gestured for Siegfried to wait; Fernandez would be witness to the contents of the safe-deposit box. The bank officer preceded Kate down a short flight of stairs into a vault sectioned off into floor-to-ceiling walls of safe-deposit boxes that looked like receptacles in a crypt. Inspecting the number on the key, Fernandez rolled a ladder on wheels over to a section of larger boxes and climbed two stairs.

Kate presented Fernandez with the key she had removed from Herman Layton's desk. Fernandez inserted that key and her own, turned them both, and then gingerly slid out the gray, shoe-box-size metal container. Holding the box level, she handed it down to Kate. She descended the ladder and led Kate to a small room with a table and several chairs. "I'll need to remain with you," she said.

"Sure." Noting the light weight of the box, Kate placed it carefully on the table.

She felt a reluctance to continue, a strange foreboding, as if she had become a participant in some occult ceremony. With her pen, she slowly, warily lifted the lid as if what had lain in this box for the past three decades might attempt to flee its imprisonment like some evil genie, and she could slam the lid back down if need be.

Leaning closer to peer into the dark cavern, she saw a small, spiral notepad perhaps two inches by three, the edges of its white cover curled and yellowed with age, tucked against the far corner. Kate opened the box fully.

"That's it?" Fernandez asked in disappointment.

Oddly, Kate felt no sense of relief. But she joked, "I was expecting gold bullion."

Fernandez smiled. "From the weight of the box, I thought maybe diamonds, negotiable bonds."

Kate did not touch the notepad; she leaned over the box, studying its interior. Over a period of nearly three decades, the safe-deposit box had been too well sealed in the bank wall to have acquired dust, but there was a faint impression, perhaps from the weight of whatever had rested in this gray metal container for so long a time, and it was the approximate dimension of the packaging found at Rancho La Brea. The dimensions of this safe-deposit box were ample enough to encompass the jawbone and its wrapping.

Kate doubted that her camera had sufficient acuity to register the faint impression but, taking time to set up each shot, she took half a dozen Polaroids of the box, including a long shot to show the position of the notepad. Then, with a pair of tweezers, she picked up the notepad, laid it on an evidence bag. She pulled up a chair, and with the tweezers opened the cover.

The first page, discolored with age, was blank. But several pages had been torn out; remnants of paper remained caught up in the spiral rings. Kate leafed through the other pages. They, too, were blank.

"Whatever information was in there, somebody ripped it out," Fernandez remarked, leaning over her shoulder.

Staring at the notepad, inexplicably unsettled, Kate

replied, "It appears so." She photographed the open notepad close up, then closed it with the tweezers and slid it into the evidence bag. She did not know what she had expected, but the blank notepad was deeply, eerily disturbing. She sealed the bag and signed and dated the evidence tag as Fernandez returned the box to its slot.

Upstairs, she thanked Fernandez, gathered up the paperwork she had requested, and said to Siegfried, "We're done here."

"Sure," he said, elbows resting on his gun handle and Sam Browne belt, the image of polite indifference.

Sitting in her Saturn, she took out her mobile phone. "It's Kate, Lieutenant," she said when Walcott picked up her phone. "I'm in my car outside the B of A on Masselin. The box held a spiral notepad, yellow with age. There was nothing in it. But there's evidence that several pages have been torn out."

Her statement was greeted with silence. Finally, Walcott said, "That's it?"

"Not quite. Layton rented the box twenty-seven years ago and visited for the first time this past July eighth. There's a faint imprint in the bottom, about the same size as the packing we found at La Brea." She pulled the Polaroids out of her shoulder bag and sorted through them. "You can sort of see the outline on the photos I took if you look at all of them and know what you're looking for."

"What do you make of this, Kate?"

Placing the photos on the seat beside her, holding the phone to her ear with her shoulder, she leaned her head back against the headrest and closed her eyes to concentrate. "Herman Layton's with a detachment of World War Two Marines in 1941, they're assigned to get a priceless collection of prehistoric fossils out of China and into this country for safeguarding from the Japanese. His platoon's captured, he spends the entire war in a

Japanese POW camp. The fossils vanish. Five decades later, we find a jawbone that appears to be part of that missing collection. We have a murder victim who's directly connected with those fossils, whose homicide looks like a contract killing. We have fingerprints on the fossil belonging to the victim, we have a safe-deposit box our murder victim's paid for for nearly thirty years—he makes his one and only visit to it last month, presumably to remove the jawbone since there's strong indication the box contained the jawbone. The only other item in the box is a notepad with pages ripped out.''

''We're trapped in some damn John LeCarré novel,'' Walcott muttered.

Kate sighed. ''I think you're absolutely right about all of us being small cogs in this particular machine.''

''Get the notepad in here, I'd like to look at it and all the other info you have before we turn it over to our good friend Nicholas Whitby. One more thing, Kate. Peri Layton's lecture tonight at UCLA. I want you there.''

''Okay. Any particular reason?''

''A hunch. Her line of work fits in with this, too. A little fame can be a dangerous thing—some people will do anything to stay in the limelight. From your notes about her, I'd say she's an aging wunderkind, a fading star over the last decade or so. Something like this could be dynamite—could put her right back in the news again in a big way. It's interesting she's going ahead with this lecture despite the death of her father.''

Disliking Walcott's hypothesis because of her own admiration for Peri Layton, at the same time Kate conceded that offspring had killed their parents for far less reason. The mode of death fit Walcott's hypothesis just as easily as it fit Cameron's theory that the killer was a pro. An ice pick in the back not only solved the problem of the attention-drawing sound effects of a gun, it prevented having to look one's own father in the eye.

"I'd like to know your take on her tonight," Walcott said. "What she says, how she handles herself."

"I'll be there," Kate said.

She folded the phone and replaced it in her shoulder bag. She was picking up the Polaroids when she saw a shadow fall over the window of the Saturn. She looked up into the lean, grim face of the CIA's Nicholas Whitby.

12

WHITBY rapped sharply on the car window; Kate pushed the power switch to lower it.

His glance raking over the photos lying on the passenger seat, he leaned in to say in his penetrating voice, "May I sit with you a moment, Detective."

"Yes sir," she said.

As he came around to the passenger side of the car, she gathered up the photos and tucked them in the cubbyhole behind the console gear shift. If he knew about the safe-deposit box, there was no point in hiding them; if he did not know, they would be meaningless to him.

Seating himself, Whitby leaned over to place his briefcase between his feet and to adjust the seat to better accommodate his long legs, then he sat back and straightened the jacket of his gray suit. He looked gaunt and tired and smelled faintly of pipe tobacco. "Detective," he said softly, "you disappoint me."

She looked at him without replying.

He added, "Lieutenant Walcott is even more disappointing. Both of you were duty-bound to report to me the existence of this safe-deposit box."

She fastened a stare on him. So he *had* placed an eavesdropping device in Lieutenant Walcott's office.

"Don't let your imagination go into overdrive, Detective," Whitby said dryly. "If we really wanted to do an audio operation, our equipment could record your every intake of breath. Our KH-twelve satellites can distinguish the dust particles on this car. Mobile phone conversations are hardly a high-tech intercept even on a digital phone equipped with the privacy protection yours has. It's an easy intercept; anyone can do it."

Furious, Kate replied in a barely controlled tone, "The point is, the 'anyone' is you. You've had surveillance on my partner and me, and now you're tapping in on private conversations between myself and Lieutenant—"

"You can't really be this naïve," Whitby said, his gaze seeming to look beyond her and into an immeasurable distance. "You have no clue at all as to what's at stake here?"

"Perhaps you could enlighten me," Kate said, and added in sarcastic respect, "sir."

A glimmer of a smile passed over Whitby's lean face. "To the extent that I can. After you hand over everything pertaining to that safe-deposit box."

Not here, not on your life, Kate thought. "I can't do that, sir," she stated. "My orders are to bring everything in to my Lieutenant."

"You're wasting precious time. My orders supercede yours in every respect."

"I have no direct authorization to that effect," Kate countered.

Whitby's face, his pale eyes, were glacier-cold. "My bona fides have been well established by your lieutenant. I don't know what else you could possibly require. It should be more than enough that I represent the national security interests of the United States."

"I represent a murder victim," Kate said. "And the oath I took as a police officer."

"Very high-minded," Whitby said.

Infuriated by the amusement in his voice, Kate struggled to remain silent, knowing she would regret anything she said.

Whitby said, "More likely you're a member of the Vietnam generation—you've got a chip on your shoulder and knee-jerk antipathy toward anything connected with the federal government. Contempt for anyone who tries to protect this nation from a host of enemies you consistently underestimate. When it comes to love of country or patriotism—"

"You hardly have the market cornered," Kate interrupted in a burst of wrath. "My father fought in Italy and Germany. My uncle died in a Japanese kamikaze attack in the Pacific. My aunt drove an ambulance during the war. I spent four years in the Marine Corps, one of those years in Vietnam."

Tapping his fingers on a knee that revealed its bony shape through the fabric of his pants, Whitby looked away from her to stare out the windshield. He said quietly, "I should have done even more homework on you, Detective."

"No, you shouldn't have. You might just watch your assumptions instead. Sir."

"Educated guesses are part of the game, Detective," he said imperturbably, his gaze fixed on her once more. "But then I'm sure you don't want anyone delving too deeply into your life—particularly since you have your own secrets to hide."

"Meaning exactly what," Kate demanded, her voice harsh with animosity. "Are you referring to my private life? Are you threatening me?"

"Only suggesting that you get out of my way, Detective. Now, are you going to hand over your photos and everything else pertaining to that safe-deposit box?"

"No," Kate replied with angry finality. "The only person I'll hand them over to is my lieutenant."

Sighing, Whitby pulled a trim, sleek phone out of his inside breast pocket along with a small address book, which he consulted; then he turned a dial imbedded in the side of the phone and punched in a series of numbers.

"Lieutenant Walcott, Nicholas Whitby here. I'm sitting with Detective Delafield in her car on Masselin Avenue . . . Yes, Masselin Avenue. The detective refuses to surrender the contents of the safe-deposit box . . . No, I was not following her. But anyone who thinks a mobile phone conversation, unless it's conducted on a phone like the one I'm using, is a private—"

He held the phone away from his ear. Kate could not make out any words, but she heard with relish the high-pitched wrath squawking from it.

Restoring the phone to his ear as the tirade subsided, Whitby said easily, "Lieutenant, we all have our jobs to do. If you'll consult the order that arrived this morning from Washington, you'll note the language covers any and all evidence collected pertaining to this case, and you'll also note the word immediate . . . Yes, of course you can speak to Detective Delafield." He handed Kate the phone.

"Yes, Lieutenant," Kate said.

"Give that pompous, imperial asshole what he wants," Walcott grated. "I'm sorry, Kate. We have no choice."

"I know. Will do, Lieutenant," Kate said and handed Whitby back his phone.

Not bothering with any sign-off niceties, he switched it off and tucked it inside his breast pocket. He picked up the photos from the console. "These are the photographs you took?"

"They are," she said. As he leafed quickly through them and placed them in his briefcase, she reached into her shoulder bag and extracted everything she had collected, including the plastic evidence bag holding the notepad.

Whitby seized the bag in undisguised eagerness. Holding it up by its corner, he studied it with a speculative eye. Kate knew that Whitby would have the note-pad undergo the most sophisticated testing possible, to see if an imprint, however faint, from what had been written on the missing pages had bled through to the next page.

He placed the evidence bag carefully in his briefcase. "I do need your cooperation, Detective. It would be much better from here on out if it were your willing cooperation. So let me offer you a few things to consider. Since you're a patriot from a patriotic family. And if you'll guarantee me that this confidential information will be kept in strictest secrecy."

She nodded, judging it a cynic's bargain. Anything he might tell her he had already deemed safe to reveal, and his "confidential information" might not be anything resembling the truth. She would guarantee him confidentiality—as much as he had accorded her thus far, and as much as her judgment dictated.

He said, "Tell me what you think at this point."

"To begin with," she answered willingly, "it would take a cretin not to see that the Peking Man fossils are the basis for your interference in this investigation."

He nodded. "You're far from a cretin, Detective."

"Thank you. So if the jawbone is real, and the rest of the fossils come to light, then three nations—us, the Chinese, and the Japanese—are very interested."

"Four nations, actually," he said.

"Four?"

"Four. Continue, please. Which nations, and why?"

"Well, China, obviously. From what I understand, Peking Man is one of the greatest discoveries in the history of paleontology—and the find was made in their country. We're involved because the fossils were supposedly given over to the custody and protection of our Marines for transit to this country. Japan, of course—when they captured our Marines at the beginning of the war, the fossils should logically have come into their possession. Who's the fourth nation? Russia?''

''No, thank the stars. Taiwan. If those fossils fall into their hands, they gain enhanced prestige and identity as an independent Chinese nation determined to remain separate from the mainland.''

Kate sat still, digesting this information, her gaze on the traffic making its way up and down Masselin, reminding herself that it was just a hot, ordinary day in August, and that she was in Los Angeles, not in some surreal fantasy.

Whitby's thin shoulders moved in a soundless sigh. ''Perhaps you can see our difficulty here, Detective. If those fossils surface, they'll precipitate a crisis. Where, is the only question. We need to know, because we'll be in the middle of it.''

Baloney, Kate thought. They're just bones, not oil or territory. This hasn't anything to do with our national defense or vital interests.

''It's a matter of national honor,'' Whitby said as if hearing her challenge. ''The Chinese consider the fossils national treasures, and if they're in this country, then China will be looking at us as bold-faced thieves of monumental proportions. Several American scientists, especially Frank Weidenreich, were major participants in the discoveries. Teilhard de Chardin—do you know of him?''

''Vaguely,'' Kate said. ''A mystic, or something?''

''That, too. He was a French Catholic priest, very controversial in his day. Also a geologist and paleontologist. He was on the scene in China and ended up living in this country. Given all our entanglement, we could lose for a significant period of time a country with the potential to become our greatest trading partner. If the fossils happen to still be in China, then we need to be prepared to answer for any role our Marines might have had in their concealment all these years.''

"I see," Kate murmured.

"If they're in Japan, we're faced with a heightening of tension between two hostile Pacific powers and the reopening of old war wounds. Severe wounds, Detective. Few Americans know about the savagery, the atrocities committed by the Japanese during their occupation of China—the rape of Nanking rivals any barbarism in history. As for Taiwan, if the Taiwanese are part of this, we're looking at a real powder keg. China's already poised to invade—they may well do so if Taiwan refuses to return the fossils, which is a foregone conclusion. They've been overtly interested in obtaining them since the days of Chiang Kai-shek. So the imperative is to learn first of all if those fossils exist. And if so, Detective, where they are, how they got there, and what, if anything, we can do about it."

"I see," she said. But it seemed blown out of all proportion to her—much ado about relatively little.

Scrutinizing her carefully, he said in a neutral tone, "If nothing else, perhaps you do see that we need to move quickly since people other than ourselves have already involved themselves."

To the extent of committing murder, she speculated. "What if the jawbone's not authentic?" she offered, knowing her statement was absurd even as she made it; why would Herman Layton hide a fake fossil for over fifty years, twenty-seven of those years in a safe-deposit box?

Whitby surprised her by nodding. "Yes, perhaps it is a fake. Just because Layton thought it was real doesn't mean it is. Copies of the fossils were made, as you know, and very good ones. We've had other false alarms about Peking Man."

"Can you tell me if the CIA suspected Herman Layton all along?"

"We came into the matter late, and at a disadvantage," he said ruefully. "You may not know that our agency didn't even officially exist till September 1947. I'm not telling you anything that isn't in the history books. The search for the fossils received high visibility in '71. A Marine Corps medical officer named Thomas Foley claimed he'd been the one personally entrusted with bringing the fossils to this country. Another man named Christopher Janus offered a reward for the return of the fossils and there was a highly publicized meeting between him and some woman at the top of the Empire State Building—''

''I seem to remember something about all that,'' Kate said, nodding.

''It was all discredited and came to nothing, but we were working behind the scenes and pursued every lead. To answer your original question, we suspected everyone. Investigated everyone. Thoroughly.''

Not much wonder Herman Layton had had bars on his windows, Kate thought. Not much wonder he was afflicted with paranoia . . .

''If we'd had half the tools back then that we do today,'' Whitby was saying, ''we'd have known about that safe-deposit box the instant he rented it. God knows where he hid the fossil for the twenty-five years before he moved it into the bank.''

Or why he chose to move it at all, Kate thought.

Whitby picked up his briefcase and grasped the door handle. ''My next step is obvious, Detective. As is yours, and I'll leave you to it.''

His next step was indeed obvious—the testing of the notepad and pursuit of any leads therefrom. Her next steps, beyond going to the station, looked to be far murkier, but she was not about to admit that to him.

''It's possible we may not meet again, Detective. But I suspect we will.''

Whitby let himself out of the car and walked off.

Kate reached over and pulled shut the passenger door. Did the man never close doors behind himself?

13

"DETECTIVE," Carolina Walcott said to Kate, "the CIA didn't know what they were getting into when they came barging into our shop. Somebody else would've handed every damn thing over to his royal high-ass without so much as a murmur."

Grinning at Walcott's assessment of the confrontation with Whitby, Kate said, "I wish I could've hung onto our evidence."

"Whitby and his cohorts, they're a bunch of little boys," Walcott said with sudden intensity, "still playing their little boy games. But it's even more fun to deploy human soldiers instead of toy ones. The whole world's a board game, everything's secrets and skullduggery. The Cold War's over, despite their best efforts, and now all they've got is crazy old Saddam Hussein and trying to make a crisis out of a missing collection of old bones."

Nodding agreement with Walcott's cynical assessment, Kate nevertheless argued, "They're considered priceless, Lieutenant. Direct evidence of the origins of man."

"I understand that," Walcott said impatiently. "What I can't see is Clinton on television—" She lowered her voice and intoned, " 'My fellow Americans, we're going to war over Peking Man . . .' "

Kate laughed and Walcott joined in. But Kate remembered Whitby's statements about this issue becoming a matter of national honor among four nations, and she knew that avenging loss of face was by no means an ancient Far East precept. Many current homicides had their roots in perverted notions of personal honor, Joey Washington shot five times just last week because his killer had perceived himself as having been, in the current vernacular, "dissed."

Walcott nodded. "So where do we go with our current info?"

"We know it's likely the jawbone was in Herman Layton's safe-deposit box. We definitely know the notepad's been in there the same length of time—Layton never visited the box till last month. It just adds more credence to the possibility that an odd little hermit of a man dying of cancer in West L.A. got himself knifed because he was directly involved in the disappearance of Peking Man."

"Maybe, Kate. *Maybe.*" Walcott's eyes seemed a luminous brown black as they bored into Kate. Her long, well-manicured fingernails tapped a staccato on her desk. "Just go on about your business as best you can, and we'll see where we go from here."

A hand on her phone, Walcott grinned sardonically as Kate rose to her feet. "Kate, our fair city's had earthquakes, fires, floods, Rodney King, O. J. Simpson, and every other goddamn thing. Get out there and make sure we don't get blamed for starting a war over Peking Man."

Kate turned the Caprice onto Santa Monica Boulevard, threading her way through heavy rush hour traffic as she and Cameron headed west toward the ocean and the Grand Slam Bridge Club.

Cameron's postautopsy choice of clothes was a button-down white shirt and light gray pants; he had tossed his suit jacket into the backseat. Fidgeting beside her, he flipped through the pages of his notebook. "No-where. We're nowhere with this goddamn case," he muttered.

"Did you ask Arlene about her husband's cancer?"

"Still haven't been able to reach her. I did interview the Kiwis. Just let me get all my notes together here . . ." Cameron turned the pages of his notebook with exaggerated slowness. "They found the body about ten o'clock yesterday morning and were horrified. New Zealand's a far more civilized country, and they hope they make it back home before they all get killed."

Grinning, Kate again checked the Caprice's mirrors, changing lanes as she looked for a car that might be tailing them. Both hands on the steering wheel, she rotated her left wrist to check her watch: 4:20 P.M.

"We're okay," Cameron said, observing the time check. "Thirteenth Street's a half hour max, even in this mess. The guy I talked to bitched about having to push the patrons out the door at five o'clock."

Again perusing the mirrors, Kate asked idly, "Ever play bridge?"

"Couldn't pay me to. My Aunt Mabel and Uncle Gerald play. All they do is fight and argue over the game. So, what've you been up to all this time, Detective Delafield?"

She was ready for the question. "Brainstorming a new approach to the Gonzales case."

"You come up with something?" he asked with interest.

"An eyewitness we can maybe squeeze with his own rap sheet." She took him through the case again and the ramifications of Torrie Holden's search warrant error, to educate Cameron and recheck her own analysis of the countermeasures she had laid out for Walcott. Then she added the news she had been saving to deflect any deeper inquisition as to how she had otherwise been spending her time: "I heard from my brother."

"No shit," he exclaimed, turning to face her. "You always keep the good stuff for last. What was he like?"

Uncomfortable under his stare, she shrugged. "He left a message on my machine. He wants a meeting."

"So?"

"So, I don't know."

He asked in genuine puzzlement, "What don't you know, Kate?"

Passing Overland Avenue, again she checked the rearview mirrors. Then, thinking about his question, she glanced beyond him at the majestic white beige Mormon Temple high on its perfectly manicured hill of green. Exactly what *was* her problem?

Cameron said, "Seems to me the guy's just looking for information on a family he never knew."

Her family. A family with him not in it. She'd been an only child garnering all of her parents' attention. Had this brother been a part of her life, had her mother not been haunted by the deadly secret of his existence, how different would her growing-up years have been? Why had this monkey wrench been tossed into her life now, this bolt from the blue affecting her whole image of her parents, her entire concept of her family? She muttered, "This feels too weird, Joe."

"So, you gonna see him?"

"I'm thinking about it, okay?"

"Sure, okay. The way you're checking the mirrors, you'd think the dude's stalking us."

"A nervous tic," Kate said, hunching her shoulders and concentrating on her driving.

The Grand Slam was located in the upper floor of a beige stucco two-story bungalow; a cleaners and tailor shop occupied the street level. Kate and Cameron climbed a staircase covered with threadbare gray carpeting to a cavernous, un–air-conditioned room lit by three rows of track lights. Approximately ten card tables were occupied by older people who played cards with such intensity of focus that only a few glanced up as the detectives made their way into the club's interior.

Behind a small desk, a bald, rotund man perhaps in his late sixties stood up to greet them, his khaki shorts and yellow seersucker shirt stained with perspiration.

Cameron introduced himself and Kate. "Are you Mr. Dixon?"

"Frank Dixon, yep." His gaze swept over Kate as he addressed Cameron: "Incredible what happened to Herman, just terrible. The people here are real upset."

Sure they are, Kate thought, taking in the rapt card players. She asked, "Which one was Mr. Layton's table?"

Dixon gestured. "The far one, way back there."

The dank, musty, close smell of the place filling her nostrils, Kate peered at the shapes of three men and a woman in the distant shadows of the room. "How come that particular table's separate from the others?"

"They play—" He broke off, then said, "They get a little loud. The other players like it quiet in here."

"I see." But she had detected evasion in his eye shift and his response. "Mrs. Layton—"

"Not here today. As you'd figure," he added, his voice lowering to an intonation of sympathy. "Her usual table's this empty one here by the door. Her foursome's collapsed in a heap, dammit." The tight, shiny skin on his forehead pinched into wrinkles of fretfulness. "Sadie Bingham moved right into Herman's foursome without so much as a how do you do, so the other two ladies went on home. Till Mrs. Layton returns and we find another member to make up their foursome."

Looking around the room at the forty or so people hunched over their cards, Kate could only imagine the difficulties in coping with the cliques and petty bickering that would arise in a group such as this.

Cameron asked, "This bunch meets once a week?"

"Right. Fridays, from one to five." He pointed to the wall behind him that held a huge No Smoking sign and a bulletin board thumbtacked with schedules and bulletins. "We have a different bridge group Mondays and Wednesdays. Our canasta group meets—"

"Anything unusual about Mr. Layton's foursome?"

"They keep to themselves." He nodded approvingly. "Never a word of complaint."

Cameron thanked him, and he and Kate made their way quietly along the periphery of the room to the back table, toward four players fully absorbed in their game.

The woman player, her body a shapeless blob under a dark blue muumuu, her gray hair tied back in a tight bun, was dealing cards, snapping them off the deck. She intoned in a Bronx accent: "Pair of fours for Barney . . . King high for Sam . . . Whoa, possible flush there, Russ. And a pair of aces for me, and I deserve them." From a stash in front of her, the woman pushed two paper clips into a pile of perhaps half a dozen other paper clips in the center of the table.

The strong scent of gardenia perfume reached Kate. Grinning, she whispered to Cameron, "This is what your Uncle Gerald and Aunt Mabel play?"

"I wish," Cameron whispered back, folding his arms as he observed the wagering. "If they played poker, I'd like them a lot better."

Barney checked the two cards that lay facedown in front of him. "I'll see you," he declared and pushed two paper clips forward.

"I'm out," Russ said, tossing down his cards. A small man, completely bald, he reared back on his chair legs and hooked his thumbs through his suspenders, peering across the table at Barney. "You're a brave man. Piddling fours against Sadie's two hammers."

Pushing a plump hand through his few strands of gray hair, Barney said with irritation, "Sam, sometimes I know what I'm doing."

"Her scare cards don't bother me neither," Sam said. With a flourish, he dropped three paper clips into the pile. "See the two and raise one."

"Well, boys, I'm impressed with your courage," Sadie said, "but it'll cost you. I'll see you, Sam, and raise you one more—"

"Excuse us, folks." Cameron stepped forward and displayed his shield and identification, Kate following suit.

Russ's chair thumped on the floor as he abruptly sat forward. "Holy God," Barney said, spreading his hands over his cards and paper clips as if to conceal them.

"Relax, folks," Cameron said, "we're homicide, not the vice squad."

"Homicide, oh that's relaxing, all right," Sadie said in her broad accent, peering up at them through hooded dark eyes. "That's a very good reason to relax." Her gaze fastened on Kate.

"Pull up a coupla chairs and siddown, people," Sam said. "I guess we know what's up."

"You catch anybody yet?" Russ inquired of Kate.

"We're working on it," she replied. "It's why we're here."

"You think one of these boys did in Herman?" Sadie said, winking at Kate.

A real mischief maker, Kate thought, wondering exactly how welcome newcomer Sadie was in this previously all-male foursome. Kate addressed the men: "I understand you three gentlemen were in Herman Layton's regular foursome," she began as Cameron pulled two chairs from against the far wall and carried them over.

"Yeah, we were," Russ said, flicking a sour glance at Sadie.

"You played poker every week?"

"Yeah." Russ gestured to the front of the club, to Frank Dixon. "We all slip Frank five bucks, he lets us."

He took a chair from Cameron and placed it beside him, moving his soft drink away and gesturing for Kate to sit down. Cameron scraped his chair up to the table opposite her, next to Sadie.

"Thanks," Kate said. "May we have your full names, please?"

Sadie raised a hand festooned with copper rings on every finger. "Don't say a word unless they guarantee not to turn us in to the vice department."

"We guarantee it," Kate said, keeping a straight face by managing not to catch Cameron's eye.

"Look," Barney said, his plaid shirt stretched across his paunch as he extended his arms in a pleading gesture. "I'm way behind, and we only got a couple more minutes left. That bastard Dixon never lets us stay a minute past five. Can we play cards and talk at the same time?"

"Sure," Cameron said, and Kate looked at him approvingly. People were always more willing to talk when they were not antagonized by an officious approach.

Sadie picked up the deck after the male card players divulged their names to Kate and Cameron. "So," she said, dealing cards, "a lady for Barney, no help with those fours. Oops, another heart to Sam, a real possible flush there, Sam . . . Oops, I got Barney's four. My aces still look good to me. I bet two."

"See that and raise you two," said Sam.

"See that and raise you another two," said Barney.

"A lot of dough—I mean, paper clips going into this pot," Russ observed mournfully, gazing down at his defunct cards.

"How long did you know Mr. Layton?" Cameron threw out to no one in particular.

Sam scratched his whiskery chin as he glanced around at his male cohorts. "Whaddya think, ten years?"

"Yeah, prob'ly," Sam said, his eyes flickering between Sadie's face and her cards. "He joined our foursome what, four years ago? After Phil passed—no, it was Eddie who passed on."

Death was not an uncommon visitor in this age group, Kate reflected, but these people seemed unusually accepting of Herman Layton's death, regardless of its cause.

"You boys don't scare me," Sadie announced, pushing six paper clips into the silver pile. "I call and raise you two more."

"Call," Sam said.

"Call," Barney said, lifting the corner of his hole cards to peer at them as Sadie picked up the deck to deal the next round. "Yeah, at least ten years, all told. Funny thing, the guy getting knifed proves it all over again: Just because you're paranoid doesn't mean somebody isn't after you."

Cameron said casually, "What do you mean?"

Barney shrugged and rolled his eyes as Sadie dealt him the five of diamonds. "No help with those fours, Barney," she said. "Club to Sam, no help with that heart flush. A deuce to me, good for nothing."

"He had all these people watching him," Sam said, again studying Sadie's cards, "just waiting for him to make a wrong move."

"What kind of people? What kind of wrong move?"

"He said we were better off not knowing," Sam said, and the three men laughed easily together.

"Guess you didn't take him too seriously," Cameron suggested, grinning.

"Hell, everything's a conspiracy these days," Russ said, winking at his companions. "Every week, somebody was out there spying on our good old Herman. But what the hell, his ex-wife Arlene seems like a real nice woman, and she put up with him all those years they were married, and every week old Herman was good as gold to come in here and drop at least twenty bucks.'' He looked darkly at Sadie. "I'll sure miss him.''

"My good-as-gold aces bet two,'' Sadie serenely announced.

"Raise two,'' Barney said.

"Barney, you sneaky bastard, you're too damn proud of that pair of fours,'' Sam said dourly. "See you and raise you.''

"I'm damn proud of my aces,'' Sadie said. "See you both and raise you two.''

Cameron said doggedly, "So Mr. Layton never went into any detail at all about these people spying on him?''

"Nope,'' Russ said, taking a sip of his soft drink. "Claimed he couldn't say anything because of his famous daughter. Me, I never heard of her.''

"Yeah, but he brought in those *National Geographic* magazines so we could see at least that part's true,'' Sam conceded. "He said we'd find out good and proper one day real soon.'' Again the three men laughed together.

Cameron said congenially, "So you never took him seriously.''

"Well, about as much as you believe all the people that get picked up by space ships,'' Barney said, his gaze fixed covetously on the stack of paper clips in the center of the table.

"Russ,'' Kate said, "why did you find Herman Layton an easy mark at poker?''

He looked at her blandly. "The man never bluffed. Show me a cautious poker player, I'll show you a loser.''

"Speaking of bluffing and losers,'' Sadie said. "Let's go, boys, last round. Down and dirty.'' She dealt a face-down card to Barney, Sam, and herself. "I bet two,'' she said.

After another round of raises by Sam and Barney, Cameron asked, "Anything unusual in Herman's behavior lately?''

"Nah, just as looney tunes as ever," Sam said, lifting the corner of his newest card.

"I'd say more looney," Barney offered. "You come in for a nice quiet game of cards, and instead you get Herman talking about history's nut cases. Lee Harvey Oswald, John Hinckley . . ."

"Yeah, you're right," Barney said. "Jeffrey Dahmer, for chrissakes. Ted Bundy."

Kate asked with considerable interest, "What did he say about them?"

"Chapter and verse on how they came from nowhere and got famous," Russ answered. "How, like, Hitler got to be more famous than Churchill."

"Yeah," Barney said, "and everybody knew Benedict Arnold but nobody had a clue about who it was he sold out."

"Did he have some point with all this?" Cameron asked.

"Who knows?" Russ answered. "His big thing was, people might be good or bad, but famous wasn't good or bad, famous was just famous."

"Show and tell time, folks," Sam said. He turned over his hole cards. "As advertised—a heart flush, king high."

"Sorry, Sam," Barney said, exposing his hole cards. "This time I had a four and queen tucked away. Full house, fours over queens."

"Well, boys," Sadie said, "those are pretty good hands. But . . ." She turned over her own hole cards. "I'm afraid I've got this embarrassment of riches."

"Jesus," Sam uttered.

"Four aces," Russ marveled.

"I didn't even have to use the one up my sleeve," Sadie said with a wink at Kate as she swept in the pile of paper clips from the pot.

"Only a royal flush beats this woman," Barney muttered.

"Excuse me," Sadie said, scraping her chair back, "I need a trip to the little girls' room before we knock it off for today."

"Tell you what I really think," Sam said, staring at his losing heart flush as she sauntered off. "I think it was Sadie who knocked Herman off so the lady could get a seat at our table."

"That's no lady," Barney said, sweeping up his queens and fours and dumping them onto the remnants of the deck, "that's a boa constrictor."

"I for one got a motive for killing Herman," Russ said, staring balefully at Sadie's back. "I'd like to kill the bastard for dying on us."

"One thing I feel bad about," Barney confessed. "The last time we saw the guy, he went away really mad. If I could change anything, I'd change that."

Cameron asked the question before Kate could: "Why was he mad?"

"We always humored him, you know. I mean, why not? Everybody's got their quirks. But last time we blew our cover and really laughed at him. I mean, we had to, we couldn't help it." A grin began to tug at the edge of Barney's mouth.

Russ picked up the story: "He tells us something big's gonna happen. Right after somebody real important, somebody we know, comes to see him so Herman can take care of the final piece. Everything's going to change, we'll find out all about him—"

"It was my fault," Sam said, his shoulders beginning to quiver as his laughter welled. "I have to ask if this really important person is arriving by chartered jet and should we watch on television—"

"And Herman says no, it's somebody coming on the bus!"

The three men burst into guffaws of laughter, slapping the table, and Kate and Cameron laughed along with them, their merriment subsiding only after angry hisses from the other tables.

"Makes you wonder what the world's coming to these days, don't it?" Sam said, wiping his eyes. "Russia falls apart and the poor spies all have to take the bus."

"Thanks, gentlemen," Kate said, still chuckling as she got to her feet. "Good luck with your game."

"We'll need it," Barney said, watching Sadie make her way back to the table.

Outside the club, in the Caprice, Kate was still smiling as she said to Cameron, "I want to be Sadie when I grow up."

"You already are," Cameron said.

He was grinning, but Kate heard an edge in his tone. She said cautiously, "Meaning?"

"Meaning you're already a good poker player, Kate."

"I'm not sure how to take that, Joe," Kate said.

Cameron shrugged. "When I grow up," he said, "I want to be you."

She didn't know how to take that, either.

14

For the third time that day, Kate stepped out of the shower. Vigorously toweling herself, she heard, faintly, the slide back of the deadbolt in the front door. Aimee was home. "Hi honey," Kate called.

A few moments later, Aimee strolled into the bathroom. "Hi yourself," she said, and bussed Kate noisily on the lips, then softly kissed the scar on Kate's left shoulder. "You're wearing one of my favorite outfits," she teased. "You look your sexiest in a towel."

"Too bad I have to leave again in twenty minutes," Kate responded with a grin. The remark was lip service; she was focused beyond distraction on the Herman Layton case. But Aimee's navy blue pants and dark blue silk shirt deepened the violet of her eyes, and Kate looked at her with a sexual stirring that had never diminished in the eight years they had been together. "You seem to be feeling a lot better."

"I am."

"How was your day?"

"Hassles," Aimee said. "Yours?"

"The same. I picked up some pizza."

"Great. Let me get out of these clothes. . . ."

A few minutes later, Kate sat in her armchair gulping coffee and wolfing down her food, reviewing notes of the interview she and Cameron had conducted of the poker players at the Grand Slam Club. Aimee was perched on the sofa with blue-jeaned legs folded yoga style as she ate her pizza, her gaze on the TV news; she knew Kate was still on the job, regardless of her presence here.

Something about the interview nagged at Kate. The poker players, inured over the years to Herman Layton's grandiose claims, had dismissed as blather Layton's preoccupation with fame as desirable no matter what its source, had heaped ridicule on his boast about someone important coming to see him on a bus. On its surface, the boast did seem ludicrous . . . but Herman Layton, it had turned out, was not as crazy as he seemed. Russ had said that Herman Layton never bluffed . . .

"May I interrupt?" Aimee inquired.

Reluctantly, Kate pulled her concentration away from the case. "Sure."

"I listened to the message on the machine a couple of times. What do you think about your brother?"

"I suppose I'll have to meet him."

"Suppose? I take it you really don't like this."

Not much, Kate thought. "His timing could be better."

"Tell me the truth." Aimee pointed to Kate with her folded-up piece of pizza as if she were administering an oath. "Would any timing be right?"

"Maybe not," Kate admitted. "But I really am wrapped up in this case."

"Aren't you even a little curious?"

"About him? A little. Curious what he looks like—I have people to compare him to. But he's got his own life. We might as well have grown up on different planets. I don't know what he wants from me. He doesn't have a clue about me or anybody he's related to by blood."

"He's come to you looking for a clue. To his identity."

"He *has* an identity," Kate argued. "A white male

baby—you know he was adopted. He has parents of his own. Who gave him a home, supplied him with identity.''

''It's not the same. I talked to Nina at work about this adoption business—'' Aimee again pointed with her pizza as Kate started to speak. ''Relax, I didn't say a word about you. She's been searching for years for her birth parents—I asked her about it. In a nutshell, she says there's a part of identity that environment alone doesn't supply. People like you and me, we have continuity with our past, family history. Even if it's checkered family history. Those connections reach right into our present. Some adopted people seem okay with everything, but Nina says most are like her. She adores her adoptive family, says they're her real family—yet there's still a part of her that feels cut off, adrift. In a fundamental way she feels estranged . . . alienated.''

''I understand all that,'' Kate said, ''I really do. The fact is, there's just nothing I can do about Dale Harrison and how he feels.''

''Answer his questions—that's what you can do. But you're unhappy about even seeing him.''

Annoyed at Aimee's perceptiveness, Kate said, ''I'm going to meet him, okay?''

''Okay.''

Kate bit into another piece of pizza, wishing that Aimee could just let some things lie and stop her nagging and prodding.

''Honey . . .''

She heard this new note in Aimee's voice with uneasiness. ''What is it?''

''Marcie called right after I talked to you today. Last night a guy turns up at her apartment to give her an estimate on her move to Sacramento—''

''Thank God. She'll be much—''

''She's not moving,'' Aimee said sharply. ''I know you think that's what she should do, but Charlie found her last time. She'd spend all that money and wouldn't feel any safer. Anyway, after that, a plumber shows up to fix leaks she doesn't have. She goes to the grocery store, Charlie follows her, follows her into the store, shadows her, does his own shopping so he has a legitimate reason to be there. Late last night a delivery service shows up with three dinners—"

"This is escalating."

"No kidding."

"Did she call it in?"

Aimee nodded. "Got the usual. He's not in violation of his restraining order if he's in a grocery store at the same time she is, and they'd gladly pick him up for malicious mischief if they can prove it's Charlie—"

Kate sighed in exasperation. "That's right. There's only so much we can do, Aimee. We've talked and talked and talked about this."

"Something has to be done," Aimee said vehemently, throwing down the remnant of her pizza.

"What do you expect us to do?" Kate demanded. She was dead tired, and she still had a long evening ahead of her. "What the hell do you want from me?"

Aimee crossed her arms. "I don't know, Kate," she said. "I guess nothing. It's obvious you've got yourself into this little box about your brother, and I'm sure Marcie's in her own little box, too. You probably think she's created the mess she's in—"

"I don't feel that way at all," Kate protested heatedly.

"Don't you? Maybe there's nothing you can do as a cop, but as a person—" Aimee plunged on, "For God's sake, you could at least show a little compassion."

Compassion. Kate stared at her. "You know how it is. You know what my job is like. You know I have to shut down some things just to keep my sanity—"

"I know that. You seem to be shutting down more and more things."

Kate shook her head. She said intensely, "You just

can't understand what it's like carrying a gun and supposedly having all this authority when the truth is, my
hands are tied.'' She was vividly seeing Nicholas
Whitby and his lofty exercise of power.

"I *know* that, Kate. You never give me credit for
knowing anything."

Kate was silent. Could Aimee be right? Had she so
gradually walled off an entire side of herself that she
hadn't realized it?

She made a crucial leap toward a decision. "Charlie—
where does he live? Can you get me his license number?" As Aimee's face lighted with eagerness, Kate
warned: "I can't promise anything. I can't promise
anything at all."

"He drives a Camaro. Red, I think. I know his license
number," Aimee said, "because it's so gross. MRCI
MYN," she spelled out. "Get it? Marcie mine. Doesn't
it chill your soul? He lives on Colgate, just off Robert-
son. I'll get the address from—"

"That's good enough. I can't promise anything,"
Kate repeated.

"Even so, somehow I feel better. I can't even imagine
how Marcie must feel."

I haven't even tried to, Kate admitted to herself. All
these years as a cop—maybe it truly had cost her a vital
piece of herself.

15

ENTERING Lockhart Auditorium twenty minutes ahead of Peri Layton's scheduled appearance, Kate took up a position in the upper left corner of the amphitheater; from this vantage point she could scan down the tiers of seats to the stage and observe the assembling audience.

Cameron, she thought, would claim that the people filing in for the lecture—of various ages and a cross-section of multiethnic Los Angeles—mirrored the universal fascination with Peri's profession and the address she would give tonight on the origins of mankind. If Kate was amused by Cameron's acute case of hero worship, she knew that she herself needed to subdue a subversive esteem for Peri: She had read through Peri's letters to her father.

That Peri herself had colluded in the death of her father might be an unpalatable hypothesis, but Kate had no choice other than to share Carolina Walcott's opinion that Peri Layton's despair over a once-brilliant career could provide the motive for an act so drastic as patricide. Until Peri was cleared as a suspect, Kate's job was to remain focused, alert, ready for any contingency; she could not afford to be dazzled by the woman who had revealed herself in elegant, poetic dimension on the fragile onionskin pages of those letters from Africa.

The diversity of the audience reminded Kate of an additional X factor, the presence of international players in this case. If Peri was actually an innocent bystander in the death of her father, she might unwittingly blunder into jeopardy.

Barney from the bridge club entered the room, a dark blue necktie cinched tightly around the collar of the plaid sport shirt he had worn to the club today, his thin hair in distinct ridges from a freshly employed comb. Spotting Kate, he made his way along the aisle above the top row of seats toward her.

"Just curious, you know." His grin was sheepish, his blue eyes ingenuous; his forehead bore a light sheen of perspiration. He did not hold her gaze but looked away to scan the rapidly filling auditorium. "You never could put any stock in anything Herman said, except about having this fancy-dancy daughter. So—it's a way of paying my respects."

"Nice of you," Kate offered, continuing to observe the audience and at the same time interested that Barney felt a duty to be here and a need to explain himself to her.

"Might even learn something," he added. "The *Times* says her talk's for the general public. I hope it's not just a bunch of boring scientific bull. So what are you up to?" Before she could reply, he answered his own question. "Right, you're on duty. Got your eye on anybody yet?"

"The investigation is proceeding."

Greg Jamison, the paleontologist from the Page Museum at Rancho La Brea, walked in accompanied by Betty Parsons, his lab manager; they were deep in conversation. Kate glanced away from them to acknowledge Barney, who was smiling and backing away awkwardly. She watched him descend the stairs, to sit several rows from the front. Jamison and Parsons, still conversing earnestly together, had taken seats halfway up from the stage. The hall, which Kate estimated to hold five or six hundred, was almost full.

Cameron slipped into the room; she caught his eye and signaled; his return gesture affirmed he would cover the right-hand side of the auditorium.

Nicholas Whitby sauntered in, gray jacket unbuttoned, hands in his pants pockets; he hesitated as if in a selection process for the optimum seat, casually taking in the entire scene including Kate, to whom he made no sign of recognition, his gaze pausing only on Cameron. Whitby strolled to a seat in the back row and lowered his lanky frame into it, propping an ankle on a knee, the picture of ease.

Arlene Layton, smartly attired in an ivory pants suit adorned with lime green costume jewelry, walked in alone; grim-faced, she strode down the tiers of stairs looking neither right nor left. But Kate observed Whitby's head swivel toward Arlene, and that he, too, was observing her progress down the stairs toward the stage where she removed the band of tape marking a seat in the front row as reserved, and sat down.

"Ladies and gentlemen," a voice soon announced over the loudspeaker. The murmur of conversation in the auditorium faded to silence.

"On behalf of the Paleontology and Anthropology Departments here at the university, we are proud to present an esteemed scholar, an explorer and researcher of great distinction and accomplishment, a highly respected scientist of international reputation. Please welcome our renowned visiting Professor of Paleo-anthropology, Dr. Peri Layton."

To a smattering of claps, the auditorium lights dimmed; the claps grew into warm applause as Peri, strikingly clad in a white jacket and pants and a black open-throat silk shirt, strode past a projection screen on the stage and over to the spotlighted podium, a leather folder in hand. She adjusted the microphone, turning it upward with practiced expertise, and placed the leather folder on the lectern. She smiled down at her mother, a gentle, melancholy, affectionate smile. "I wish to dedicate this evening's program," she said so softly that the words scarcely reached Kate, "to my mother . . . and to the memory of my father."

Scattered clapping from the audience quickly ceased as Peri raised her somber, acute gaze. "I am a time traveler," she declared. Her bold statement echoing in the auditorium, she looked up to where Kate stood unobtrusively shadowed in the rear corner of the chamber.

Disconcerted, feeling as if an X-ray machine had moved into position over her, Kate held Peri's gaze, wondering if this could be some sort of optical effect, whether she could be imagining that Peri had singled her out in this audience of hundreds.

"And," Peri continued in a tone that contained an undercurrent of intimacy, "I, too, am a detective."

As Peri's gaze released her and again encompassed the audience, Kate felt an erotic hotness suffuse her over this surprising and oddly private interaction in so public a place.

"I am a time traveler," Peri said, "moving through the centuries. I am a detective hunting for clues. I am a hunter of fossil people."

A slide of workers on a barren, dusty dig appeared on the screen to the right of Peri. "I am drawn to the hunt, driven to it—because of the clues the fossil people have left for me, because there are questions that demand answers. The discoveries in Clovis, New Mexico, and in Monte Verde, Chile," she continued as slides of excavated huts, fireplaces, and tools on a wooded hillside flicked past on the screen, "tell us that humans emerged in our own hemisphere about thirteen thousand years ago. I'm intrigued by those humans and the history they tell us as we continue our excavations, but I'm also fascinated by the fossil people we're finding in Siberia."

On the screen, a slide appeared of a shaggy figure swathed in animal skins, discernible as human by its upright stance and fur-covered boots. Peri pointed in challenge to her audience: "Surely you join me in wondering how these early Siberians got to that frozen place three hundred thousand years ago, how they controlled fire and made clothing and boots and had a survival strategy in so lethal an environment. How could they manage such a feat—when today it requires our greatest effort and determination to uncover these remarkable ancestors through the permafrost?"

Audible reaction from the audience died away and she continued, "What about the much earlier discoveries of Java Man and Peking Man in Asia, what about the Leakeys' discoveries at Olduvai Gorge in Kenya, what about Lucy, some of you may say—after all, those finds go back much, much farther than three hundred thousand years."

She briefly consulted her notes. "In 1974, when Donald Johanson found Lucy in Ethiopia, she became our superstar fossil." The depiction of arranged fragments of a skeleton appeared on the screen. "Three million years old—she's indeed a miracle. Lucy's told us a priceless amount of information about our earliest ancestors. Lucy was very short—only about three and a half feet tall—thick through the waist and full-bellied. We learned from her that we walked upright three million years ago, a fact confirmed by Mary Leakey's electrifying discovery of the footprints at Laetoli—"

Interrupted by enthusiastic applause, Peri paused to smile and nod at this recognition of her connection with this discovery.

"My lasting pride," she said in a soft tone. "How fortunate I was to be a young student on that team with Mary Leakey at the discovery and initial excavation of so thrilling a find, that seventy-five-foot trail of forty-seven hominid footprints. Footprints three and three-quarters of a million years old—" She broke off as an image of another skeleton flicked on, then off the screen.

"I'm getting ahead of myself and the slides."

Again she glanced down at her notes. "Ten years after Lucy, in August of 1984, Alan Walker unearthed the Nariokotome Boy in Kenya. He, too, is one of the most exciting discoveries of this century." Her voice was animated, her austere face lighted with exhilaration.

"A million and a half years old, the Nariokotome Boy is the most complete *Homo erectus* we've found." The slide, of a virtually complete skeleton, reappeared. "An adolescent male, and coming along after Lucy, he's told us he was considerably taller, he had narrow hips—"

In the darkened auditorium, hypnotized by Peri's voice, Kate found herself remembering the letters. Peri's communications with her father and the vividly described world beyond the world Peri was now dramatizing with slides on the screen. A primitive world of heat and dust and teeming human commerce, of contrasting, exotic cities: Nairobi, Addis Ababa, Johannesburg. In reading those letters, she had become Peri's clandestine companion, traveling to remote excavation sites—Sterkfontein, Olduvai Gorge, Koobi Fora, Lake Turkana, Laetoli—once, on a bone-shaking ride on a camel, but most often in the same ancient, faithful Land Rover, its every crevice packed with supplies, bouncing over a bleak, rust-colored landscape of searing heat, under a sun so fierce that the strongest skin lotion was ineffectual.

A horizon dotted with lions and zebras and giraffes and wildebeests. A panorama of landscape: forests and bushland of every conceivable shade of green; thorn trees, coco palms, mango, papaya, lianas. Intoxicant fragrances of acacia blossoms, frangipani, hibiscus, jasmine.

At work sites, many times having to quickly seize and fire a rifle over the heads or in front of stalking lions to urge them from the excavation area or the camp. Nights at the edge of the bush, in the open, sheltered by a fragile tent under a vast silvery canopy of stars, smoke from the great campfires acrid in her nostrils, the night winds singing, lions roaring into the dark, predators prowling all around, hyenas and snakes just beyond the tent flaps, poisonous insects butting against the mosquito net, the muffled, mysterious sounds of gunfire in the distance . . .

Awakening to the singing of the cicadas, the tree frogs, the chittering of tiny mousebirds, the rising heat of another suffocating day. Painstaking, dusty work in the digs under a relentless glare of white sky, sweat collecting under the brim of her hat, dreaming of a summer northerly, the pelting Kenyan rains . . .

A photo in one of those letters had seemed to burn in Kate's fingers and now burned in her memory: Peri in riding boots and jodhpurs, a khaki shirt, a safari jacket, and holding an ancient skull . . .

"—right here in our own city," Peri was saying, and Kate realized with a startled glance at her watch that she had been woolgathering for a full half hour. Furious with herself over her inattention to her surroundings, she looked over to Cameron on his side of the auditorium; but he stood transfixed, arms crossed, utterly engrossed in Peri's words.

Behind the podium, Peri leaned toward her audience. "You're blessed with a remarkable Pleistocene deposit right here in Los Angeles." A slide came up, of the entrance to the Page Museum at Rancho La Brea. "The single richest, most densely packed cache of Ice Age fossils in the world. This Los Angeles basin was once a pine-covered forest, and much of its history is contained right here, at the tar pits in Rancho La Brea. Walk through the doors of the Page Museum and see twenty-five-thousand-year-old Pleistocene animals, some of them extinct before the Chumash Indians first ventured into the region. See a replica of La Brea Woman, the oldest human we've found on this coast, our first carbon-dated human. She's nine thousand years old, and we're still speculating over the ambiguous circumstances of

her death. Her skull fracture suggests a violent end—
and yet she was buried with a dog and jewelry.'' A grin
lighted Peri's face. ''Some of you might argue that the
residents of Los Angeles haven't really changed too
much over the centuries.''

As the audience laughed, she gestured to the screen
and its rapidly changing series of slides. ''Consider the
spectacular dimensions of Rancho La Brea. A million
and a half vertebrate fossils—vertebrate meaning having
a spinal column—and two and a half million inverte-
brate fossils have come from its depths. More than a
hundred and forty species of plants. More than four hundred and twenty species of animals—''

Kate's gaze jerked to Nicholas Whitby; he was rising
to his feet.

''—all of this in addition to the world's largest collection of Ice Age birds, not to mention microfossils—
insects and pollen—''

Fully alert, Kate watched Whitby make his way unhurriedly along the back aisle toward her. He gave not
a sign of recognition, turning away from her to travel
the far outside aisle and down the steps toward Peri.
What had he seen? Kate stared as if to somehow penetrate the maddening enigma of this man.

She glanced back at Peri, who was smiling broadly
and pointing into the audience. ''Every summer, under
the direction of that man right there, paleontologist Greg
Jamison, another thousand fossils are pulled out of the
tar pits for cleaning and study, and you, you fortunate
residents of this city, you can go there and watch it all
happening.''

There was a smattering of applause. A dozen rows
down from Kate, Whitby bent his lanky body over the
shoulder of a stocky man who reclined in the aisle seat,
and spoke to him. The man stiffened, then rose, hastily
buttoning his suit jacket. Whitby stood aside; the man
preceded Whitby up the aisle.

"—our tar pits are not unique, but they're very rare, one of a dozen locales throughout the world. And unlike normal fossils, which solidify into stone over the centuries, La Brea's bones are preserved in asphalt and therefore are close to their natural state—"

Kate's scrutiny of the man who climbed the stairs toward her produced little beyond a generalized impression of a husky, older Chinese male approximately five foot ten, with sparse graying hair combed straight back, a mole on the left side of his broad forehead, thin lips tightly drawn; aviator-style, reflective sunglasses covered his eyes. The slight bulge along the left-hand side of the jacket suggested a firearm. The rigid body language signified tension, if not hostility. But as the two men passed her, Whitby again making no sign of recognition, he placed an arm around the Asian's shoulders and leaned toward him, as if to give him some fatherly advice. They exited the auditorium.

"And finally," Peri said, "before I leave you: wonderful news. And this is the first public announcement. By far the most difficult aspect of the quest for our origins has been to gain the funding to finance the sites that feed our research. But funding for a new site has come through—"

Applause rippled through the audience.

"Major funding," Peri exulted. "Enough to sustain our research for the next two years and possibly beyond—"

The applause grew in enthusiasm.

"—and so I'll be leaving within the next several days to arrange for supplies for a team at a highly promising locale in Tanzania. Thank you for your kind attention tonight and for your interest and support throughout the years. I hope, when we meet again, that I'll have new finds and more pieces of the puzzle to explain our origins. In the meantime, the search continues for the full definition of what it means to be human. Thank you and good night.''

Gathering up her notes to a clatter of applause, Peri smiled once at the audience, blew a kiss down to her mother, and strode from the stage.

As Kate watched the crowd file out, Cameron shouldered his way through the throng and over to her.

"Wasn't she great?"

"She was." Kate was watching Arlene Layton climb the stairs to the stage, presumably to go backstage to visit her daughter.

"The news is great, too. I wonder who's funded the dig."

You and me both, Kate thought.

"If it was *National Geographic*," Cameron said, "she'd have said so. Great timing, too. It'll help her deal with her father's death."

Interesting timing, Kate thought. Peri Layton's career gets a major transfusion the day after her father dies. Who, indeed, was the mysterious donor? Walcott's suspicions looked to be soundly based. Knowing Cameron would think it odd if she did not mention Whitby leaving with the Chinese man, Kate said, "Those two men who left—"

"Yeah, I saw them. Was that about anything?"

Kate answered truthfully, ruefully, "I have no idea."

16

BACKSTAGE at Lockhart Auditorium consisted of a small, nondescript area of gray carpeting and muted walls, with a disorderly array of stacked folding chairs, a long, metal-topped table, and a worn corduroy sofa along one wall. Peri had taken off her jacket; her black silk shirt was neatly tucked into her white pants. She stood with Arlene Layton at her side, surrounded by perhaps three dozen people; but Peri's eyes met Kate's as if she had been waiting for her, and the penetrating gaze seemed to fix Kate to the spot. An upraised index finger and quizzical look formed the question as to whether Kate would wait a few minutes, and Kate replied with a nod.

She took a seat on the sofa and observed the mixed, mostly young group surrounding Peri, which was Kate's purpose in being here; but her glance was repeatedly, involuntarily drawn to Peri. Hands on her slender hips, she answered questions, accepted compliments on her speech with a modest ducking of her head, and congratulations on the new funding with a pleased grin.

As the crowd thinned to what appeared to be a few students of Peri's, Arlene came over and greeted Kate by gesturing to Peri: ''A fine talk, didn't you think?'' Pride in her daughter had transformed her face into radiance.

''Very fine,'' Kate agreed.

Then Peri strode over to Kate, a hand extended; and her grip seized Kate in an electric current of physical awareness. She sat down beside Kate, leaning back, an arm stretched along the top of the sofa behind, an ankle crossed over a knee.

"I enjoyed your talk, I learned a few things," Kate said.

"Thank you."

Stirred by Peri's nearness, her sensual perfume, feeling even more vulnerable in Peri's charismatic presence because of what she knew and could not reveal, Kate cleared her throat and fumbled with her notebook, trying to focus her thoughts and project some composure. "I wanted to bring you both up to date on the status of our investigation, especially now that you'll soon be leaving the country, Peri."

Peri said easily, "I'd have called before I left. But I'd have been disappointed not to see you again."

Kate clearly heard sexual suggestion in the low tone of Peri's voice. She said neutrally, "I only wish I had more information to give you."

"It would be surprising if you had any news," Arlene said, unfolding one of the metal chairs and perching on its edge. "Random acts like this one—I'm sure they're the hardest to investigate."

"Yes, ordinarily," Kate said, concentrating on Arlene's remark; she needed her wits about her. "But there seemed to be enough complicating factors here to . . ." She paused, seeking to complete the statement without arousing more questions than she could answer.

Peri was nodding. "Of course you were right to assume the find at Rancho La Brea had to be connected to my father. The poor man had no idea his fossil was a copy—"

"What?" Arlene said.

"Yes, Mother—the CIA says so."

"The CIA?"

"Yes. In the person of a man named Nicholas Whitby. The fossil failed authentication."

"Is that a fact," Arlene said, the skepticism in her tone belying her words.

"I didn't get a chance to tell you, Mother. He came to see me just before I left to come here—" She broke off, her vibrant green eyes searching Kate's face intently. "You didn't know either?"

Kate recovered quickly. "I didn't know you knew."

Peri was still searching Kate's face. "The rediscovery of *Sinanthropus pekinensis* would be an international story with enormous political and scientific repercussions. China considers the fossils a lost national treasure. Beyond that, modern study of the actual fossils could reawaken debate as to whether humankind originated in Africa or China. I'm not surprised in the least that the CIA is involved. You seem to be."

"I am," Kate admitted warily. "Their stock in trade is secrecy."

"And of course lies," Peri added. "But actually, they seemed quite candid."

"Did they," Kate said. How much had Whitby told Peri? An equally important question: What, if anything, had Arlene Layton revealed to her daughter about Herman Layton's cancer?

Peri said, "I always suspected—well, you figure at some point if there's that much smoke surrounding someone, even your father, there has to be at least a small amount of fire. It's what you've always thought, too, isn't it, Mother."

"I did wonder," Arlene said mildly, staring at her daughter.

"All those government people . . . My poor father . . ."

"What's your theory about this?" Kate probed, hoping to see a path through the morass of what Peri did and did not know.

"Somehow my father got hold of one of the copies and all this time believed it was the real thing. I'm convinced he took it inadvertently, maybe he considered it a war souvenir. My father wasn't a thief, I assure you."

Again Kate nodded. Peri could hardly be expected to believe anything else.

"When he found out what he had," Peri continued, "he couldn't bring himself to destroy it, bless his heart. He hid the fossil to protect mother and me. If anyone learned the truth, he'd be considered a traitor, he'd disgrace us. Nicholas Whitby says the CIA believes the same theory. Then Father discovered he was dying—"

Arlene said to Kate, "I told her this morning that Herman had terminal liver cancer."

"Peri, I'm very sorry about this added tragedy," Kate offered.

Peri nodded her thanks. "Mother wasn't sure whether my knowing about Father's cancer would make his death easier or harder. What it does is explain things. He couldn't go to his grave believing he had one of the Peking Man fossils in his possession. So he made a plan to make it public, thinking it wouldn't be traced to him or us or—well, God knows exactly what he was thinking, but that's my guess. Then this grotesque attack occurs, this mugging . . ." Peri said, "I take it the fossil was what he kept in his safe-deposit box?"

"The box was empty except for a blank notepad, but I think we can assume so," Kate said.

"I haven't had time to think about this, but maybe you're right to be skeptical about authentication of that fossil, Mother. They've had time to run only the most preliminary X-ray and composition tests. Maybe I should put off Africa this year and do my own authent—"

"*You can't!*" Arlene's vehemence surprised both Kate and Peri. "The CIA wouldn't lie to us about this."

Of course they would, Kate thought.

"Sure they would," Peri said, grinning. "They'd lie about anything. They may be wrong—"

"Why on earth would you do anything to jeopardize your funding for this year? For God's sake, Peri, don't be a fool. What difference does it make whether it's real or fake? Will we know anything more about where the rest of them are than we did before?"

Peri looked thoughtful, then shrugged.

"Go to Africa. Go now. It's what I want, and you *know* it's what your father would want."

"You're probably right," Peri conceded. "Mother, you need your rest. Go on home. We'll talk tomorrow."

Obediently, Arlene got to her feet. "You're leaving for Africa on Monday. And that's final." She picked up her purse and walked off.

"Mothers," Peri said.

"Yes," Kate said.

With the room emptied of everyone except the two of them, Peri turned to face Kate, her hands clasped around one knee. "I know you're doing everything you can."

"I wish I could offer more."

"Well . . ." Peri's eyes met hers; Kate could not look away from her gaze. Peri said, "I'm glad you came back to see me. I think you know I . . . have a very high regard for you."

Afraid of what her own eyes might reveal, Kate lowered her gaze and found herself staring at Peri's delicate collarbones within the black silk shirt, her golden skin, the visible cleavage at the top of Peri's breasts. Kate quickly looked up and saw that Peri had observed her stare.

"I'm very attracted to you," Peri said huskily.

Warm fingers traced Kate's cheekbones. Peri whispered, "I think we're attracted to each other."

Then, through the fabric of the black shirt there was the heat of Peri's slender body in Kate's hands. Kate did not know who moved next, only that Peri's mouth was against hers, Peri's thigh was pressing into hers, then Peri's lips parted and her tongue touched Kate's and their bodies were tightly together on the sofa and they were thrusting passionately inside each other.

Kate gripped the taut flesh of Peri's back, moving her hands down, then up over the silk shirt to cup Peri's small breasts; her hands sliding up and down, she felt the nipples swelling hard under her palms. Peri's mouth left hers and she gasped; desire was a heaviness clotting Kate's throat, a dull pulsing in her ears. Peri's thighs were undulating into Kate's, Kate's tongue was inside Peri, and Peri's body was arching in her arms.

"Not here," Peri groaned against Kate's mouth, "let's go . . ."

The words brought shocking awareness to Kate that this was a public place and the woman in her arms was not supposed to be in her arms.

She sat up, released Peri, pulled away from her. "I'm sorry . . . I . . . I have to go," she stammered.

"You can't—"

"Yes. I have to." Or she was lost. Beyond recall.

Peri seized Kate by the arms. "Stay with me. Come home with me."

"I have to go," Kate repeated dully, unwilling to meet her eyes, sitting rigidly until Peri's hands dropped away from her. Kate stumbled to her feet.

"Leave now," Peri whispered. "Or I'll do whatever I have to do to make you stay."

Kate fled.

"You're out of your so-called mind," she lashed herself as she sat in her car in the UCLA parking lot. "You fool, you *moron*. A public place—someone comes in and that's it, you're history, your career is over. You stupid, stupid damn fool, Peri Layton is a *murder* suspect."

She started the Saturn, gunned the engine in fury.

Tired, she thought. Too goddamn tired. Too tired can be worse than being too drunk.

"I thought you said you were tired," Aimee murmured a half an hour later.

In Aimee's arms, cocooned in the delicious sleepy warmth of her body, Kate answered by putting Aimee under her. Aimee's legs rose, and Kate surrendered to the full embrace of Aimee's naked body under her own, the voluptuousness of Aimee's breasts and warm, soft, silken skin. Aimee's hands slid up Kate's back and into her hair to bring Kate's mouth to hers, Aimee's mouth parted under hers, and Kate's tongue was inside her. Fitting herself between Aimee's fully open legs, suffused with sensation, her every subtle motion intensified pleasure until Kate finally took her mouth from Aimee's, gasping, her body rocking, Aimee's writhing hips riding up into her, and Kate climaxed, fully, quivering with waves and waves of ecstasy.

Still moaning with the exquisiteness of her release, she slid down Aimee's body to the wetness within her upraised legs, slid her hands under Aimee's hips, and with Aimee's shivering thighs against her face, she drank and drank her fill.

17

THE next morning, Kate pulled herself away from Aimee's warmth to dress and meet her brother.

At exactly nine o'clock, giving a final adjustment to her jacket and slacks, Kate entered the Vagabond Motel coffee shop. Smelling richly of cooking bacon and toast, the room was crowded; but had she not been armed with a description, the vague familiarity of the man sitting alone in a small booth across the restaurant would have identified him to her.

Dale Harrison saw similar elements in her as well, or perhaps saw her look of recognition; smoothing back his thin gray hair, buttoning his sports jacket, he maneuvered his way out of the booth and stood up, never taking his eyes from her, a hand extended as she walked toward him.

"Dale," she said, gripping his hand.

"Kate. My God." He pumped her hand vigorously. "My daughter looks like you."

"The poor thing," Kate bantered, a wash of goose bumps passing over her at his resemblance to her father. *His* father . . .

"Sit down, sit down," Harrison said heartily, lowering himself into the booth, picking up a menu and handing it to her. "Thanks for meeting me. I know you have better things to do with a Saturday morning. Let's get some breakfast. I don't know about you, but I'm starved.''

Kate was touched by his evident nervousness and wondered if the shaving nicks in his chin and neck had been caused by anxiety over meeting her. She herself had a tendency toward clumsiness when she was emotionally disquieted. Although she always ordered the same breakfast, she opened the menu, allowing him time to settle down and to glance surreptitiously at her as he fidgeted with his own menu.

A rail-thin, brunette waitress addressed Kate: ''Coffee? Like to order?''

''Yes, thanks. Bacon and two eggs over easy and a short stack,'' she said, glad for the temporary distraction.

''Ham and scrambled eggs, double order of white toast for me. Thanks.'' Harrison closed his menu and handed it to the waitress, and Kate saw that the glaze of fine gold hair on the back of his hand was laid out like soft bent grass, exactly the way her father's had been.

''So what's your daughter's name?'' Kate asked as the waitress left.

''Dylan. Nan loved the name. Nan's my wife,'' he explained.

So he was in a presumably intact marriage. ''How old is Dylan?''

''Thirteen, and is she ever a handful.''

''So was I at that age,'' Kate said. With a daughter that young, he must have a youngish wife. ''Your message said you live in Red Bluff. A nice town.''

He nodded. ''Growing up in Chicago I always felt I was a small-town boy. Maybe it's in the genes.''

''Maybe not,'' Kate said affably. ''I guess you know I'm from Greenleaf, Michigan—a real small town—and here I am in Los Angeles, been here for years. So what do you do for a living?''

''Real estate. Been in it since the get-go. I do pretty

good for a guy who left school three years short of a degree."

She was still the only Delafield ever to graduate from college. She was gratified at retaining the distinction.

"What about you?" he asked.

Not sure if his question referred to whether she had a degree or to her occupation, she answered, "I'm a police detective."

"No shit. Sorry, I mean no kidding. What kind of detective?"

Kate smiled. "Don't fuss over your language, Dale. I hear it all day long. I'm in homicide."

"No shit. How long you been a cop?"

"About twenty-five years, all told."

"That kind of work—I take it you got a degree."

"University of Michigan."

He nodded. "How'd you get into . . . what you do?"

"One thing led to another. Police work seemed like a logical idea after four years in the military."

"What branch?"

"Marines."

"No shit." He leaned on the table toward her, crossing his arms, hands gripping above his elbows. "I was Army. Got real lucky, didn't go to Vietnam, but some of my best buddies—"

"I know. I was there. Da Nang. I lost some good friends, too," Kate said.

"Damn," Harrison said, shaking his head. "My sister—you've had quite a life. God, I can hardly believe it, here I am, fifty-five years old, and I finally get to meet my sister." He glanced at the band on the ring finger of her left hand. "You're married?"

Not by his standards. She shook her head.

He studied her face. "I don't look very much like you. Do I look like . . . anybody?"

"Your . . ." She struggled with her reluctance to

share parentage with him. "You look like your birth father."

He leaned back, clasped his hands together, and started to crack his knuckles, then abruptly stopped himself, laying his palms on the table. "How so?"

He was fidgety like you, she thought, but not a knuckle-cracker. "Same height, same build and coloring," she said, "same color eyes. His nose was a little thinner through the bridge—"

Harrison chuckled, and Kate thought she heard a note of her mother's throaty laugh. He said, "I busted my beak twice. Football." He blinked rapidly, as if clearing a cinder from his eye. "It feels weird that you know stuff like that and I don't."

She met his gaze directly. "Dale, I can't imagine what it would be like to be in your shoes."

He seemed like a nice enough man, a regular, pleasant person, and she realized how rarely she saw a Dale Harrison. The men and women she came into contact with on a daily basis were either police professionals case-hardened into wary self-protectiveness, or sullen antagonists on the other side of the law, or the bereaved, stunned facsimiles of the people they ordinarily were.

"I brought pictures," Kate said, pulling them out of her shoulder bag.

"You did? That's great. It's terrific you thought to do that."

She hadn't. She handed him the two photos she had hastily pulled out of a desk drawer, wondering whether it would have occurred to her to bring them had it not been for Aimee's prodding.

Harrison placed the photos carefully side by side and examined them, his gaze constantly shifting from one to the other, looking up once at Kate, to search her features. "I do look like him," he said. "You look a little like both of them."

"So I've been told," Kate said. She had her mother's

mouth and facial shape, her father's eyes and some of his husky build.

"The detective I hired told me they've both passed on. Leukemia for her. Him, a heart attack."

"Your detective got it right." She hoped he did not want further details.

"That's real young," he said, shaking his head. "I mean, he was only fifty-seven. Makes you wonder about our own genes—"

Their breakfast arrived. He put the pictures down on the seat beside him and tended to his food.

Kate thought, He'd better not assume those are his to keep.

"Your adoptive family," she said. "How do they feel about this?"

"My folks? They feel okay. I mean, they're my family. My sister doesn't like me coming here, but I don't give a damn what she thinks. Agnes Delafield sure gave me the bum's rush," he added, forking egg and a piece of ham into his mouth. He talked around his food: "Didn't want to talk to me, couldn't get rid of me fast enough."

"She's an old woman," Kate said, digging into her hash browns. "She wants history over and done with, a settled issue."

"You're the one I really wanted to see anyway," Harrison said. "What can you tell me?"

An open-ended question a cop would ask, Kate thought. "Where do you want me to begin?"

"What kind of people were the Delafields? What were they like?"

"Good people, all of them. Fine people. Salt of the earth—"

His nod was impatient. "What did my father do for a living?"

"He was a sanitation worker," she said. The shift of his gaze away from her, the slump of his shoulders, told her his keen disappointment. "He was crew chief when he died. He dreamed of owning a landscape business. Mother never worked away from home."

Again he nodded and ate a few more bites of food. "There's a question I need to ask. Maybe you can't answer. Like . . . They kept you. But not me."

Kate understood how important her answer was to him. "It wasn't 'they' making the decision," she said. "It was Mother. There was a reason. Thanks to Agnes Delafield, I can actually explain it to you."

As Harrison slowly lowered his fork and waited for her to continue, she saw the lines around his mouth deepen, saw his lips thin with tension, saw him again begin to crack his knuckles before he could stop himself.

She, too, put down her fork. Quietly, she related the story her Aunt Agnes had told her four days ago, recounting every detail she could remember, including her father's conversation with her on the day they had stolen together to go fishing.

Harrison did not speak until Kate concluded: "No one knew except Agnes Delafield and the town doctor. Your birth mother took her secret about you to the grave."

"So you never knew any of this till now."

"No."

"So Andrew Delafield never knew he had a son."

"No."

"Jesus." He swallowed coffee with an audible gulp. "Is this weird, or what." He picked up his fork and proceeded to consume his food as if he were programmed to do it.

Knowing he was assimilating the information she had given him, Kate silently ate her own meal, glancing frequently at him, occupied with her own assimilation of a man who bore so eerie a resemblance to her father.

"Well," Harrison said after the waitress cleared away their dishes, "now tell me about my sister."

"Not that much more to tell," she deflected. "You have the one daughter?"

"Yup." He grinned. "I got a young wife—she keeps me going."

"Do you happen to have pictures?"

"Yup. Dylan'll be real interested to know she has a cop for an aunt. She'd be thrilled to meet you." He was pawing through the briefcase beside him.

"I'd like to meet her, too."

"Good. Good, glad to hear it. Like I said, you've had one hell of a life. Ever fit marriage in anywhere? Kids?"

"I thought about it," Kate said, impatient with his fumbling. She was eager to see Dylan. Her niece. Who looked like her.

"That's it? Just thought about it?" He fished out two photos, slid them across the table.

"That's it." Assuming one of the pictures would be of Nan Harrison, ready to give it a polite perusal, she instead lingered over the image of a fortyish, trim-figured, grinning blonde, her dark-framed glasses the dominant feature on her friendly face. A solemn teen-aged girl was also in the photo and was clearly Dylan Harrison, and Dylan Harrison was the image of Kate at thirteen. Kate could tell from the awkward, V-like bend of Dylan's body that her mother had suddenly pulled her close as the camera lens clicked. Against the background of a tent in a forested area, Dylan and her mother wore jeans and identical sloppy, oversize green T-sweatshirts with a *Tyrannosaurus rex* on the front. Dylan appeared to be several inches taller than her mother.

"No surprise in this day and age," Harrison said.

She blinked in confusion and then remembered that he had been asking about her marital status.

"So, you live with somebody," he said. "Is that it?"

She looked up at him. She could not divide her attention between him and the photos because she had to decide how to respond to questions that were so easy for heterosexuals to answer but so complicated for gay people when they had no way of foretelling or gauging reaction.

"I've had relationships off and on," she replied and added a shrug, hating herself for the glib ambiguity.

"Look, we've got an awful lot to talk about, but I've got business down here today, Kate," Harrison said apologetically. "An easement approval, I need to get it signed this morning. The property owner lives in Carson, he's a drunk. If I don't get to him by eleven, he'll be blotto."

"Seems we draw from the same client base," Kate said absently, still studying the photo. "I'm tied up with a case myself today." She focused now on the photo of Dylan, a head shot; she stared at the mass of unruly, wavy, fine-textured hair, the lock falling over the wide forehead, the hair the same brown black color as her own before early onset of gray, the eyes the same shape and pale blue color as her own, the broad cheekbones the same. Kate picked up the photo, held it wonderingly between thumb and forefinger. But—had her own eyes ever been so bold, had her own mouth ever been set in so defiant a line back then? No. Not then. She had been an obedient daughter, a dutiful daughter—she had been dutiful all her life. She remembered Harrison's remark that Dylan was a handful. "When were these pictures taken, Dale?"

Harrison pointed. "That one, back in May, a camping trip. That's Dylan's most recent school photo." He asked eagerly, "So what's your case about?"

"A fatal stabbing." For once she did not mind the universal fascination with police work; at the moment, it was an advantage. "At the La Brea Tar Pits."

"No shit." He looked crestfallen. "Here I was going to bring Nan and Dylan down here in a couple of weeks, and Dylan's crazy to go there."

"No problem, Dale. The place is safe, trust me. The

occasional weird thing happens at Disneyland, too, you know.''

"Guess you have a point. You should know.''

She smiled. "I'll be your police escort when Dylan comes down, if you like.''

"Sure would. Look, I've got to leave tomorrow morning, I've got afternoon appointments back home. How about this afternoon? Tonight? I'd love to see more of your photos, talk about stuff. Maybe I could barge in for a drink at your place, we could spend the evening together? You look like a woman who likes a drink.''

Wondering why he thought so, she said agreeably, "I do. I wish I could do it tonight, Dale.'' She did and she didn't. It was all too complicated right now, revealing Aimee's existence too big a risk if there was a possibility she might meet her niece in the near future. "Being here is all I can do right now. With a new case, we have to move fast. I need to catch up with my partner.''

"Guess I can understand that.''

"Now that we've made contact—''

"Yeah, that's the important thing. We can set something else up.'' He extracted a business card from his jacket pocket, slid it across the table to her. He pointed to the photos. "How about a swap?''

It was hardly an even swap; his opportunities to photograph his family were legion, while the number of photos of her parents were finite. "It's a deal,'' she said, and reached into her shoulder bag for one of her own cards.

The waitress approached with the check; he reached for it. "I got this one, Kate.''

"The next one's mine.''

"A deal,'' he said.

Kate drove directly to Wilshire Division; she knew better than to risk any conversation over her mobile phone. The station was quiet, the homicide table deserted on this Saturday morning. She picked up the phone.

"So how was it?" Aimee asked eagerly. "You didn't take much time with him."

"He had to leave for a business appointment. So, I have a nice-guy brother who's a real estate agent, a young sister-in-law, and a thirteen-year-old niece who looks just like me."

"The poor little thing."

Kate managed a chuckle. "That's what I told him."

"So, are you getting together again?"

"They're coming to L.A. in a couple of weeks. I didn't come out to him, Aimee. I didn't tell him about us."

"So what? Honey, you just met the guy."

And I denied the existence of the most important person in my life.

Brother and sister had found each other after half a century of separation, but she knew very well that they might lose each other again. Because she would tell Dale Harrison the truth as soon as she could. She had to. She was sick of secrets, sick of hiding.

Kate said fervently, "Believe me, I understand first-hand what you went through with your family. For sure I'll tell him, but I hate to think it'll turn out the way it did for you. I hate to think I'll have to wait fifteen years to hear from him again."

"Maybe it'll be okay. The world's changed a few degrees since I told my family, thank God. A news item from this end: Marcie went out to get the paper this morning and found a knife stuck in her door."

"Marcie mine," Kate said, remembering Marcie's ex-husband's license plate.

"His or nobody's," Aimee agreed. She asked, "Do we get to have a piece of the weekend together?"

Kate knew it was a simple query, not an attempt to apply pressure. As a paralegal, Aimee had her own deadlines and occasional erratic hours; she fully understood the time demands of Kate's job. "I don't know yet," Kate said. "Tomorrow looks good, but don't hold me to it."

"Okay. Later, alligator. And honey? All these years you never dreamed you had a brother, much less a niece. Be glad."

"Okay."

But thoughts of her brother slipped away as she focused on the Herman Layton case.

After stacking and moving files and other paperwork to make room, Kate spread out maps of central and west Los Angeles. With a yellow marking pen she traced lines that converged on Herman Layton's house on Tilden, and with a green pen, another line to the La Brea Tar Pits on Wilshire Boulevard.

Logging onto the department computer, she called up the web page for Los Angeles Metropolitan Transit Authority, and its map of Metro bus lines, then the complete schedule. She printed out all fourteen pages.

Squinting at the fine print of the weekday schedules, she circled key segments. Then she consulted a department directory and called the MTA, threading her way through levels of bureaucracy until she reached Vera Perkins, who asked in a pronounced Southern accent for Kate's badge number and patiently and courteously went over Kate's list with her, matching the times of buses with the drivers. Afterward, Kate called the major taxi companies.

Still trying to fit the bits and pieces of the Layton case together, she absently stacked her paperwork in a file. Her theory about this case was tenuous, farfetched, and it would be Monday before she could begin to chase this probable wild goose.

An hour later, Kate glanced up from a report to see Cameron fling his jacket onto the clothes tree and drop his lean frame into a chair across from her.

"What are you doing here?" Kate greeted him.

"Hello to you, too. Details. Loose ends. Crapola." Cameron loosened his tie. "I just reinterviewed Arlene."

"Ah yes, the prime suspect."

"She did know about her ex-husband's cancer, and Herman made her promise not to tell Peri till it was necessary, and Peri knows about it now, and I understand you know all about them knowing about it."

"Yes. I saw them both at UCLA after you left."

Cameron looked at her as if not quite sure whether he should express annoyance at this freelance activity of hers. Then he said, "Layton's phone records show two calls to Arlene. Arlene denies she went to see Layton."

"She does?"

"She does."

Interesting, Kate thought. Why would Arlene deny it?

Cameron said, "If that older woman Meyer Silverman saw wasn't Arlene, who could it be?"

"Who indeed?"

"I'll finish up my case reports," Cameron said gloomily. "I don't know about you, but I think we've shot our wad."

Kate was also preparing herself for that eventuality. "Could be," she said.

"Joe Cameron's first case, unsolved."

"Not without historical precedent," Kate said with a faint smile.

Cameron looked puzzled, then caught on. "La Brea Woman and Herman Layton. Two homicides at Rancho La Brea ten thousand years apart. Both unsolved. Historical symmetry. Bookends."

"Don't sweat it. We'll have plenty of business to improve your stats."

After looking around to ensure they were alone, Kate said, "I met my brother this morning, Joe."

"Hey, no kidding." He leaned toward her. "So how did it go? Does he look like you?"

"No, but his daughter does."

"The poor kid."

"A consensus of opinion seems to be forming about that," she said wryly. She related the morning's events to Cameron.

"It's looking real promising," he said with a smile. "Maybe you'll end up having a family again, Kate."

She shrugged in response. I already have one, she thought. One I can't reveal.

"For whatever good a family might do you," he muttered as he pulled out the Layton murder book.

"I guess every family has its problems," she said, and was not surprised when he did not reply. Some families also have their secrets, she reflected, studying her enigmatic new partner. About personal matters, he was reluctant with his trust. Well, so was she. If she had her reasons, she could only respect his reticence, whatever its cause. If this partnership grew in rapport, over time she would learn a great deal about him. Many police partnerships became a bonding as close as a marriage. Right now, she had no choice but to extend some preliminary trust.

She took a small piece of paper out of her jacket pocket. "Joe," she said, and handed it to him.

He glanced at it, then at her, in surprise. "I thought you weren't going to do this."

You and me both, she thought. "This morning he stuck a knife in her door."

"She's in big trouble," Cameron said, his face somber. "The cork is about to pop."

"That's how I read it, too," Kate said.

Cameron looked more intently at the paper, then handed it back to her. "Destroy it."

She nodded. "What happens now?"

"Expect a phone call. When it comes, we move. You drop anything you're doing. Agreed?"

"Agreed. I don't like not knowing, Joe," she said.

"It's how it has to be," Cameron said. "It works better if you don't know."

18

THE call came on Sunday night.

"It's show time. Meet you at the station," Cameron said and hung up.

Half an hour later, amid the growling static emitted by the Caprice's police radio, a phone rang. Kate was confused; then, as Cameron reached into his inside jacket pocket, she scolded herself for being a dimwit. She received all the calls when they were out working together, but of course he had a cell phone.

"Cameron." Then, tersely, "Got it. ETA five minutes."

Not looking at Kate, he sped up with a faint screeching of tires.

Her pulse escalating, she automatically checked her shoulder holster. "So what's the plan, Joe?" Surely he would tell her now.

"This goes down only if we can get to him on a quiet street." Cameron placed his phone on the console between himself and Kate. "You're background furniture. Don't draw your weapon under any circumstances. If I say anything to you, all you say is, 'That's right, partner.' Got it?"

Kate nodded, repeating with an effortful grin, "That's right, partner."

"One more thing, Kate. Trust me."

"I've already done that."

"It goes further. How this may look to you—you need to trust me."

She did not reply. Unconditional trust she gave to no one. Not even Aimee.

He, too, lapsed into silence as he drove through the night, and Kate sat perfectly still beside him. His tension was palpable and all too familiar; he was gathering himself in the same way she did when she had broken a case and was leading a team in for an arrest. Despite his assurances of her noninvolvement in the upcoming incident, she knew better. She felt a growing pressure in her chest, surges of adrenaline. Confrontation with anyone, regardless of circumstance, regardless of thoroughness of preparation and planning, always held unpredictability and peril. The bullet she had taken in her left shoulder was permanently aching proof.

Five minutes later, after they left the bright lights of nighttime West Hollywood and were cruising along Lexington Avenue near Plummer Park, Cameron's phone rang again.

He snatched it off the console. "Yeah." He listened for a few seconds. "Got it," he said. He placed his right hand back on the wheel and, still holding the phone, sped up, turned onto Lexington Avenue, sped up again.

Again he lifted the phone to his ear. "Got him, visual sighting. Thanks, buddy." Cameron tucked the phone back into his jacket.

Ahead of them, Kate saw a black Ford Ranger signal a right-hand turn; it disappeared onto Formosa Avenue, revealing a maroon '94 Camaro, its license plate MRCI MYN.

Cameron maneuvered the Caprice in behind the car, which held a single driver, a male. As the Camaro turned off Lexington onto Mercer, Cameron glanced out both side windows, hunched forward to scrutinize the street through the windshield; it was deeply shadowed by overhanging trees, their branches whipping in the night wind. "Perfect," he muttered. "Thanks, asshole."

He turned up the volume of the police radio, flipped the dashboard switch to activate the rear-window light. Kate braced herself. The radio loudly crackling with dispatch calls, the swirling red of the rear light slashing through the dark night, he floored the accelerator and gunned the Caprice around the Camaro, cutting the car off, forcing it to the curb in a screeching of brakes and burning of rubber.

Seizing the flashlight from its bracket, Cameron leaped from the Caprice and trained it on the driver who was rolling down his window. "Hands on the wheel! On the wheel! Do it!"

"What the hell—"

"Now!"

"Sure sure. What the *hell*—"

Striding up to the Camaro, shining his flashlight directly into the eyes of the driver, Cameron held up identification. "Sit still. Don't move a muscle. Don't even blink."

"You got the wrong guy! I didn't—"

"Shut up. I said don't move a muscle. That means your mouth."

As Cameron shifted the beam of his flashlight to the interior of the Camaro, Kate got out of the Caprice to move in behind Cameron for support; she could see the driver's thinning dishwater-blond hair, his wide, flat, dumbfounded face, his dark eyes bright with apprehension, his white-knuckled hands clutched on the wheel. He could not, Kate thought, possibly feel more apprehensive than she did.

"Okay. Step out of the car. Nice and slow," Cameron commanded. "I'll open the door. Get out with your hands up high. Got it?"

"I don't—"

"Shut up, goddammit. Do exactly as I say. You're starting to make me nervous."

"I got it, okay, I got it."

Cameron swung open the car door, and the driver climbed out awkwardly, arms raised, blinking against the flashlight beam that was full on his face.

"Turn around," Cameron ordered. "Hands on the car. Legs back and apart."

"Wait—"

"Do it."

The driver spun around and spread his feet and leaned forward, his agitation expressed in the slamming of his palms on the roof of his car. Cameron kicked the man's feet further backward and then patted him down with his free hand, running it swiftly over the yellow polo shirt and then down his baggy jeans. He reached into the right front pocket and removed an object; it was not until Cameron passed it through the beam of the flashlight that Kate saw it was a red-handled Swiss Army knife. Cameron stuffed it into a pocket of his jacket.

"This is crazy! I didn't do anything. I'm gonna bring charges—"

"Shut up. The wallet in your back pocket. You have ID?"

"Yeah, sure."

As he started to bring his hand down, Cameron kicked at his spread legs. "Look, asshole, are you deaf or just stupid? Do what I say—not one thing more. Now take one hand off the car and very slowly pull out the wallet."

Cautiously, the driver obeyed; and Cameron snatched the wallet from his fingers. "Hands back on the car," he ordered. He flipped open the wallet. "Charles George Grissom," he read from the license. "This your car, Charles?"

"Damn right."

"Registered to you?"

"Yeah."

"Registration?"

"Sure. Insurance, too." He shifted his right hand on the car, then stilled it. "In the glove compartment."

"Okay with you if I check, Charles?"

"Yeah. Christ. Whatever."

A permissive search, Kate thought. The first lawful thing that had occurred here. Then she caught herself: None of this was lawful.

"You gonna tell me what this is about?"

"Don't you move, Charles. My partner's watching you."

He looked over at Kate and she uttered, "That's right, partner."

Cameron, standing behind Grissom, gestured to the whirling red light and made a sign to Kate to douse it; Kate moved to the car and gratefully flipped off the switch. If another police car cruised past the intersection, they would be less noticeable. Cameron strode around the Camaro to the passenger side, opened the door and then the glove compartment, searching, his flashlight trained, through the papers within.

But the police radio in the Caprice continued to squawk into the night, and Kate could see lights go on in adjacent houses and people gathering at their windows. An elderly man and woman, in pajamas and slippers and yellow chenille bathrobes, shuffled down the sidewalk of the nearest house toward the street. Shit, thought Kate. She did not dare turn off the radio without Cameron's instruction; she did not know what factors were a part of his scenario. Approaching the two people, she said courteously, "Everything's under control, folks. Please return to your house."

"You betcha," the old man said, staring over to where Grissom stood with his hands pressed to the roof of his car. "You get that scum off our street." Taking the arm of his wife, whose pale eyes were fixed on the spread-footed Grissom, he turned her away, and the two old people shuffled away, the hems of their bathrobes dragging on the sidewalk.

Cameron had returned to his position behind Grissom. "You're right, Charles, the car is definitely registered to you."

He closed the distance between himself and Grissom and shone the flashlight onto the floor of the backseat, behind the driver's side. "So you're telling us we got the wrong guy, right, Charles? That's what you're saying, right?"

"What the hell is *that?*" Grissom asked in bewilderment, his gaze following the radiant beam of Cameron's flashlight.

"Pick it up," Cameron ordered. "Be real slow while you do it."

"I don't know what the hell it is," Grissom protested.

"Are you deaf, asshole?" Cameron roared. *"Pick it up."*

Grissom stooped, reaching into his car. When he rose, he gingerly held a pliant, transparent sack the size of a pound of coffee; it contained a white, powdery substance.

Jesus, no, Kate thought.

"Okay, Charles. Now, put it on the roof of the car."

"It isn't mine," he protested vehemently. "I don't know anything about it."

"That's what they all say."

"What the hell is this stuff?"

Cameron said in a suddenly congenial tone, "I think we both got a pretty good idea, Charles, but let's find out for sure, shall we? Let's take care of this right now. With my field test kit. Stay where you are. Don't even think about moving."

Keeping Grissom in her line of vision, Kate stared at Cameron as he walked over to the Caprice and unlocked its trunk. But he did not look at her; he opened a case and a moment later strode back to the Camaro carrying a metal rack of test tubes with cork tops.

"What the hell's going on here?" Grissom demanded as Cameron set the test tubes on the roof of the car. "I don't know anything about this. I've got rights—"

"And so do we, Charles."

Cameron removed the cork tops from the test tubes. Then he picked up a large needle from the metal rack and pierced the top of the plastic bag of white powder. He lowered the needle into the first test tube, then inserted it again into the package, repeating the process for all six test tubes, muttering, "Charles, Charles, Charles," as each test tube changed color, reds, blues, greens.

Finally, he emitted a brief whistle and a marveling, "Wow! Charles my boy," he declared, "it's been at least five years since I saw H this pure."

This can't be happening. How did Cameron get this much heroin? No matter what Grissom had done, how dangerous he was, she could not let Cameron plant drugs and frame this man. Taking a step forward, she remembered Cameron's admonition: *How this may look to you—you need to trust me.* She held her ground.

"What the hell's going on," Grissom said, rocking back on his spread feet as if he were suddenly dizzy.

"You tell me." Cameron's tone had changed, was harsh. "How about you give yourself a break and tell us exactly where you got this package and exactly where you're delivering it."

"I was just going out to—just out—" He broke off. Kate realized that he was probably on his way to pursue his obsession with Marcie and could not admit this to Cameron.

"I was just going for a drive, man," Grissom stammered, staring at the package, "Man, I mean Officer, I don't know what this stuff is—I never saw it before."

Cameron sighed audibly. "Fine. You play it your way, Charles."

"I'm not playing it any way!" Grissom screeched. "I never saw that stuff! I don't know how it got in my car!"

"You really think that's gonna fly someplace, Charles? Courts don't listen to that crap. They just look at the size of the drug bust."

"I'm telling you, somebody put this stuff in my car!"

"Sure, Charles. And who'd want to do that?"

"My wife," Grissom said immediately. "She did it. Goddammit—the bitch put it my car and called you guys!"

"Your *wife?*" Cameron said, his voice rising with his incredulity. "That's a good one. Okay, Charles, tell us about it. What did you do to your wife that she'd do this to you?"

"Nothing. Not a goddamn thing. She's the one who did it all, the fucking, two-timing little whore, the—"

"Cut the bullshit, Charles. She could get a pro to take you out for five bills. She's gonna toss away more than half a million bucks in pure grade heroin?"

"Half a million—"

"Okay, I'm a conservative guy. Maybe twice that much, depending on who's cutting. So what the hell did you do to her that's worth pissing away a million bucks?"

Kate watched in disbelief. How had Cameron managed to get his hands on this much dope? From her side angle on Grissom, she saw him gape at the package of white powder, a liquid brightness spreading over his wide, staring eyes as his confusion mutated into fear.

Cameron said, "Let's have a serious conversation here, Charles. My partner's run you through the computer—" He looked over at Kate.

Staring back at him, she hesitated. *The way this may*

look to you—you have to trust me. "That's right, partner," she supplied.

"And you've come up clean—"

"That's right, partner."

"I told you," Grissom said, his voice shaking. "I
didn't do this—"

"Which means nothing, asshole. So it's your first
strike. A bust this big adds up to twenty-five years, man-
datory. You can look for parole—"

"Twenty-five years!"

"Hey Charles, didn't the people who put you up to
this caper happen to mention that little item? You
chump, being a courier for this much dope is a class A
felony."

"I'm not a courier! I didn't *do* this! I didn't do *anything!* I want a lawyer!"

"Sure, you do. But we got *this* package in *your* car,
it's registered to you nice and tidy, and we got your
fingerprints all over the package—"

"You made me pick it up!" he shrieked.

"That's what *you* say, Charles. We got you stitched
up with a Do-Not-Pass-Go ticket to San Quentin, maybe
even Pelican Bay. A soft first timer like you—I hope
you really like cock, Charlie."

"I'm dreaming," Grissom whispered. "This is a
nightmare."

You got that right, thought Kate.

"Yeah, a nightmare it is, Charles. You have no idea,
you schmuck."

Grissom lowered his head, and Cameron stood back,
his flashlight trained on him; Kate could see Grissom's
tears drip from his face to splash on the pavement.

Cameron finally said, "We're gonna give you a break,
Charles."

"What do you mean?" His voice shook with sup-
pressed sobs.

"You notice we didn't put any cuffs on you yet."

"Yeah . . ."

"So we're not going to arrest you."

His head jerked up. "You're—"

"We're not going to arrest you."

Grissom's body lurched; he started to turn around.

"Don't move. You keep those hands where they are till I tell you. We need to explain a few things."

"Hey," Grissom said, his head twisting toward Cameron, "you don't need to explain one damn thing. You guys want this stuff, this whole million dollars or whatever the fuck it is? Take it. It's yours. I won't tell anybody, not a soul. Is that a deal? You got it."

"No, that's not a deal. Here's how it works, Charles." Cameron moved to Grissom's side and poked a fingertip into the cellophane bag that sat on the roof of the Camaro. "My partner and I don't want any part of this shit." He looked over at Kate.

Kate said fervently, "Damn right, partner."

"So let me tell you what's gonna happen now, Charles. There's some people already looking for this shipment." Cameron's quiet tone contained a glasslike edge of menace. "They're already looking for *you,* my man. Because even if you're telling us the gospel truth, you're still the guy. The guy who had it last. They'll find you, Charles. And when you don't have what they want . . ."

Cameron pulled out the Swiss Army knife he had taken from Grissom; he tucked the flashlight under his arm and extracted one of the knife's blades. "Let me tell you what happens, Charles. These particular guys don't kill people. They don't do that. They use guys who cross them to leave messages. Last guy that crossed them, he's still alive. Jake's living in Bakersfield, matter of fact. If you call it living. Jake's balls are missing. After they finished with that, they cut his eyes out, too." He displayed the knife to Grissom, the open blade gleaming in the flashlight's beam.

"Jesus Christ," Grissom said, his body flinching as he watched Cameron with the knife. More tears fell from his face.

"You're not going to have what those boys are looking for, Charles. Nobody will. Because looky here."

Cameron jabbed the blade of the Swiss Army knife into the sack of white powder, slashing the bag open. Holding up the sac, he dumped out its contents. The powder blew around in the wind, into the shrubbery and on down the street.

"Jesus Christ," Grissom uttered.

Kate sagged back, leaning against the Caprice.

"Let me explain ourselves to you, Charles. We're sick to death of assholes like you. We're sick to death of busting fucks like you and taking your poison away and dragging you into court and spending our good time testifying about how your slimebag ass belongs in jail. We'd just as soon take care of scumballs like you the easy way. Let your own people do it. The bottom line for you is, you're history."

"Damn right, partner," Kate offered unprompted.

Cameron said, "If you got any brains left in your shit head, you're gonna get in that car and get as far from here—"

"Please, look, I'm telling you, I had nothing to do with this—"

"Then listen, asshole. Listen up. Get the fuck out of here. Way out of here. You understand what I'm telling you?"

"Okay, I could leave for a while," Grissom said, lowering his head to wipe his eyes on his sleeve. "I got a friend with a cabin, I'll pack up—"

Cameron laughed; he looked over to Kate and she obediently forced a few barks of laughter.

"What a schmuck. What a sweet little lamb this guy is, right partner? Sure, Charles, you go on home. Maybe they're not waiting there for you—yet. They waited six years for the last one. He made the mistake of coming back to L.A. at three in the morning to visit his mama. Now he's with mama all the time—he's got no knee-caps, no eyes, no hands.''

''Give me a break,'' Grissom pleaded.

''We already did, Charles. What more do you want? It's a free country, you're a free man. What else is there?'' Cameron extinguished his flashlight. Strolling to the Caprice, he called back, ''You're free to go, Charles.''

Grissom stood within the open door of his car, his body haloed by the interior light, his hands on the roof of his car as if cemented there. ''Wait, wait—wait just a minute—''

''Have a nice life, Charles.''

Cameron climbed into the Caprice, slammed the door, and pulled away from the curb, gunning the engine and roaring off down the street.

Kate did not speak until they reached Santa Monica Boulevard.

''Judas Priest,'' she finally said.

''Had a few doubts back there, didn't you, partner?''

Kate gave an elaborate shrug. ''Who, me? No problem, never a doubt.''

Cameron chuckled, then said, ''Think he bought it?''

''Yes. Oh yeah, for sure he bought it.''

''Till he mulls it over, Kate. We won't know for sure for a couple of days. Call your friend,'' he ordered. ''In case he decides to take care of unfinished business. Tell her to get out—''

''She has. After that knife in the door yesterday she packed a few clothes, she's staying with a friend.''

''Good. If he does leave town and then comes back to test the waters, we may have to follow up, but it'll be easy to put the fear of God in him, just put a real visible tail on him—''

''Joe, what if—what if he looks for police protection—calls in a complaint? You showed him ID—''

"You kidding? I put the flashlight in his eyes and showed him my driver's license.'' He lifted a hand from the wheel and raised one finger at a time. "Neither one of us identified ourselves as police, ever drew a weapon. I never cuffed him. The search of his vehicle was permissive. I never arrested him. We got witnesses looking out their windows to prove it. What's his beef—that I took his drugs and threw them away?''

Kate began to laugh. After a moment, Cameron joined in, and the two of them laughed uproariously, Cameron beating on the wheel, Kate rocking back and forth, fully giving into this shattering of tension, her sheer relief.

"Joe," she finally said, wiping her eyes, "have you and your buddy done this before?''

"Yeah," he said, slinging an arm along the seat back as he drove. "I planted the package and—my buddy ran the scene.''

Kate noticed the careful use of "my buddy" to avoid use of a pronoun. "So what's in the package? It looks like the genuine article.''

"Flour and confectioners' sugar.''

Kate chuckled. "Nice recipe. Your field test kit?''

"Don't know. You'd have to ask my buddy. There's chemicals in there that turn different colors when you add flour and sugar. That's all I know.''

"Impressive.'' Kate shook her head. "Amazing.''

She sat back and said after a moment, "This is very personal to you, isn't it, Joe. This is closer to home than those killings in Victorville—''

Again he held up a hand—to silence her. "Some day," he said. "We all have our secrets, right?''

In view of the past days' events, she could hardly argue. "I just wish . . .'' She did not finish.

Cameron asked, "Is this so bad, Kate? So we put the shoe on the other foot, so we show this piece of shit how it feels to be stalked. How it feels to have somebody think they own you. How it feels to be looking around every corner every goddamn minute of your life. Give me another way to solve a problem like Grissom before he goes on to kill the woman he claims he loves. It's like my mother talked about women going into back alleys for abortions—it was the only way. The only way, Kate. Yeah, I stepped over a line. Somebody had to.''

She nodded. She had stepped over that line along with him. And the choice to do it was profoundly grave and would have its consequences. She had irrevocably betrayed her oath as a police officer. Somewhere along the line, maybe not now, maybe not tomorrow, but someday, there would be consequences.

19

SITTING in her Saturn on Kenmore Avenue for what had turned out to be the second time that Monday, Kate reviewed her strategy. She had taken a day of comp time, deciding it was the least complicated way of continuing her investigation without having to lie or account for her activities to Cameron. But the results of day-long effort had been as minimal as she had suspected they would be. At this point there seemed to be nothing to lose in directly pursuing the woman who could prove or disprove her theory. Kate tossed her keys in her shoulder bag and got out of the car.

Arlene Layton answered her apartment buzzer so promptly that Kate wondered if she was expecting a visitor. "It's Detective Delafield, Mrs. Layton. May I come in?"

"Certainly."

Except for a few butterflies idly floating above the pots of daisies in the courtyard, the building was as quiet as it had been earlier in the day, its stucco seeming baked to its beige color by the late-afternoon orangey hues of unremitting August sun. Kate made her way up the staircase to apartment two-nineteen on the second floor.

Arlene Layton waited in her doorway just as she had when Kate had first been here with Cameron. Her face was composed, the slenderness of her body accented by a pale green crepe tunic and matching pants. Walking toward her, Kate thought that the swept-back gray hair and erect, dignified posture added the illusion of height; you had to actually stand next to Arlene to realize her petiteness.

"No Detective Cameron today?"

"Not today. I thought we'd just have a talk."

Arlene nodded. "Come in and sit down, Detective. I'll be right back."

Kate seated herself on the sofa. The oscillating fan whirred at high speed and the tranquil orderliness of the apartment gave an illusion of coolness, but the living room did seem more comfortable, Kate thought, than when she had last visited four days ago.

Her gaze fell on the doctorate degree hanging on the wall, and on the small framed graduation photo of Peri, the same one that had been in Herman Layton's wallet. The strongest bond between Herman and Arlene Layton had been pride in their daughter, epitomized by the graduation photo prized by both parents. Yet, that graduation had meant the end of her parents' marriage; Arlene Layton had filed for divorce the day afterward. . . .

Arlene returned with a tray holding a pitcher of lemonade and glasses, and placed the tray on the coffee table. "Detective, may I serve you a cold drink?"

"Thank you, I appreciate it." Kate observed the unhurried movements of her hands, the calmness of the bluish green eyes behind the thick lenses of her glasses. Twenty years from now, Kate thought, Peri will be Arlene.

"Mrs. Layton," Kate said, opening her notebook, "did you visit your ex-husband last week?"

"Detective Cameron asked me the same question."

Based on her first encounter with this woman, Kate had no expectation that this interview would be any easier. She took a swallow of her lemonade and then followed up patiently. "Did you?"

"No."

"The day of your ex-husband's death—would you explain again where you were last Thursday between the hours of nine and ten in the morning?"

Arlene settled herself in the armchair facing Kate, crossing her legs, and nesting both hands together on her thigh. Her magnified eyes met Kate's. "I believe I told you and your partner I was here," she said with conversational ease.

Kate kept her own tone equally casual. "What if I told you I have a witness who places you at Mr. Layton's cottage last week?"

Arlene shrugged. "People make mistakes."

"People—who do you mean? The eyewitness, or yourself?"

"I think the answer to that is obvious."

"We have phone records of calls between you and Mr. Layton. . . ."

Arlene picked up her drink in long, pale fingers, the manicured nails coated with clear polish. "Yes. I confirmed that to Detective Cameron."

"Right." Kate's tone was courteous; she did not want to convey the impression that she was conducting an interrogation. "We've established a pattern of recent and significant contact between you and the man you divorced more than two decades ago."

Again Arlene shrugged. "Herman and I were never enemies."

Kate played one of her trump cards. "I did some interviews in this building earlier today, Mrs. Layton, because we need to verify your alibi. You had a visitor to your apartment last Wednesday. A member of your Gang of Eight mentioned him."

"Which member?" Arlene looked displeased.

Kate ignored the question. "She identified our photo of Mr. Layton. Why did he visit you last Wednesday?"

"To bring me that." She gestured to the degree hanging on the wall. "And to prove what a very sick man he was. He said he was giving it to me for safekeeping. Peri's doctorate degree always belonged with her, not with him or me. He insisted on hanging it there, it didn't matter what I said."

Kate doubted the story. "I think the truth is, you and Mr. Layton were much closer than we've been led to believe."

"Do you?" A brief smile flickered over Arlene Layton's face; she remained silent.

Impressed by her self-possession, Kate said, "This is what I've figured out so far. Your ex-husband was involved in the disappearance of the Peking Man fossils, and you've always known about it—"

"You're wrong," Arlene said.

Kate said doggedly, "If you didn't know about it initially, you recently found out about it—"

To her utter astonishment, Arlene nodded and said, "You don't know the half of it."

Quickly recovering her composure, Kate said, "I probably don't." When Arlene did not respond, Kate pushed on: "According to our eyewitness, you were at your ex-husband's house last Tuesday. You went there to confront him. He admitted his involvement. He told you he was planning to make a public disclosure—"

"That's not it at all," Arlene said irritably and shook her head as if Kate were a backward pupil; Kate remembered that Arlene had indeed once been a teacher. "No notes," Arlene said, nodding toward Kate's notebook. "I'll talk to you only with no notes, and with the hope that you'll leave me and Peri—especially Peri—alone."

Kate immediately tucked her notebook into her shoulder bag. The imperative was that Arlene continue talking; a written record could come later.

"I sensed it all along," Arlene said. "Years ago, I suspected he was hiding something from me. He lied to me."

Her eyes had narrowed; two vertical lines deepened between her eyebrows. "All his life he lied to me. He swore up and down he never knew what happened to the fossils, and neither did anyone else in his unit. All those years I stood by him, all those years the son of a bitch looked me right in the eye and *lied* to me."

Kate knew it was not the lying but the mistrust implicit in her husband's betrayal that enraged Arlene Layton and impelled her to speak. "Tell me about it," she said. But she scarcely needed to encourage Arlene, who held her glass of lemonade to her lips with a tremulous hand and quaffed down the liquid as if it were fuel stoking an engine.

"Those government people hanging around, I knew they weren't here just to get a California suntan. Persistent, they were just too persistent—there had to be something. But Herman swore everybody was after poor innocent him and he didn't know a thing. Then all these years later," she said wrathfully, "all these years later, he comes barging back into my life and has to see me right now, he's going to tell me God's truth."

She gestured to the harmonious furnishings of her apartment. "This is mine. It has nothing to do with him."

"I can understand that," Kate said.

"You don't understand a thing," Arlene snapped. "Please," she added in a tone only slightly less sharp. "You really don't. He wouldn't meet at a public place, so that meant going to that . . . fortress of his. I didn't want to, but he said Peri was involved, and so I had no choice."

She sagged back into the sofa, laying her head back as if overcome by exhaustion. "That airless, pathetic, barred cage of a house . . ." Her voice was pitched just above a whisper. "He told me he had cancer. Liver cancer, kidney cancer. The doctors were saying he'd go quickly. In a matter of weeks."

She closed her eyes. "He had one of the Peking Man fossils. . . ."

She did not speak for so long that Kate finally ventured, "Did you see it?"

Arlene's eyes flew open, but she did not lift her head from the back of the sofa. "No. God no. He tried to show it to me. I saw the box, the stenciling on the package—that was enough. I knew—God, I knew it was real. . . ." Again she lapsed into a lengthy silence.

Kate thought: Not much wonder she reacted so skeptically about the CIA calling it a fake. She said, "Then last Tuesday was the first time you knew."

"Yes. The first time I knew. He'd had the fossil the whole time since he was in China, of course."

Kate asked cautiously, "What about the rest of the Peking Man fossils? Did he say anything about them?"

"He said he knew how to track down all of them." Heaving a deep sigh, Arlene again closed her eyes. "He'd kept the fossil hidden for years. He thought it was the best thing to do. And it was—the stupid fool at least had the brains to figure out that much. He was right to protect us, protect Peri. But he couldn't let sleeping bones lie. Oh no, all of a sudden he has to expose everything. He'd spent a lot of time figuring out how to do it to attract maximum attention. He said he knew the CIA would step in and contain the situation till they could figure out how it might affect American interests. He was sure right about that. You know about the CIA already claiming the fossil is a phony."

"And you're convinced it's not."

"Of course it's not. I know it's not."

Why and how had Herman Layton become mixed up in this affair in the first place? Out of her many questions, Kate selected the simple, obvious one that would elicit a reply from Arlene: "Why?"

"Why indeed. Herman said he kept the fossil with him the whole time he was in the POW camp—"

"How did he manage that?"

Arlene abruptly sat up as if reenergized and poured herself and Kate more lemonade. "Apparently it was never a problem. The Japanese soldiers guarding the camp thought it was just an old bone, a souvenir. They only took what they knew was valuable or what they thought the prisoners could make into a weapon. According to Herman, all the prisoners had a few personal items."

"I don't understand," Kate said. "How did he get the fossil in the first place?"

"I'm not entirely sure, Detective. I didn't ask him every question, you know—I was far too upset. It was before the cases of fossils were turned over to his Marine Corps unit for safekeeping, that's all he said. He knew what he had but didn't find out till he got back home that the rest of the fossils had vanished. He also knew he'd be branded a traitor for being involved in the disappearance of a priceless discovery—"

"Why?"

"Because he knew where the entire cache of fossils was hidden, and if our government was questioning him and the other Marines, then the fossils were gone from that location. Because he'd conspired with someone and revealed their location—"

"Who?"

"I have no idea. Maybe somebody else from his unit. Maybe some of the Chinese researchers working on the Peking Man site. Maybe someone from his POW camp. I don't know. What I do know is, he couldn't bring himself to destroy his fossil. I believe that, Detective. Also that he'd lived in fear all these years he'd be tracked down and it would all come out."

"Tracked down by whom?"

"Our government, I presume—although who really knows?"

Kate's fingers itched with the need to make notes.

There were questions upon questions, and they needed to be asked in some sort of logical, coherent order. She said, "This doesn't make sense—"

"It doesn't have to make sense if it involves Herman. He claimed everything he did was always for me and Peri—but things were different now that he was dying." She shook her head.

"How did he explain himself? Why did he want it to come out now?"

"He was crazy, he had to be," Arlene said firmly. "The progress of his cancer affected his brain. All of a sudden he's claiming he has to clear his conscience and he's going to have Peri make things right for him."

"Being branded a traitor no longer bothered him? He wasn't concerned about collateral damage to his own daughter?"

Arlene turned up her hands in a gesture of helpless despair. "He had this theory. According to him, any kind of fame was okay, it was still fame. Hitler's more famous than Churchill, there's Lee Harvey Oswald and Benedict Arnold and Ted Bundy, Jeffrey Dahmer—well, you get the picture."

Kate did. Herman Layton had espoused the same theory and the same names to his cronies at the bridge club. "Can I go over this again, Mrs. Layton?" She was hoping for more details and a clearer narrative. "As I understand it, Mr. Layton got hold of one of the Peking Man fossils before the rest of them were consigned to the care of the Marine Corps unit. You don't know how he came into possession of the fossil—"

"Let me say this: I agree with Peri that he got it legitimately. I'll never believe Herman stole it. He may have been a liar, but he wasn't a thief."

Kate put no credence in this claim. If Herman Layton had deceived Arlene over his possession of the fossil and had revealed the location of the rest of the fossils to a conspirator, then Arlene could be equally deceived about the possibility of larceny. But if Arlene was right and Herman had not stolen the fossil, then someone involved in the packing and/or delivery of the fossils had given one to Herman for some purpose—and that someone had to be either Chinese or American. . . .

Kate said, "So Herman came back from the war with the fossil in his possession. Do you know what he did with it then?"

"He buried it. For more than twenty years."

"Where?"

"I have no idea. For some reason he eventually decided it was no longer safe. By then he'd figured out how to get it into a safe-deposit box without it ever being traced back to him, even if something happened to him and the safe-deposit box was opened. So there it sat till he got this insane idea . . ."

Kate asked cautiously, "Did he mention anything about writing something in a notepad?"

"No."

There had been the slightest hesitation, and then emphasis on the denial, and Kate knew she was lying. But she nodded. "Did Mr. Layton go into specifics as to how he planned to make the fossil and its origin public?"

"Yes, he told me," Arlene said flatly. "He was arranging to have it found at Rancho La Brea last Thursday. He knew the staff people there, knew they'd identify the fossil as *Homo erectus*. The press would be on the scene—a jawbone millions of years old being found in Los Angeles at the Tar Pits would be a sensational story. Then Herman would step forward and tell them that one of the world's leading paleoanthropologists had the information that would lead them to the rest of the fossils."

"And how would he accomplish that?"

"He was going to give Peri the name."

"And did he?"

"Of course he didn't. Do you think she'd have believed the CIA's claim the fossil was fake? She'd be investigating this thing for all she was worth. He died before he told anyone."

"Did he say where the fossils were?"

"No, Detective, he didn't."

"Did he tell you the name?"

"No, he didn't." She added coldly, "To the very end he wouldn't trust me with the whole truth."

Kate believed her; it was totally consistent with Herman Layton's behavior pattern. "And his motive as you understood it—"

Arlene's mouth thinned and turned downward. "Peri Layton would be the paleoanthropologist daughter of the man who restored to the world the Peking Man fossils and cleared his conscience."

Carefully, Kate led her: "And you didn't want that to happen."

"Of course not," Arlene said emphatically. "Herman's legacy to Peri would be disgrace—his disgraceful behavior."

Kate said softly, "So you attempted to stop him, Mrs. Layton. And that's what happened on Thursday."

"No, that's what happened on *Tuesday*. Attempted was what I did on *Tuesday*. I couldn't change his mind. When he was here Wednesday, he told me the fossil would be found at La Brea the next day, it was a fait accompli, nothing could stop it."

"And so you went to the La Brea Tar Pits on Thursday—"

"No. I did not."

"You did, Mrs. Layton. You went there to stop him, permanently."

"That's ridiculous."

"What you didn't realize was that it was indeed a fait accompli. He'd already placed the fossil at Rancho La Brea. You didn't know that the observation pit where he'd planned to put the fossil opened only once a day at two o'clock in the afternoon, so he had to go there Wednesday, he had to be the last person to leave the observation pit in order to linger behind and place the fossil. He planted the fossil at Rancho La Brea on Wednesday in order to have it found on Thursday.''

Remembering the first interview with Arlene, Kate said, ''When we told you about the discovery of the jawbone, the first words out of your mouth were, 'Too late.' Because when you realized you couldn't stop Herman, you went to Rancho La Brea on Thursday to stop him then and there. Isn't that what happened?''

Picking up an arrow-shaped polished fossil that decorated the coffee table, Arlene contemplated its sharp point. She did not speak.

''When he didn't have the fossil with him, you thought perhaps he'd postponed doing what he said he'd do, or maybe he had second thoughts. But you couldn't afford to give him another chance.''

''He *was* plainly crazy, you know . . .''

''So you came up behind him . . .'' Kate said, ''You killed him.''

''An interesting theory that you can't prove. But, for the sake of theory, Detective, you'd kill a mad dog, wouldn't you?''

''You did kill him.''

''I deny it, of course.''

Kate stared at her. ''This investigation is only beginning, Mrs. Layton. It's just a matter of time. You know that, don't you. I'll find someone on the Wilshire Boulevard number twenty bus line who saw you, someone who saw you at Rancho La Brea—''

''No, you won't. Not if I was in disguise, which I'm not saying I was.''

Still staring at Arlene, Kate could not resist asking, ''Mrs. Layton, did it never occur to you that you were destroying perhaps the last chance to recover the bones of Peking Man?''

Arlene Layton's voice did not waver. "All I care about—all I've ever cared about—is my daughter."

A thought suddenly occurred to her. Kate said, "And all Herman Layton cared about was his daughter. . . ."

She remembered the square white patch on Herman Layton's wall where something had recently been removed. Then she looked at the doctorate degree. It was the same size as that white patch. Peri Layton had said that she was her father's heir, his only heir.

"If Mr. Layton brought that degree here for safe keeping, and he knew giving you Peri's degree meant you'd simply pass it on to her—"

Arlene sprang off the sofa, but Kate was ahead of her, snatching the frame off the wall.

"Give that to me! It's mine! This is my home! You need a search warrant!"

Kate ignored her. Any evidence in plain view was fair game. Carefully pulling at the edge of a paper protruding between the degree and its cardboard backing, she already knew from its torn top edge that it was from the notebook in Herman Layton's safe-deposit box. With Arlene still screaming protests, Kate unfolded the small piece of paper. Then Arlene flew at her.

Holding the paper high to protect it, holding off Arlene's clawing fingernails, at the same time Kate heard a key scrape in the lock of Arlene's door.

"What on earth—" Then Arlene screamed again as the door was violently slammed open.

Kate dropped into a crouch and was reaching for her weapon when Nicholas Whitby, followed by two burly men, burst into the room, slamming the door shut behind them.

Gaping at Whitby and his men, Kate withdrew her hand from the .38 inside her jacket. Arlene again sprang at her, this time snatching the paper.

Kate and Whitby rushed her, Whitby tackling Arlene as she was tearing the paper to pieces.

Whitby grasped her hands, but not before Arlene managed to stuff the shreds in her mouth, and swallow, gagging as she did so.

"You stupid, stupid, stupid—" Whitby seized Arlene's throat with both hands as if he would choke the
paper out of her.

Kate attacked Whitby, to pull him off Arlene, but it
was Whitby's men who succeeded in prying Arlene
loose.

"Get out! Get out of my house!" screamed Arlene,
coughing and massaging her neck. "I'll sue!"

A farce, thought Kate. I'm trapped in a French farce.

"The name," Whitby barked at Kate. "Did you read
the name?"

She could not speak; she was suppressing the almost
irresistible urge to howl with laughter. The scene with
Cameron and Charlie Grissom and now this, this surreal
thwarting of her attempt at an arrest for murder. The last
two days had surpassed anything in her entire police
career.

You're losing it, she told herself sternly. Get a grip.

She stalked to the door of the apartment and flung it
open.

"The name!" Whitby roared at her. "Did you read
the name!"

"That depends," Kate managed to say, and marched
off, leaving the door ajar just as Whitby always did.

20

"THE name, Detective. We need the name."

Her pulse beating in her temples, Kate turned away from him and peered out the windshield of her Saturn. "I've fallen into a time warp. This is Russia under Stalin." She focused on the row of apartment buildings arrayed neatly along this quiet, sun-splashed block in Mid-Wilshire as if to reorient herself. "You told Lieutenant Walcott that the CIA's domestic operations don't involve spying on the domestic activities of Americans. You virtually broke down the door of an American citizen's house—"

"Our charter does apply when a foreign—"

Kate talked over him, "—planted listening devices and God knows what other surveillance, came charging in with your goon squad, compromised my arrest of a murderer—"

"What arrest? There's nothing you can prove, from what I heard."

"Probably not any longer," Kate spat, "thanks to you."

"I keep trying to tell you. This is much larger than you and your murder case, Detective."

"Bullshit," Kate barked. "Pure and utter crap. We're not talking about national security. This isn't oil or territory, or some ungodly religious war. This is a collection of bones nobody gives a fuck about. Nobody but you and a few scientists—''

''Wrong, Detective,'' Whitby retorted. He rested his left hand on his knee, bony fingers working at the crease in his pants. ''You just don't—''

''I'm not wrong. It's just a stupid game. One more time before you die you want to wave your CIA credentials around, make people dance—''

The sound from Whitby was something between a chuckle and a snort of exasperation. ''We're wasting—'' He was visibly struggling to maintain his composure. ''We need the name, Detective.''

''So I can help you cover up the truth like you did with Layton's fossil? And this murder—not to mention Arlene Layton committing a hideous premeditated murder, taking an ice pick to Rancho La Brea—''

Whitby held up both hands. ''We've had no choice but to exercise caution with you. I know you believe you hold the high moral ground—''

''Me? *You* hold *no* moral ground. I'm not as stupid as you think. The funding for Peri Layton's new project—you're it. You pronounced the fossil a phony and then arranged for the paleoanthropologist who'd know the truth to be removed from—''

''We needed to know the full dimension of what we were dealing with. Calling the fossil a fake—we could always say we made a lab error. And as for Peri Layton's funding, we gather intelligence—that's what we do, that's our job. We monitor the internal politics of countries so Americans can sleep at night. Placing an asset among the workers in a paleontological dig—''

''Christ. You people. The CIA loses more credibility every single day. You've made enough mistakes—''

''And LAPD hasn't,'' Whitby snapped.

''We're *accountable*. Unlike you, we can't sweep everything under a carpet and throw the carpet away. We know we don't have a patent on the truth—''

"The only patent we hold is on the security interests of the United States."

The statement spurred her rage. "My country right or wrong," she sneered. "You must have slept all the way through Vietnam."

"Some of us were paying attention," Whitby said in an even tone. "Look, Detective. We're talking about a man who would in any case be dead in three to six weeks—"

"*That's* your rationalization?" Kate demanded incredulously. "How much lifetime do we get to steal from someone? Six weeks? Six months? A year? What's your cutoff?"

He held up both hands. "None is acceptable. I'm only trying to make the point that everything is not nearly so black and white as you make it. We act according to the mandates of our job—just as you do. Every organization has its secrets, even yours. Not everything you do is released for public consumption—"

"What we're talking about is not being adult enough to play with you so-called grown-ups at the CIA—that's all this is."

"It isn't paternalism, Detective, far from it. It's about having limited options. Right now, you're our last option. You're our last remaining link to those fossils."

"I'm *not* giving you the name." She thought of *Los Angeles Times* reporter Corey Lanier. Lanier would love to get her teeth into a story like this.

"Are you thinking the press will get out the truth? You trust the press, do you?"

The question sobered her. The press always had its own agenda. In her experience, the press always went sniffing down its own byways in unprincipled pursuit of the most sensational possible story. "I need to think it over," she said. "Right now, I've given you all the information I intend to give."

He turned away to gaze out the side window and muttered, more to himself than to Kate, "I've consistently misjudged you. Underestimated and misplayed you and your Lieutenant Walcott. . . . "

Because we're women, Kate wanted to say.

"We thought the best strategy was avoiding your Robbery-Homicide detectives—they'd be more likely to probe into things than a supervising detective from an inner-city division." He shook his head. "We never anticipated anyone like you."

This insult to the rank and file detectives of LAPD was no compliment to her, and Kate did not bother to reply.

"Detective, let me tell you what I know, everything I know—and then you can decide whether you should tell me that name. Is that a deal?"

"It's a start," Kate said.

"It all begins in 1941—of course. The Peking Man fossils, I assure you, were and still are counted among the treasures of China. You do know something about the contingency plans that were implemented to protect them."

"They were placed in the care of a Marine Corps detachment assigned to our embassy."

"That's the information released for public consumption," Whitby said. "The truth is, more than one copy was made of the Peking Man fossils besides the one sent to the Natural History Museum in New York. That was the copy packed into footlockers and placed in the care of our Marine Corps."

"You're telling me the fossils given to our Marines to safeguard were fake?"

"I'm telling you they were fake," Whitby said. "A scant few people knew the truth—"

She shook her head. "Then what happened to the real ones?" The machinations around these fossils rivaled the intrigues of a royal court. "Did Herman Layton know?"

"You're way too far ahead of me. The Chinese were reluctant to have the fossils leave the country. Too many nations come into possession of another nation's treasures and then refuse to give them back. A trip to any national museum will tell you that, like the British Museum and the Elgin Marbles. Turning over fakes to our Marines was a diversionary tactic. Carefully thought out, well-planned, well-executed."

He smiled wryly. "Or at least it would have been well-executed had Pearl Harbor not occurred that day, had the Japanese not seized the train carrying our Marines. Had not both sets of fossils—the real ones and the fake ones—disappeared."

"Okay, so copies were turned over to our Marines instead of the real fossils. What happened to the real ones?"

"They were hidden. In plain sight. Reburied at Zhoukoudian, the locale just outside Beijing where they were first discovered, in a hillside cave, an area so completely excavated it wouldn't be explored any further."

"Ingenious," Kate murmured. "Arlene Layton said Herman claimed he got hold of that jawbone before the fossils were turned over to us—"

"We believe he did. As part of the fail-safe plan, only two Chinese working at the Cenozoic Research Lab knew the Marines were given copies instead of the real Peking Man fossils. We learned from Layton, and confirmed it from interviews with other Marines in Layton's unit, that he had friends at the lab. We know Layton had an amateur's interest in paleontology, and from those two facts we deduce Layton's access to the real fossils. He must have known about the reburial plan. Maybe one of the Chinese confided in him or he discovered the plan by accident or was included in the plan for some other reason; we don't know. He probably lifted the jawbone as it was being packed for reburial at Zhoukoudian. Not even the Marine Corps commander knew the two foot-

lockers contained fakes. Colonel Ashurst was simply another part of the fail-safe preparations, a red herring who
didn't know he was a red herring.''

''So the real fossils—''

''Were dug up sometime before the war ended. Beyond that, up till now we weren't sure who did it or
when or what happened to the fossils afterward. You
can be sure we've looked into this with the greatest possible scrutiny. We have the names of every single person
who came into contact with those fossils at the Cenozoic
lab, everyone Herman Layton ever served with, every
single soldier at the POW camp. Who did Herman Layton tell, and what did that person do with the fossils?
You hold the answer.''

Whitby fixed his gaze on her. ''If you give me the
name, I'll make this promise: You'll know what I know
when I know it—and I should have at least some information immediately. Who was it, Detective Delafield?''

Kate's chest hurt; her tension seemed to grow expo-
nentially until it threatened to burst her skin. This man
was perfectly capable of breaking his word and pursuing
yet another avenue of cover-up and betrayal. Yet . . . in
her fragile memory was the answer to an enduring mystery of the world of paleontology. She, above all, knew
the vagaries of fate, that on her way home a truck could
come through an intersection . . .

She said: ''Lieutenant Shigeko Kuroda, two hundred
and thirty-second Regiment, thirty-ninth division.''

Whitby seized his cell phone, turned the wheel in its
side, punched in a code. ''Japanese. Lieutenant Kuroda,'' he said. ''Shigeko Kuroda.''

Whitby placed the phone down beside him. He closed
his eyes and swallowed visibly; Kate thought she could
see his lips tremble. She suddenly and fully understood
that this moment, for Whitby, was the culmination of a
lifetime of searching for the Peking Man fossils.

After a moment, he looked at her and said in a calm

voice, "Thank you, Detective. Now that the final piece is finally in place, I can tell you a bit more while we wait."

But she had a question: "You suspected Herman Layton all along?"

"Not at all. At first we went with the theory that one of the Chinese had been forced to collaborate with the Japanese. Because of logistics. It would be extremely difficult for a Chinese to remove the fossils from the dig at Zhoukoudian when it was in Japanese hands. And if a Chinese somehow did succeed in removing the fossils, why did they never surface, why were they never offered for ransom in their own country or for sale on the international black market?"

"Isn't it possible a private collector—"

"Of course. Art masterpieces aren't the only items to vanish into someone's private collection. But the Peking Man fossils weren't hanging in a museum for someone to covet, for someone to pay somebody else to plan and carry out a robbery. They were buried by insiders in a place occupied and guarded by Japanese, and we found no linkage, or rumor of linkage, between the burying of those fossils and a thief who was a go-between with a collector."

It all seemed logical, and Kate nodded.

"We know both of the Chinese involved in the diversionary tactic died, one of a heart attack, the other, we're not sure of the cause. We can only surmise neither one broke under questioning—"

"Why?"

"Because the Japanese never located the fossils and never stopped searching. We put together what information we had, went from there. Eventually, we suspected everyone. The possibility of an American collaborating with a Japanese became more likely."

Before he went into this explanation, Kate had to satisfy her curiosity on another point: "What happened to the fakes given to our Marines?"

"We can only guess. Certainly the Japanese soldiers who captured our Marines would open any footlockers. But there's some ambiguity as to the locale of those footlockers after our Marines took possession of them. The last time we met, I told you the story about the ex-Marine named Foley claiming to be the last one to see the footlockers and how he'd been able to hide them at various places in Beijing including the Swiss embassy. But his story didn't fully match up with the facts—the number of footlockers, how the fossils were packed. So we don't know for sure. It's also possible the fake fossils were stored with American guns and supplies in the train's boxcars, and the Japanese inadvertently shipped the entire load to one of their outposts in China or an island in the Pacific."

Whitby smiled faintly. "I happen to be a believer in the simplest explanation being the likely one. So my guess is either the Japanese found out they were fakes and dumped them or, more likely, they didn't know what the hell they were and just threw them out of the train."

"But—"

Whitby talked over her. "In which case, Chinese peasants probably gathered them up thinking they were what they called dragon bones. Zhoukoudian actually means Dragon Bone Hill. In those days there was a thriving market in China for all kinds of bones to be crushed for potions and medicine—and there still is today. All we know is, the fakes vanished along with the real Peking Man."

Her question answered, she nodded. "How in the world did you link Herman Layton to this?"

"Interviews with him and the other Marines, intuition, and guesswork, the process of elimination, the passage of time, piecing the whole thing together. He's topped our suspect list for years. The other Marines at his POW camp at Tientsin despised him—even though he had no strategic military information to give the Japanese, they suspected he was a stool pigeon.''

Kate smiled faintly. ''We Marines are good at sniffing out things like that.''

''Yes, I suppose you are.'' Whitby sighed and briefly, tiredly, rubbed both hands over his face. ''Thanks to you, we know now that he told a Japanese officer, Lieutenant Kuroda, what he knew about the Peking Man fossils. We suspected as much, suspected he'd told one of his Japanese captors. Layton was probably trying to save his own skin. Some of the stuff the Marines told us— conditions in that POW camp were beyond brutal. Then Layton arrives home, finds out he's bottom-line responsible for the complete disappearance of Peking Man. But as long as Lieutenant Kuroda makes no move with the fossils, the connection can never be made to Layton, never be verified, unless Layton admits his role and submits the evidence of the fossil in his possession. Today we know he buried the evidence till he could place it in a safe-deposit box untraceable to him. Today we know he changed his mind, decided to involve his daughter in the process of discovering exactly what happened to the fossils. I'm sure Layton wondered what Kuroda did with the fossils, why they didn't surface even if the man died. And of course he didn't dare try and find out—not with our suspicions of him. We couldn't understand it, either, until now. The name you provided is the link that's been missing all these decades, Detective.''

''Arlene is a murderer,'' Kate stated. ''What about her?''

''What about her? Even if we hadn't been on the scene, you couldn't arrest her—not from what I heard. You have no witnesses, she's too smart, she's covered her tracks too well.''

''You have her incriminating admissions on tape—''

Whitby's smile broke the grimness on his face. ''And

of course our taped surveillance of Arlene Layton will be deemed fully admissible in court.''

Kate smiled in return.

Whitby asked with a trace of facetiousness, ''Will Arlene Layton be the only murderer to ever escape prosecution in your city?''

Kate was thinking of Torrie Holden's mishandling of the Gonzales case, how close that first-degree murder case had come to being thrown out of court. And it still might be.

She said, ''I'm curious about . . . the Chinese man I saw you with at UCLA.''

Another smile crossed Whitby's face. ''A colleague from Beijing. From the old days. Who shares my abiding interest in the Peking Man fossils and for the same reasons. I assured him that the discovery at La Brea was another false trail. I'm sure he doesn't believe me.''

''Peri Layton—''

''She's completely in the dark. About all of this. She—''

Whitby's phone rang. He snatched it up, listened. ''Coordinates two zero three four, confirmed.'' He turned a dial in his phone, then said, ''Whitby here.''

For the next several minutes he simply listened, and Kate watched in mounting anxiety as his body sagged, as his face acquired a grayish pallor.

Whitby muttered an indecipherable sign-off, turned the dial in his phone, dropped it into his pocket.

''What is it,'' she said.

''You have a right to know, Detective,'' he said heavily. His low, penetrating voice seemed to bore into her. ''Just remember, you wanted to know. Our information is, Lieutenant Kuroda left the POW camp at Tientsin on a five-day leave six months before the end of the war. He had to have taken the fossils at that time. Only a Japanese officer could perform such an operation without challenge or questions being asked.''

His shoulders slumped, Whitby sighed, and he turned his head away from her as if what he would say next was too painful for him to meet her gaze. "We have every reason to believe he took the Peking Man fossils with him . . . to his next post, which was also where he lived. And that next post . . ."

Whitby's voice was trembling, and he was swallowing audibly. Kate watched in shock and with a bone-deep chill of foreboding.

Finally, Whitby asked, "Does the date August 6, 1945, mean anything to you, Detective?"

Kate managed to say after a moment, "Yes. Of course."

Whitby turned to her, his eyes awash with tears, and Kate knew that neither of them wanted to, or even could, utter the word *Hiroshima.* She knew that her own face mirrored the anguish on Whitby's face.

Whitby said, "He was virtually at ground zero."

"I see," Kate said faintly.

"Yes." After a moment he added softly, "I hope you can also see clearly where we are with this, now."

What she saw was a historical tragedy involving two nations, compounded by the fact that her own country now bore responsibility for the loss of a third nation's priceless historical discovery.

She nodded.

Whitby said quietly, "Arlene Layton committed a heinous act to protect her daughter. Our country committed a heinous act to end a war. . . . The most terrible of modern weapons has destroyed a vital link to our origins."

After a while, Whitby said, "This is my last case—my last assignment, Detective. The end of a quest spanning my entire professional life. You may not believe this, but I have always shared your . . . moral difficulty with this. And perhaps we both now share some . . . compassion for all the parties involved, whether they be nations or individuals."

"I do need to know one final thing," Kate said quietly. "Herman Layton possessed the last existing Peking Man fossil . . ."

". . . and could never bring himself to destroy it," Whitby finished for her. "Nor will . . . anyone else."

Whitby held Kate's gaze. "This tragedy has gone well beyond national security interests or any personal quest of mine. You're now privy to one of your nation's secrets. You were once a soldier. I ask you to continue serving your country. I ask you to keep that secret."

"Yes, sir," Kate said.

"I can say this." Whitby extended a hand, and Kate took it. "Some day, Detective Delafield, this story will come out."

Whitby opened the door of the Saturn and walked away without looking back. Leaving his door ajar.

21

AT the station, Kate sat dully at the homicide table, still immersed in the aftermath of what felt like a blow to the solar plexus. Idly, she examined a mailing tube that had come in addressed to her, turning it in both hands; there was no return address.

She opened one end, extracted a tightly rolled poster, unfurled it. An attached yellow Post-it read: *I'll be back. Remember me.* The poster was of Peri Layton, the one that had awed Cameron in the house on Ophir Drive, of Peri kneeling with Mary Leakey at the footprints at Laetoli.

Kate removed the Post-it, ran a fingertip over the angular writing. Peri had been like a forest fire, she mused. Or maybe more like Aimee's flu—a virulent onslaught passing irresistibly through and now gone. Almost gone. She opened her notebook and pasted Peri's message against the inside back cover.

Seeing Cameron enter the squad room, Kate tossed the mailing tube out of sight under the table.

"How you doing, Kate?" Cameron inquired in a perfunctory tone.

"Okay, how about you?" Kate replied, equally perfunctory.

Studying her face, Cameron pulled out the chair next to her and lowered his lean frame into it. "So . . . how do you feel, after a night's sleep?"

There was no ambiguity about what he was referring to, and she met his gaze frankly. "Lousy," she answered.

His light brown eyes held hers. "First time you ever did anything like this," he said. It was not a question.

"Or anything even remotely like it," she confirmed.

"I figured," he said. "I needed to be straight with you about . . . being able to do something, but what I knew about you, what I heard about you, I was surprised as hell you gave me the info."

She could not divulge the duress she had been under—her guilt over deceiving Cameron throughout the Layton investigation, Aimee's disdain of her inability to take action about Marcie. In any case, she had risked enough with this new partner to last the rest of their partnership, not to mention her career.

As Kate remained silent, Cameron said, "Look. We don't know very much about each other yet. I'm not the kind of guy that—I'm not all that good at talking about myself—"

"I noticed," she said with a fleeting smile, then added quickly, "It's fine, Joe. Neither am I."

Cameron's grin was equally fleeting. "I noticed that too." He leaned toward her. "You put a lot of trust in me, Kate. Let me tell you straight from the shoulder, I value it more than you know. It's not wasted, believe me. I figure I owe you. I figure I really lucked out getting you as a partner."

Speechless, she remembered how her father had always instructed her to respond when she received a compliment. "Thank you," she said.

Cameron sat back. "Tell you what amazes me. You've been a cop twenty-five years, it took all that time before you did something like this. One thing I know for absolutely sure: Any cop eventually gets squeezed between a rock and hard place. Between the rule book and needing a way to live with yourself. Most of us get to that place one hell of a lot sooner than you did, Kate.''

"Maybe I was luckier than I knew." She added earnestly, "We need that rule book, Joe. We need that blueprint to be good cops."

He said quietly, "I know we do, Kate. But what we did last night—it had to be done. It was the right thing to do."

"Maybe it had to be done," she conceded. "But it wasn't right. It will never be right."

Kate reached for the curled-up poster and handed it to Cameron. "From Peri Layton."

His attention instantly distracted, he rolled it open, then held it reverently between his hands, gazing for a long time. "Aren't you the lucky one," he finally said.

"No, you are."

"I am?" he said unbelievingly. "It's for me?"

"It is."

"How come?"

Kate smiled. "Maybe both of us appreciate you."

"Damn," Cameron said, his face lighted with pleasure as he carefully stashed the poster beside his chair. "This is the best thing to happen in the last five days. Speaking of things happening, Lieutenant Walcott wants to see us."

Walcott was at her desk working her way through a six-inch stack of paper. "Sit down, Detectives," she said, moving the stack to one side. "I have news on a couple of fronts."

Obediently, Kate and Cameron scraped chairs up in front of the desk.

Walcott gazed at them over steepled fingers. "Kate, you're back in court tomorrow on the Gonzales case. You were right: Lopez gave us the shooter to save himself from a third strike."

"Good," Kate said fervently.

Walcott's smile was sardonic. "Yeah. All you and the

DA have to do now is convince the jury that a piece of shit like Jose Lopez has any credibility.''

''It's still a better chance than we had before,'' Kate said. The Lopez testimony would be useful as leverage on other potential witnesses.

''Detective Cameron,'' Walcott said, ''I know you'll be sorry to hear that the feds have taken jurisdiction of the Herman Layton case—''

''The *feds?* What the hell for?''

''You're looking this gift horse in the mouth?''

''No, Lieutenant, I don't understand—''

''Even though the fossil found at the La Brea Tar Pits has been deemed a fake—''

''What? It has?''

''Detective, interrupting people is not a desirable quality in a homicide detective. It has. The so-called fossil in our evidence locker has been examined by CIA experts. Apparently some officials in Beijing have a few questions. So the case is gone, Detective. I want all your reports, I need all your notes, any other pertinent scrap of paper you and Detective Delafield might have. I need it before you leave tonight.''

''Jesus,'' Cameron muttered.

''Consider it done,'' Kate said.

Walcott glanced at her, and Kate shared with her the barest instant of communication, of complicity.

''My very first case, gone,'' groaned Cameron.

''I've looked over the reports. You did good work,'' Walcott said.

''And you still have perfect stats,'' Kate reminded him.

''True,'' Cameron said in a brighter tone.

''So get busy,'' Walcott said briskly. ''One more thing—I have this feeling about the two of you . . . I think you may make interesting partners.''

So do I, Kate thought.

Walcott caught Kate's eye and spoke as if she had read Kate's mind: "Try not to be too interesting."

Just before midnight, Kate let herself into the darkened condo, switching on a lamp and wearily calling, "I'm home." She went into the kitchen.

Aimee hurriedly joined her, pulling a robe around her nakedness, smoothing her disheveled hair. "How come you didn't call?"

"Couldn't," Kate said. "Then it got to be so late—"

"Dickhead Charlie's left town," Aimee said excitedly, her face elated. "Marcie got a call from somewhere in the desert, it was him claiming somebody mistook his car to stash a bag of heroin, he's in big trouble, he sounded really scared."

"Did he? That's good," Kate said. She dumped ice cubes into a glass. "That's very good."

"It's so late—come to bed."

"I will in a minute," Kate said and filled the glass with scotch. "Right now I need this, sweetheart. Like medicine."

"Kate—honey, whatever you did to make Charlie hightail it out of town—"

"What you don't know is better for me, okay?"

"Okay," Aimee said in a deflated tone.

"Sweetheart, will you keep me company?"

"Sure. I'll heat up some coffee in the microwave."

Kate dropped into her armchair in the living room. Miss Marple padded delicately in from the bedroom, tossed a green-eyed glance at Kate, then yawned, stretching her front paws straight out, her back arched and quivering; she trotted to Kate and leaped into her lap.

"Hello, sweetie pie," Kate whispered, scratching under her chin. Miss Marple purred, and Kate rested her hand on the cat's soft fur, comforted by the sound and the cat's want of simple contact. Kate took a mouthful of scotch and savored its sweet sharp burn all the way down her throat.

Aimee came into the room, coffee mug in hand, and perched on the edge of the sofa. "So tell me what's going on."

Kate took another deep swallow of scotch. "Nothing much to tell," she said. Except, she thought, for risking our relationship and my career in a passionate embrace with a female murder suspect in a public place, except for deceiving my new partner, except for denying your existence to my brother, except for betraying my oath as a police officer, except for aiding and abetting a government cover-up.

"Your murder case," Aimee prodded, "the guy who got it at La Brea. What was that about?"

"Well," Kate said, "it turns out he took a prehistoric fossil from a foreign country. The prime suspect ate the piece of paper that was the key piece of evidence, the feds got involved and took over the case, and now it's an international cover-up."

"Oh for God's sake," Aimee said disgustedly. "You and your secrets. This wouldn't even make a decent episode of the *X-Files*."

"Isn't that the truth," Kate said. "Honey, I'm just really bushed."

"That's what you said last night, and look what happened," Aimee said impishly. "If you put that drink down, get that cat off your lap, and come to bed, I have something special in mind to thank you for what you did for Marcie."

Kate put down the scotch, gave Miss Marple's fur a last stroking, then gently lowered her to the carpet. "It's a deal," she said.